D

C000150528

WITHDRAWN

PEZ
Com.mdb
(F)

one and all ~ onen hag oll

**CORNWALL
COUNCIL**

24 HOUR RENEWAL HOTLINE 0845 607 6119
www.cornwall.gov.uk/Library

NICK HOLLIN

DARK LIES

bookouture

Published by Bookouture in 2018

An imprint of StoryFire Ltd.

Carmelite House
50 Victoria Embankment
London EC4Y 0DZ

www.bookouture.com

Copyright © Nick Hollin, 2018

Nick Hollin has asserted his right to be identified
as the author of this work.

All rights reserved. No part of this publication may be reproduced,
stored in any retrieval system, or transmitted, in any form or by
any means, electronic, mechanical, photocopying, recording or
otherwise, without the prior written permission of the publishers.

ISBN: 978-1-78681-337-4
eBook ISBN: 978-1-78681-336-7

This book is a work of fiction. Names, characters, businesses,
organizations, places and events other than those clearly in the
public domain, are either the product of the author's imagination
or are used fictitiously. Any resemblance to actual persons, living or
dead, events or locales is entirely coincidental.

To my family

PROLOGUE

He stands in quiet contemplation of his work, the warm glow of satisfaction lingering as the body ahead of him starts to cool. There is frustration there, too; she'd deserved better, deserved him to be at the top of his game, but instead he'd stumbled and very nearly missed her throat with the knife. He'd gone a little too deep, and the blood had sprayed to places he hadn't intended, like onto the corner of a child's painting pinned by a magnet to the fridge door. *It looks like a signature*, he thinks. But that crude little picture is not his art. His masterpiece will be something far more ambitious.

The naked body is carefully arranged, and the skull-shaped mark has been drawn at the top of her thigh. The shape he's piped in chocolate icing is beautiful, exactly as he'd wanted it to be. His hand as steady as the smile on his face.

He reaches into a plastic bag and removes the final piece of the display: a tin of beans. He pulls carefully at the ring, peeling back the lid to reveal the contents. The sauce is a satisfying red. He starts to pour, shaping a speech bubble close to his victim's head alongside lips that remain parted for a final breath that never came. He tilts her head towards the carving knife he's placed behind her and positions her limbs to give the impression she's running.

When he's done, he stands back and takes it all in, wishing the lights above him were brighter and the tiles on the floor cleaner so he could enjoy the contrast between white and red. Nobody else will ever know it wasn't perfect, just as they will never know about the mistakes he's made. And there's always the next time, of course.

Sarah stares at the living room window, unable to see past the reflection of a frightened woman. Tonight, for the very first time, she will be without her children. She glances down at her phone, wondering if it's too early to call her husband and check they're okay, to make sure they're not suffering as badly as she is, but she remembers his last words when he'd given her a squeeze and told her to enjoy herself. If only he'd been better at reading her feelings. If only she'd been better at talking about them. Finally, she'd admitted she needed a break, and he'd sweetly arranged to take the boys to his parents', swearing that he'd follow every one of the two dozen instructions on the list. Now the freedom she's dreamt about so frequently over the last three years seems like the worst possible kind of nightmare.

She forces herself to move, to look away from the window and give up on the hope of seeing her children suddenly appear, running up the path, arms spread wide. As she turns, she stops, certain for a moment that she really has seen a pale face out there in the darkness. She shakes away the image, putting it down to her nerves, or the two glasses of red wine she's gulped down to try and ease them. She slumps onto the sofa, trying to remember what she used to do in the evenings when she wasn't washing clothes, thinking about fun activities for the following day, or worrying about how to put weight on the younger boy, Tate. She stares down at her stomach, lifting her shirt to reveal the scar through which her youngest had emerged. From that very first day she'd known he wasn't right. It wasn't science, it was instinct.

It's also instinct that's telling her she really ought to get up and investigate the noise she's just heard at the front door. Has something been pushed through the letterbox? It would explain the draught that's now fluttering the flame of the candle that was supposed to bring her calm. It might also explain the face she thinks she's seen.

It'll be another bloody takeaway menu, she assures herself, pushing up onto her feet and moving past the entrance to the kitchen where she can see a stack of them on top of the microwave. A proper meal out with the family would be nice, but it would have to be a restaurant where she could be sure they would understand Tate's needs, and where it could all be served and eaten before the older boy, Felix, got bored and ran off in search of trouble. She checks her phone again, wondering what Felix is up to right now, sedated by the television, perhaps, or pestering Tate, who ought really to be getting ready for bed.

As she turns the corner into the hall she spots a small plastic tractor tucked up against the side of a little pair of shoes. She reaches down to pick it up, not only fearful of the tantrums if it's lost, but wanting to squeeze it in her palm, as if it might bring her closer to the boys. She feels the draught again and looks up at the front door, expecting to see the letterbox her husband has never got around to fixing stuck ajar, but she finds the door is partly open. Her initial thought is a happy one: the boys have returned and are waiting to jump out and surprise her with their cheekiest grins. The absence of a car in the drive she can see through the gap in the doorway is telling her otherwise. As is her instinct, which is telling her to run.

She feels something strike the back of her neck. Hard. The darkness rises as fast as the floor, giving her just long enough to see the glint of a knife. The last thing she sees are Tate's little shoes, carefully arranged by her just minutes before, ready for a tomorrow that will never come.

CHAPTER ONE

Katie is woken by an elbow to the face. When she finally manages to pull things into focus the elbow looks to be the only part of the body beside her not covered in hair. Disgusted, she searches for the man's name, but her thoughts are as twisted as the bedsheets under her, and it's enough of a struggle to remember her own. She notices the curtains are still open as she peels her cheek from the pillow and rolls over, searching for her phone. A fluorescent alarm clock tells her it was just five hours ago that she was dragged into bed, and perhaps as little as three hours ago that she started trying to get some sleep.

She continues her retreat, slipping off the side of the bed and onto a pile of clothes that look like her own. They stink of smoke, booze and sweat, and she has to hold her breath against the smell as she fights her way into them. The body on the bed doesn't move.

She slips into the bathroom, taking the briefest of glimpses in the mirror. Her shoulder-length dark hair is matted on one side and stubbornly resists being untangled with her fingers. Her make-up is a state, but she can feel the reassuring lump of a lipstick in her trouser pocket and hastily smooths it on, wiping the kohl from under her eyes. The rest is most likely in her handbag, but she has no idea where that could be. She stands perfectly still, replaying as much as she dares of the previous night. She's sure she left her bag in her car; she's also fairly certain she drove that car to just outside this flat. The thought makes the room swim and leaves her leaning over the edge of the sink.

She walks as quickly and as silently as she can manage down the stairs and out to the street. As she feared, her old Rover is parked a few feet away, one wheel up on the kerb in a residents-only space. She's relieved to see there's no ticket on the windscreen, just a splattering of bird shit and a spidery crack she hasn't got around to fixing. She's equally relieved to find a set of keys in her other trouser pocket and her handbag wrapped around a handbrake she'd failed to put on.

She climbs behind the steering wheel, pushing aside several cardboard fast-food containers to make room. For once the Rover's engine starts first time and she stares into the taped-on mirror at the seemingly endless stream of traffic passing by. The people of London are heading to work, and she's reminded she should be doing the same. She fumbles around in her handbag, pushing past all the familiar objects, before finally spotting her mobile. As her fingers draw it out she feels its vibration. The call ends the moment she looks at the screen, but she can see it's the latest of twenty, all from a number she hurriedly redials.

The answer is instant: urgent and breathless. 'Is that you, boss?'

'What's wrong, Mike?'

'We've got one. Walton Road, West Molesey. Just behind the reservoirs.'

From the map in her head she instantly knows where she needs to go. The difficulty is working out where she is right now. Squinting at a street sign in the distance, she can make a vague approximation. 'Fifteen minutes,' she says. 'Who's there with you?'

'Just Stu and a couple of PCs. We've sealed off what we can and tried to protect the scene.' She waits for him to continue, but he doesn't. Were it not for his short, sharp breathing, she'd think she'd lost the line.

'Is there a problem, sergeant?' As she asks, she realises his voice had sounded different before, constricted by something. 'Tell me.'

She feels the urge to get going, to drive closer to the answer before it slips away, but the traffic to her left has slowed to a crawl, and she has no magic light to throw on the roof. Distracted by practicalities, she almost misses the words at the end of the line. She opens her mouth to ask DS Peters to repeat himself, but by that point it's too late; she's taken in their meaning. The effect is immediate, making her feel like she's slipping through a hole in the floor of the car. She grips the steering wheel tightly, desperately trying to hold on.

'You're sure?'

'I am.'

Terrible images flashing up in her mind, terrible possibilities pushing her down. Then, just as she's certain she will have to let go and sink to a place she knows she'll never escape, she finds herself standing in the hallway of a stranger's house, staring at a photo on the wall of two young schoolgirls, smiling broadly, eyes shining with innocent joy. She blinks, and the vision disappears, but the feeling does not. It lifts her, straightens her, pushes her forward, and suddenly she's revving the engine, forcing the Rover out into the traffic, ignoring the horns, ignoring the twisting in her gut, ignoring the little voice screaming at her that she's lost her edge and can't be trusted to do what is right.

CHAPTER TWO

Nathan opens his eyes and immediately the desire takes hold. Some days, the best days, it doesn't come for hours, but today it's there the very moment he wakes. He sits bolt upright, muscles twitching, desperate to run away and hide. It's only when he finally considers his surroundings that he remembers he already has.

He uncurls his hands and places them lightly on the tops of his thighs, focusing on his breathing as he works his way through the usual reassurances. Then, when the desire has slowly faded, he falls back onto the bed, as drained as if he hadn't slept at all.

He stares towards a shuttered window where sunlight is streaming through a narrow gap. He can just make out the tops of trees on the hills in the distance, bending in the usual north-easterly. He doesn't need to see the rest to know exactly what's out there, nothing ever changing but the colours and the sky.

When he eventually rises he does so in stages – sheets pulled back, one foot towards the floor, the second leg swung round till he's sitting up straight, tying up his shoulder-length hair with an elastic band. As soon as he's up he's down again, working through a rigorous exercise routine that leaves him with a splinter and in desperate need of a shower. That shower is hot and long, and he scrubs himself until his skin is flushed pink. Then he returns to the bedroom and pulls off the sheets, taking them down the narrow staircase to the equally narrow kitchen to throw them in the wash.

His first meal is as every meal, a tin of something warmed on the hob. When he's finished, he cleans his teeth in the kitchen sink with a splayed brush and the tiniest dab of toothpaste. Then he walks, still naked, into the living room, flicking on the light to reveal a tiny wooden-beamed space with a high-backed leather armchair in the middle of two piles of books. Without looking he reaches for the top of the taller pile, sits himself down and starts to read. The only distraction is the sound of birds at the top of the chimney and a strengthening wind rattling the locks on the door.

*

Several hours later, the height of the piles has been reversed, three children's novels read from cover to cover, a quarter of a million words he's worked his way through so many times he could almost recite them by heart. Nothing too thrilling. Nothing with crime. He almost laughs when he considers how different it had once been.

He pushes himself up from his chair and flicks off the light, reaching for his trainers, the soles of which are worn paper thin. He slips them on and prepares to go outside. Before he pulls back the final bolt on the door he takes a deep breath and reminds himself of the emptiness of the landscape around, of the distance to the nearest village and of the promise made by the only person in the world who knows that he's here. These days it's more a ritual than any kind of necessity – like saying his prayers before he goes to bed – because there can no longer be any doubt: he is alone.

He walks a few paces then starts to run, following the well-worn path around the house. He doesn't look up as he makes his circuits; sometimes he doesn't even need to open his eyes. He finally collapses after a couple of hours, crawling through the dirt and back into the house, using the last dregs of his strength to reach up and draw the bolts across the door.

It's a while before he's able to eat any dinner. Even longer before he's willing to attempt the stairs. When he does, he pauses halfway up to drag a filthy finger across the wall. All around him are the marks he's left: one a day, every day, covering virtually every inch of the plaster. What had started as an ordered line soon became a tumbling circular smudge, spiralling towards the centre. Now, after three hundred and sixty-two days, he's almost at that centre, just three more stripes and he'll have reached his goal. He smiles as he runs a thumb alongside the inside of his left wrist, feeling the narrow band of raised and hardened skin, evidence of the many occasions he didn't think he'd make it.

CHAPTER THREE

The house is a small, detached 1960s property tucked away at the end of the street, the front of the house hidden by an overgrown chestnut tree, the back leading out to the reservoir. She waves her warrant card at a young PC as she slips through a gathering crowd and ducks under the perimeter tape. As she approaches the front door she glances across at a carefully maintained rose bed, spotting two flower heads that have been knocked off in their prime, perhaps by the rushed arrival of her team. The vivid red of the petals seems to soak into her, as does the sense of dread at what's about to come. She crouches down, certain if she doesn't she'll be falling that way. She hopes it appears to those behind as if she's had to tie a shoelace, and she decides while she recovers to do exactly that, but when she squeezes her eyes shut and pictures those two schoolgirls she feels the shoelace snap in her hand.

A moment later the door ahead of her opens and she stares up at all six feet five of DS Mike Peters, wearing a paper forensics suit and a comforting smile. He offers a hand and she takes it, wishing she'd thought to wipe the sweat from her palm, wishing he didn't so remind her of her dad.

'It's okay,' she says unconvincingly. 'It's just...' She can't think of anything to say, no excuse for her appearance, nothing that she hasn't used before. Peters simply nods as she starts to move forward. He passes her a suit to match his own, and she feels, not for the first time, like an actor putting on her costume, playing the part of someone in control.

She tries to keep her head down as she moves along a dark, narrow hallway but she can't resist looking up at a photo that she somehow knew would be there. It's of two young boys, both with cheeky grins, both utterly oblivious to the horrors that life can bring. She wonders whether she had ever been like that, or whether she had known the truth from the very beginning.

She estimates the older boy to be about three. Three more years with a mother than she ever had. But she knows he won't remember that time, beyond the photos that his father shares. He'll never be certain how much his mother loved him. The younger boy, two, perhaps, is far smaller. She knows about that, as well. She'd also been sickly and small as a child, a worry to her dad and a target at school, at least until she'd proven herself ready and willing to fight. And fighting is what she wants to do now when she considers not only what has just ended in this house, but what, for the boys, has only just begun. Having lost her own mum a long time ago, Katie knows only too well what comes after, likely even worse given the violent nature of this death; she knows about the gradual curdling of knowledge and understanding inside of them. She knows how, even if everyone thinks they're coping, there'll be moments that prove them all wrong, flashes of anger, of reckless behaviour and blame.

She turns away, eyes blurring, nails digging into her palm. On the floor to her left is a stack of shoes, all carefully arranged with the exception of the smallest pair. Beside them is a toy tractor, crushed flat and with a wheel missing. She steps around this whole area, following the markers instructing her to do so, reminding her to stay on the right path, reminding her just how late she is.

In the kitchen at the end of the hallway lights are set up and people are moving around busily as they go about their various assignments. She can still feel the heat of alcohol in her blood and wishes, for the hundredth time, that she'd listened to her boss's advice to stay at home and get some sleep. Not that she will have learned her lesson. Most likely she'll be doing the same thing tonight; anything, to try and wash away the collection of memories she knows she's about to add to. She feels she ought to say something as she steps into the kitchen, something to break the oppressive silence, but when she finally gets a glimpse of what they're working around, it's all she can do not to cry out and run.

The victim is young, possibly younger than her own forty years. She meets the eye of Kieran Smith, a young detective new to her team. She knows he's looking for reassurance, but there's nothing she can say to convince him they're going to win here.

'Name?'

'Sarah Cleve.'

She glances across at Sarah's wedding finger. 'Husband informed?'

'A couple of hours ago,' says Kieran before looking away, as if he's the one that should feel guilty for drawing attention to her tardiness. 'DS Peters and I tried to… But he… But you can't…'

She knows exactly what he's trying to say. She'd been the one to inform the husband of the first victim, Sally Brooks, a week ago. He'd refused her request to sit down before she told him the news, and when he'd started to fall she'd only just reached him in time. He'd cried on her shoulder and then squeezed her as if it might bring his wife back to life. If Katie could have swapped places at that moment, if she could have been the one carved up on the floor while the mother continued to raise her smiling children, she would happily have made that deal.

'You've done well,' she says to Kieran, managing half a smile. 'You all have.' Her voice barely carries to the rest of the room. Once, she'd have easily commanded the scene with clear and precise orders and everyone would have listened, knowing that it was going to get them what they all wanted, but that seems a very long time ago now.

The forensic photographer steps aside to give her a better look. The woman's naked body has been contorted to look as though she's finishing a golf swing, except her hands have been wrapped around a carving knife instead of a club. Most likely it is the same knife that has been used to cut her neck from ear to ear and spilt a life's worth of blood across the kitchen floor. Across her bare stomach, part hidden by the now-congealing blood, is a long caesarean scar, around which are hundreds of fresh, tiny slits, starting in a vertical line just beneath her breasts then spiralling round towards the belly button. Baked beans have been used on the floor to create a speech bubble from her mouth and written in the centre, in capital letters, is a single word:

SLICE

Someone moves alongside her. She doesn't need to look across, knowing who he is from how close he's standing.

'Good night last night?' he whispers. 'When's it my turn?'

'Just a couple more billion first,' she says, through gritted teeth. 'Tell me what you know.'

'I know you shouldn't be here in this state. I'd hate to think what might happen if word got back to the Super.'

'Well, you've seen a lot of terrible injuries,' she says. 'I'm sure you can imagine.'

'Is that a threat?'

'It's a request for you to stick to what you're supposed to be good at, Dr Parker.'

'And what are you good at now, DI Rhodes? Not such a star working on your own, are you? Not Daddy's little protégé anymore.'

She turns to look at him for the first time, lifting her stare past his jutting chest and up to his unbearable grinning face that others have described as handsome, but that she has only ever wanted to punch.

'About forty years old,' she says, this time with enough volume for the rest of the room to hear, her eyes still locked on his. 'A blow to the back of the neck out in the hall, which knocked her out. She was then dragged through here, and her throat was cut with a serrated knife, likely the same knife which has been placed in her hand. Judging by the blood splatter and angle of flow I'd say the rest of the wounds were inflicted *after* death. Time, probably late yesterday evening. Eight o'clock-ish?'

Dr Miles Parker blinks and takes a step back, almost treading on another forensic examiner crouched behind him taking photographs of a stain on the kitchen floor. He says nothing, but the look of surprise turning to anger is clear on his face.

'Just remember who has the qualifications,' he says, quietly. 'From what I hear you barely went to school.'

'If you think this job is about qualifications,' says Katie, with a sigh, 'then you clearly still have a lot to learn.'

She returns her attention to the body, running her eyes across the figure until they fix on the inside of the woman's right thigh. She's poorly shaved up there, perhaps expecting such an area would not be seen by anyone, not even her husband now the young kids are dominating their lives. It feels like a crime in itself to be staring, to be focusing on such an intimate spot. But she has no choice. She has to know.

She contorts her body to get a better view, her back starting to protest as it remembers a slipped disc from a reckless but successful pursuit in the past. It had earned her both a medal and a reprimand, but she knows she would be just as reckless now if it meant she could catch the bastard that did this.

'It's not there,' says DS Peters, nodding towards the victim then looking away. 'Perhaps the other mark didn't mean anything.'

Katie is sure she knows better. She doesn't believe in coincidence. What she has always believed in is working as a team, sharing every thought and feeling, no matter how insignificant it might seem, and yet what she's thinking and choosing to keep to herself right now is far from insignificant.

'Could something have leaked?' she asks, weakly. 'Could this be a copy?'

DS Peters nods towards the kitchen. 'Do you really want two people out there to be capable of that?'

She lowers and shakes her head at the same time, embarrassed by her suggestion, by her desperation. She's known all along that Sally Brooks' killer would strike again, and yet now that it's happened she feels utterly unprepared. She has no idea where to begin, no instinct to go on other than to do what she's never done in her eighteen years of service and walk away. Even when she pictures the other victims – the parents, the husbands, the boys and the girls – she finds no strength, no inspiration. All she can think to do is apologise. She turns towards the body, intending to do just that. She crouches down, struggling to keep her knee from the floor, and starts to whisper something in private, stopping abruptly when she spots a mark below Sarah's right nipple. She blinks a couple of times and inches closer, focusing on two tiny dots on the skin. They could so easily be ignored, dismissed as two more among the many moles on this woman's body. But just as with the first victim, Katie knows better.

She reaches out to point, to share, then quickly pulls her arm back, lifting it to rub the back of her neck which has broken out in a sweat. The significance of her discovery is hitting home, bombarding her with possibilities that leave her breathless. Wordless. The room around her is starting to spin, and she stands up quickly for fear of contaminating the scene. She stumbles forward and for a moment believes she's going to fall on the victim, but at the last second, a powerful arm grabs hold of her, stands her up and leads her out into the garden.

DS Peters gives her time. He's always given her time, as well as trust and respect. All the things she'd struggled to earn from the others. When he does speak, it's with a soft and understanding voice.

'This isn't easy for any of us,' he says, swallowing hard, and she's reminded that he was the one who had to break the news to the husband. 'Which is why we need to work together.'

She steps back from his grasp and considers his stare, wondering if he knows that she's been holding back, but all she sees in his eyes is concern.

'The team is still with you,' he continues. 'Those that you aren't always winding up.' He nods towards Dr Parker, who's watching her closely from inside the house.

'It's the one thing about him that's hard to resist,' she says, giving him a grin and a wink, before turning back to Peters.

'We all know what you went through with—' He breaks off, not needing to name the case, even though it's been more than a year. 'Perhaps this is your chance to get back on track. I mean, you saw those little boys. And the girls, last week…'

Katie nods; she's already there, thinking of the previous body, of crouching down to inspect the skull-shaped mark on the mother's inner thigh. There can no longer be any doubt of what it had represented, not now she's seen and recognised the two little marks on the second victim. The only certainty in all this swirling madness is where she needs to go. She'd thought it would never happen, that she would stick to her promise; it was the least she could do after all she'd put him through. But this – she stares through the open door into the kitchen, seeing the flash of a camera from the forensics team, then an image of the scene just as sharp in her mind – *this* has changed everything.

CHAPTER FOUR

Nathan sits alongside the wall of muddy stripes, staring at the tiny centre of the spiral and telling himself out loud over and over that he's very nearly made it. He's perched on the edge of the uppermost stair, and his legs and arms are drawn in as if trying to stop himself from leaping forward. It's a thought which has certainly crossed his mind, and the daydream had been a bad one. He's had several of late, moments of madness in between the routine, but this was so terrible, so vivid, so real, that the moment he'd woken from it and found his breath he'd started searching his entire body for cuts. Not that it was *his* body that had been under attack.

He stares at the filthy lines on the wall and counts them again, just to be sure. Perhaps knowing there's only three more days is the source of the problem, because some part of him, *that* part of him, isn't going to go without a fight. In a container in his hand is the last of the sleeping pills. He'd come here with hundreds, four hundred to be precise, legally, and not so legally, acquired. He'd foolishly believed that one a day would do the trick, but some nights he'd needed to swallow down two or three just to keep things quiet. Now there aren't enough.

A week ago, he was in the middle of heating a tin of beans and sausage – an old favourite, a treat – and was absent-mindedly playing with the lid, running the sharp edge across the inside of his wrist, remembering the last time, thinking of the next time, when he'd felt himself drifting away suddenly, drifting into a vision, and to both his horror and delight he realised there was nothing he could do to stop it. The lid of the tin had become a knife, and ahead of him was a woman, just visible through a cloud of filthy stripes spiralling towards her centre where he knew, without a trace of doubt, that he was going to plunge every inch of the blade. Either side of the woman was a child, seemingly identical in almost every way except that one wore a look of absolute horror while the other was smiling just as broadly as he was.

After it was over, and the excitement had left him, he'd cried his eyes out on the kitchen floor as he drew the tin lid across his wrist, following the lines he'd made there before. He'd known he had to stop before he'd even started. It was still too early; he hadn't reached the centre of the circle; he hadn't achieved the perfect symmetry.

CHAPTER FIVE

Katie pulls the car to the side of the road, telling herself it's to give the car's suspension a break, but in reality she's having doubts and needs a moment. She's been playing DS Peters' words over in her mind, convincing herself that this case could be her salvation, the one that will bring her back from the edge. But to do so she will have to work with someone who's already fallen over it. She pictures him and tries to remember the good times, but it's like that period of their lives has been erased, overwritten by everything that followed.

She very clearly remembers the last time she drove this road, gripped by a similar fear and on that occasion unable to stop, not until she had put more than a hundred miles between them. Now she estimates there's less than a mile until she returns, and she wonders what's waiting for her out there in the dark. Would she even know before it was too late? She used to trust her instinct, would have seen the truth the moment their eyes met, but she's started to question that judgement of late.

She turns on the light above her and finds herself checking her hair and make-up, as if adjustments to the surface might settle the mess that's underneath; as if looking like the person she was might somehow make the transformation complete. Her tired eyes reflect back, and she considers turning the light off, tipping back the chair and catching up on a few hours' rest. Surely it would be better, perhaps even safer, to find him in the daylight? She looks over her shoulder, as if she can somehow see back to

London, several hundred miles away in the dark. It reminds her there's no time to waste. The threat of what might be happening in the city matches with her desperate desire to do something about it, and her whole body stiffens, her foot catching the accelerator and making the engine in her dad's old car roar.

She turns, facing the front, and tries to take hold of the steering wheel but stops to stare at one finger: she is taken instantly back to the moment, more than a year ago, to that other case, when they had discovered the body of Steven Fish, whose wedding-ring finger had been torn free of the others, tendons snapped along with the bone. It was only a small detail of a bigger, more harrowing crime scene, but it has always stayed with Katie as a representation of what that case did: it broke her off from her most trusted partner, led to her losing her grip.

CHAPTER SIX

Nathan wakes with a dull thud echoing at the back of his mind. He stares at the ceiling, wishing he'd taken another pill, but he only has two left, one for each of the next two nights: his last two nights. He doesn't know what time it is; he hasn't known the exact time for almost a year, but through the gap in the shutters he can see that it's dark and his body clock is telling him it's somewhere near midnight. The unmistakable crunch of gravel makes him sit bolt upright in his bed. He tries to listen harder, but now the only thing he can hear is his heart.

The questions present themselves, urgent and loud. Who? How? Why? Are they lost? Could anyone ever be *this* lost? And what the fuck are they doing here now, with just three days to go until the year is up, with just three days to go until it's over?

He knows he needs to stay calm. He needs to stay still. If he remains where he is and says and does nothing, maybe they'll go away on their own. He starts to picture the outside of the house, rising as if he were a buzzard spiralling above it on the thermals, looking down on the circular path he's created from running. He'd planned to get rid of the tracks on the final day, to kick them over and cover them up, but it's too late now; someone is out there looking at them, trying to figure out who or what might have been responsible: the restless footsteps of a wild animal driven mad from being kept inside a tiny enclosure. Perhaps that's exactly what he is. Perhaps they'll feel uneasy and leave him alone. Perhaps they'll call the police.

The thought creeps up on him, as is often the case. He could easily kill this intruder. He could take a tin lid, the only sharp object there is in the house, and slice it across their neck. He could feel the hot blood pour out onto his hands and watch their eyes slowly cloud over. In one simple stroke he could change everything, bring about a beginning, not an end. He tells himself that he doesn't want to hurt this innocent stranger, but, as always, he knows what he *wants* might have nothing to do with it.

He looks at the gap in the shutter again and more rationally starts to wonder what sort of person would come to a house in the middle of nowhere in the middle of the night. Are they running from trouble? Are they looking for trouble?

Two knocks on the door. He can feel the sheets sticking to his skin. He'll wash them again when this is over, when they've realised he's not going to answer – never going to answer – when he's saved their life by doing nothing. Then he'll bury the sheets; he'll bury everything deep in the ground, just as he'd always intended.

Another knock, and the sound of a high-pitched shout. He drags the sheets from the bed and wraps them around him as he slumps down into the corner of the room. He feels the urge to shout out, to plead with them to leave him alone, but his hand shoots up to his mouth to stifle any words. He cannot afford for them to hear him.

The blood is thumping so loudly in his ears he almost misses the sharp clink of something striking the wall outside. The second one is louder, closer, and he realises they're throwing stones up at the window. He cowers again, as if the next one might strike him, as if it might bring the whole house down. At the same time his mind is whirling, working far faster than it has done in such a long time, calculating probabilities, possibilities and impossibilities. Another stone, a direct hit on the wooden shutter. He moves to stick his fingers in his ears, but he doesn't get there in time.

He hasn't heard the name in so long it takes a moment for him to realise that's what he can hear, and it's unmistakably her voice.

The whole of the outside world is pressing in on him, suffocating him in the corner of the room, but, like the true evil that it is, never finishes the job.

The desire is rising like he knew that it would: his only surprise is that it's taken this long. Perhaps it's the sleeping pill, or the shock of the unexpected, or maybe it's down to the swirling lines on the stairway, a visual reminder that he needs to hold on. The problem is, he's not seeing that wall anymore. He's seeing images of the woman outside, terrible, twisted, blood-soaked images in which she's crying, images in which she's screaming, images in which she can no longer do anything at all. And they're coming faster and faster, like he's running through a reel – click, click, click – desperately seeking the perfect snapshot to feast his eyes on, to act upon. He looks down at his hand and finds his fingers fully extended, and a name on his lips: Steven Fish. He should have known it would come to this, should have known that his worst nightmare, the discovery that had led him here, would return to guide his actions.

Suddenly he's up on his feet, the sweat-soaked sheets falling away. He's naked, as always, but his body doesn't feel like his own and he's no longer in control; he's moving forward, towards the door, down the stairs, into the tiny kitchen. He's picking up the lid of the tin from the side and passing through the room with the children's books that can't help him now. When his arm reaches out to open the locks he tries to order his other arm to make it stop, but a decision has been made without him. Before the final bolt is pulled back he feels for the edge of the tin lid, feels its sharpness and its potential.

This is it, he thinks, unstoppable, irresistible; but, as the door swings open and he steps out into the moonlight, he starts to feel something else, something so strong that it loosens his grip. On the lid. On the doorframe. On everything.

Katie.

CHAPTER SEVEN

'Nathan?' Katie almost trips on the ridge of gravel she'd stepped over to get to the door as she takes two paces back. 'Nathan, what's wrong?'

She already knows the answer, and she knows she won't be hearing it from him. The evidence is there in his eyes – eyes that had once sparkled brilliantly but now hold the same flat stare as the bodies that have brought her here. She thinks of those victims again; she's been thinking of them for most of the six hours it's taken her to get up here, talking to them, making promises she knows she can't keep. Not without Nathan.

He's completely naked, standing with his hand held high above his head, his knees bent as if he is carrying a great weight that's pushing him down, even though his fingers appear to be empty. She ought to feel threatened, but the sight just makes her sad.

'Can you hear me?'

No reaction, just a slow descent to the floor. She wants to move forward and grab him, to hold him up, but something makes her stop. He looks so different to how she had imagined, and she's pictured him plenty of times over the past year. He had always been small and slight, but now he looks like a marathon runner, with skin pulled tight over every muscle. No, she corrects herself, not a marathon runner, not with hair past his shoulders and a beard to match; he looks like a castaway. She uses the tip of her shoe to prod the strange circular track she's seen around the house, wondering if this might represent his island, the very edge of his world. She takes another step back, wanting to run from what she now sees has been a terrible mistake, one for which she holds herself entirely responsible. Looking down she spots her shoelace, snapped after she had very nearly snapped herself, when a photograph of two little schoolgirls had come to her rescue.

'You know who I am,' she says, moving forward again, feeling braver. 'You know what we've been through, *together*. I'm sorry I had to break my promise, but I had no choice. I thought you were in danger.' This had not crossed her mind before, and now she starts scanning her surroundings, searching for movement, searching for a sign that she might have been followed. There's nothing. Not a breath of air, not the tiniest twitch in the leaves on the trees.

She's just a couple of feet away now, staring down at his face and able to see a little of the man he had once been. His raised arm is shaking. She tentatively reaches out towards him, uncertain of what she hopes to achieve but acutely aware of the dangers. Her hand makes contact with his chest, and she can feel his heart beating at an impossible speed.

'Go!' he says, through tight lips. 'Before you get hurt.'

'But it's me, Katie,' she says. 'You wouldn't hurt me.'

Even as she says it she's no longer sure. She'd told herself she'd know the truth when she looked into his eyes, but she feels just as blind to the threat as she had in all their years working together. It was only at the end, when they'd found the tortured, headless body of Steven Fish that he'd allowed his mask to slip.

When she'd left him here, she hadn't even said goodbye. As she climbed into the car she'd caught him looking at her the way only a few individuals in her life ever had; people even Nathan, for all his loathing of over-simplistic terms, would have described as psychopaths. He'd told her to never come back, and she'd happily promised not to.

He's not looking at her that way now; he's not really looking at anything, but she fears at any moment his stare could sharpen.

She's been attacked before, she's been punched, and kicked, and strangled, and shot at; she's even been stabbed and left for dead on the street. The difference, she considers, with a brief glance over her shoulder, is that help was always minutes away. Nobody is going to be able to help her here. Nobody even knows where she is.

What a difference a year makes; once she would have done everything by the book, told her whole team where she would be and had backup on standby. But Nathan is not the only one who has changed since the Steven Fish case.

'You're not going to hurt me,' she says again.

Her professional training starts to kick in at last, as the little voice at the back of her head insists that something isn't right. She begins working through what she's seen and what she might not have seen, crouching down to peer at the shadows below Nathan's waist. The first and only time she'd seen this part of his body was when he'd showered back at her flat, and she'd been unable to resist peering through a gap in the door at a man she had always been fascinated by. This time there's nothing sexual about her search.

The skull shape at the top of his thigh emerges from the darkness. She's transfixed by it, just as she had been when she'd spotted an identical mark drawn in chocolate icing on the body of the first victim. The memory of it makes her stumble backwards, reaching for her breast, for the two moles, for her own connection to the second victim. The action triggers a thought, a possibility she can't believe she hasn't considered. What if she's been tricked? What if her every action has been predicted? What if two mothers had died purely to bring her to this place, to bring her and Nathan back together? She can barely bring herself to ask: 'Are we alone?'

No response. Not even a flicker. Even in the daylight there would be so many places for someone to hide: behind a tree; behind the boulders on the bank of the river; round the side of the small stone house; *in* the house. And she is unarmed.

'Where?' she manages to ask in a whisper, hoping he might give her a clue, just the tiniest twitch. He offers nothing. She can feel the anticipation of attack crawling across her shoulders, but she won't back down, won't run, no matter what. She rises to her full height and takes a step forward.

'Let's cut the crap!' she barks out at the darkness, her words stronger now and echoing deep into the valley. She holds her arms out and is relieved to find they're not shaking. 'It's just me. No weapons. No way of contacting anybody else. So, let's talk.' She can hear the tiniest of fractures in her voice as her mind flashes up a series of images. She stretches her arms wider and finds her head tipping back as she slowly spins, her feet scuffing the dirt. She's opening herself up for a gunshot.

But there's nothing. After a while she starts to feel ridiculous, lowers her arms and lets out the breath she hadn't realised she'd been holding. She turns back towards Nathan and is shocked to see him slumped in the doorway, his head so far forward it's almost touching his knees. Without thinking, she rushes forward to him and then freezes; her instinct is telling her to pull her arm back before she loses a finger, a hand, her life, but she knows there's something more important, something she will not leave without: Nathan.

She searches the shadows behind him, seeing only a chair and two piles of books. She swallows hard and grabs Nathan's forearm. He flinches at the touch, but nothing more. She inches her way towards the wrist and stops just short, letting out a gasp. There's a jagged line on the surface of the skin, but no blood. She lets go of his wrist and moves to his neck, pressing her fingers against it, trying to find a pulse beyond her own.

She never finds it. She doesn't need to. Nathan's hand is crawling across the carpet like a spider towards an object she can't yet make out in the darkness. She shifts to one side to get a clear view and can see it's a circle of metal, the lid of a tin can, perhaps.

Small, but sharp. Sharp enough to kill. Once more, everything is rewritten in an instant – the skull-shaped mark, the words of warning, the hand posed above the head. What if Nathan knew she'd caught a glimpse of him through the bathroom door? What if he's as damaged as she'd feared he might be when she'd agreed to leave him in this prison? What if he's taken that next step from fantasy to reality, from criminal psychologist to killer?

She shoots out a hand and pushes the tin lid away and he grabs her arm, suddenly strong again.

'What have you done?' she says, pressing her face up close to his, so close he cannot avoid her stare. The connection is instant, frightening, thrilling as his eyes finally focus on her. She'd always believed she could spot a killer; she looked at a suspect and felt the truth in her gut. Now she's not so sure. Seeing the change in Nathan had been bad enough, knowing she'd fooled him for all those years. Then came the conversation with her ailing dad. Not a conversation, just three mumbled words, but words that had made her doubt everything.

She's about to ask Nathan again what he's done, to push a finger into his chest and pressurise him the way she has so many suspects in this past year, but she can't escape the fact that he isn't like the others: he's like nobody else that she's ever known.

'I need you,' she says.

She can hear him draw in a long breath, the first breath she's heard him take, and it seems to instantly bring him back to life. He wraps his arms around his legs and draws them in so tight she half-expects to hear something snap.

'I'm not coming back,' he says firmly.

'Just one more case.' She wants to put some distance between them, some room to explain, but she knows if she moves that he could slip back inside and bolt the door. She'd never get him out again, not on her own, and the last thing she wants to do is involve anybody else.

Her next move is swift and precise. Slapping his hand off her arm, she reaches round and grabs him by the ponytail and drags him out into the gravel. When she forces his arm behind his back he does little to resist as she pushes his skinny arm up high onto his shoulder blades and shoves him towards her car. As she moves, she hears herself saying out loud, over and over, 'It's for the best…'

He thumps into the side of her Rover. There's a tiny struggle, but nothing she hasn't dealt with a hundred times before in her job, and, within a matter of seconds, Nathan is sprawled across the back seat. She gives up telling herself it's for the best, focusing instead on what she might have missed, returning to the possibility that the real killer is out there hiding in the darkness, laughing at the things he's pushed her to do. She retreats quickly, spinning round to search for any movement in the moonlight. There's nothing. And back in the car Nathan's fight is over, slumping into something that she hopes is sleep.

Before Katie climbs into the driver's seat, she rushes round the car to check the boot, which is full of the clothes she tossed in there a few weeks ago: filthy clothes from a filthy night with another man whose name she can't remember. She feels a flush of embarrassment at the latest bit of evidence of her life's decline. *At least these clothes might now come in useful,* she thinks, climbing back in the car. She turns the key with a whispered prayer, and the Rover coughs a couple of times before roaring into life.

CHAPTER EIGHT

Nathan opens his eyes, feels the pain and closes them instantly. Something is terribly wrong. He is not in his bed. In fact, he's not in his house at all. He lies still, barely even daring to breathe, but the headache and the churning in his stomach compel him to draw into an even tighter ball. He becomes aware of a steady rocking, of something digging into his back and of the surface beneath him falling away at the side. If he moves, he would slip over the edge.

There's a smell beyond his own that he is fearful of. It's a smell from his childhood. He opens his eyes at the familiar crackle of wrapping.

'Chocolate?' comes a voice from out of nowhere that instantly feels too close. He can hear rustling, and he moves to cover his ears. 'Are you okay? Do you know where you are?'

He does, finally. He's recognised the whine of an engine and the suspension creaking under him. He's also started to remember where he was before: he was standing naked in the doorway to his house, and she was in front of him, her face only inches away. He was holding the tin lid above him, ready to drive it rapidly down.

'Take me back!' he cries.

'I'm sorry,' she says. 'I can't.'

Under the edge of the blanket he can see the door, and imagines it being flung open and his body tumbling out onto the road. He doesn't care about the damage to himself – as long as it's terminal – but he can't bear the thought of her standing over him, thinking it's her fault.

'I don't want you getting hurt.'

It's the truth. He doesn't want anyone hurt, but especially her, because he knows who she is; he can picture her as clearly as she was a year ago. And he knows it was a year, almost to the day, because she was there at the beginning of what was supposed to be the end.

The car jumps and shudders underneath him and he can feel the swell of blood in his head as they turn sharply and pull to a stop. He hears her seat belt pop.

'I need you with me because I need your help. A new case… a final case.'

Her words continue to tumble over and over in his mind. It's like hearing a foreign language. The only voice he has heard in the last year has been his own, as he worked his way through the pile of children's books or found himself shouting at his own reflection.

'I don't know what he wants from us,' she continues. 'But this is definitely about us. He left some clues, some terrible…' she pauses again, and he knows she's filtering out the bad stuff. 'You have to believe that I didn't want to come here. I was going to stick to my promise. I keep my promises.' She clears her throat, and her voice moves further away. 'But this is, this is… as soon as you see you'll understand.' He can hear the emotion thickening her voice, and he wants to reach out to offer comfort, but one hand is firmly gripped within the other. 'What do you need?' she asks, her voice firming. 'A drink? Food? I've got some clothes in the boot. They're not clean and most likely a little big, but they'll do for now.'

He can hear something being placed down in the footwell. The proximity of her fingers makes him roll away so that he's pressed against the back of the seat, but also so that the blanket gets twisted and his legs and the top of his head are revealed. At least the things he fears most remain covered – his sharpening eyes, his darkening thoughts. The desire has been there from the moment he woke in the car, a threatening whisper in the background that is now beginning to find its voice.

He reaches out and touches the edge of a plastic water bottle, snatching it back under his blanket.

'Have some chocolate, too,' she says.

'I need to go back.'

'You're the only one that can help me with this.'

'I need to go back!'

'It won't be long. Just give me a day or two. Three at most.'

'Back!' he says. The focus had been on nothing but keeping his hands under control, but now he finds he's let go of the water bottle and is bending his fingers back further and further. It's an act that takes him to the crime scene that had changed everything.

'I know this is a risk,' says Katie. 'For you and for me. But it has to be taken. There is no choice.'

He can hear the aggression and remembers the danger he had seen in her too. He feels something approaching fear and this time embraces it.

'You don't understand,' he says.

'Of course I fucking do! Do you think I would have left you back there otherwise? It's you that doesn't understand. This case can save us.'

'Only one thing can save me…' he says softly, releasing the tension on his fingers and moving to the scars on the inside of his wrist.

'Three days,' says Katie. 'That's all I'm asking. And you know me, you know I can keep you out of harm's way for that long. I won't let you out of my sight. And then I'll bring you back.'

Three days. It can't be coincidence; she had taught him not to believe in those. He can also see an opportunity. He can trust her. Up until her breaking the promise to never come back, he'd trusted her more than anybody else. Perhaps this visit was meant to be. One last chance to do something right.

'Cuffs,' he says.

It takes her a moment to understand, even longer to agree. When the cuffs are on he starts to breathe more easily. He can only see the back of her head as she fumbles for something in the centre console, but it's clear she's changed. She's always looked so immaculate, a reflection of the precision of her work, but now her hair is tangled and her clothes look like they've just been lifted from the floor.

'I've got to phone in,' she says, revealing what she's been looking for. 'I had no reception before, and if someone has been back at your house my colleagues will need to take a look.'

'No!' he says, reaching out. 'No calls. No colleagues.'

He can picture them now, picking through his stuff, filthy fingers on previously spotless surfaces; touching his books, wondering, and perhaps laughing at the life he had been living; nothing dirty, nothing sharp, no temptations, no links to the past. Although it's the future he's thinking of now, of the perfect plan that must be protected at any cost.

'I was alone,' he says. 'There was never anybody else.' He checks the cuffs again and tests their strength as he sneaks another glance from under the blanket. It's more than her appearance that is different; now she's taking risks she would never have taken, acting out of desperation, not desire. He wants to understand what's wrong. And he can't resist the urge to help.

'You have to promise me three things.' He doesn't wait for her to agree, but continues while his voice still holds firm. 'First, you will not tell anyone about that place. Not now. Not ever. Second, I will be back there in three days whether or not I've helped you. Finally, you will never come and check on me again.' As he waits for her reply he buries his head in the blanket, shutting out any trace of light.

CHAPTER NINE

They arrive in London at a quarter past five in the morning, having driven for more than six hours. For the final three Nathan has been sitting upright, staring out of the window like a child seeing the world for the first time. He's wearing the clothes she found in the boot – handed over with a blush and no explanation – and the cuffs he'd demanded. He seems far more relaxed since she put them on him and agreed to his terms. She, on the other hand, is having trouble wrapping her head around what might happen when her three days are up, unable to ignore the lines of thickened skin she'd felt on his wrist.

Her most basic questions have gone unanswered so far. It makes her want to shake him. It makes her want to scream. What holds her back are the glimpses, the occasional moments when she glances in the mirror and sees who he used to be, sitting up straight, his eyes wide and alive, seeming to catch and process everything. This was how she'd seen him the first time they'd met; it was what had willed her to approach him.

'I'm taking you to my flat,' she says. It's not what she wants to do; she wants to get on with the investigation straight away; if they have less than three days to try and catch this monster then every second counts. But they'll have to wait to visit the crime scenes, and by making contact with her team she's given up a number of freedoms already.

She's been ordered into the station at 11 a.m, which means they'll be staring at Nathan, wondering and drawing their own conclusions. Despite his betrayal, despite her fear of him, she feels protective.

'You can get washed and dressed into clothes a little better fitting.' She hates that there are more men's clothes at her flat, but she's not about to waste her breath on lies, not when all she has to do is look in the rear-view mirror to see how far they both have fallen.

They're on the edge of the city now, fields replaced by street-lights, tower blocks, high walls, fences and graffiti. She remembers how he'd told her once that he loved the city at night, loved walking while it slept and soaking up the stillness. It reminds her of what she would have done as a child, sitting at her bedroom window, looking out at all the shimmering lights below, wondering when, and sometimes *if*, her dad would return.

They arrive half an hour later. She's taken a couple of calls from DS Peters during the journey, keeping up to speed with developments, but remaining vague about her own movements. She feels herself getting sucked back into Nathan's draw, like she needs to be fully committed to him, to his craziness, to his secrets, and everyone else is pushed to one side. It used to be a winning combination; now there are no such guarantees.

*

Her home is not a home. Six months back she was forced to move from her beloved riverside apartment in Kingston to a far cheaper part of town. Inside the poky seventh-storey flat are half-unpacked boxes piled up in the tiny entrance, food and plates spread across what little surface space is available in the kitchen and empty booze bottles that have even made it to the bathroom. She thinks of the other guys she brought back (before she started insisting on going to their places instead) and the look on their face as they took it all in in the light of day. If they'd known what she'd done for a living they might have asked questions, wondered where all the money had gone, but she'd kept quiet about that, kept quiet about everything, other than her desire for them to hurry up and leave.

She's annoyed to find she cares far more about what Nathan thinks than any of those strangers. Not that she tries to explain. She can put on an act, just as he had done, pretend this is normal, pretend this doesn't bother her, pretend that she doesn't blame him for his part. Not that there's any need; he seems totally oblivious as she guides him to the sofa still clinging on to the blanket she'd thrown over his cuffs, her every touch making him flinch.

She thinks for a moment about turning on the TV like she normally would on returning from work in the early hours and knowing there's no chance of sleep, but she worries it might be the news, or a violent thriller, and what such scenes might trigger in Nathan.

Leaving him curled up in the corner of the sofa, Katie goes to the kitchen where she pulls out a tin of beans, pausing as she peels back the lid. She runs her finger along the edge, pressing far harder than necessary to test its sharpness and feeling the skin part, just as it might have done on her neck. She shakes off the image and puts on a plaster as the beans start to boil, then, apologising for not having anything else in the house, places the food in front of her guest, watching carefully for his reaction. The smile makes her skin crawl. It's the same smile she'd seen when he'd finally let his mask slip, when they'd stood together over the headless body of Steven Fish. In all her years as a detective she'd never seen a crime scene like it, and when she'd turned to Nathan for support, that same terrible smile had appeared before her.

He eats slowly, his cuffed hands rising and falling, and when he's done he pushes the plate away. He yawns, and she points a shaking arm at the bathroom, wondering what kind of monster she's invited into her house.

While he's in there she stands with one ear to the door, listening to him scrub at his skin. The water stops, and she hears him open the medicine cabinet. She's about to knock, to ask what he's up to, when he appears in the doorway holding out his hands, one of which contains two white pills.

'To help me sleep,' he explains, looking at her with heavy eyes that suggest he'll need no assistance.

'But we've only got a few hours.'

'Before what?'

'Before we begin.'

He nods and turns away, carefully placing the pills at the back of the sink.

When he's in bed and wrapped up under her dirty sheets, she reaches for the light.

'One more thing,' he calls out, lifting his cuffed hands.

'Of course,' she says, reluctantly stepping forward and reaching into her pocket for the key.

Nathan shakes his head and jabs his hands towards the door. 'I want that locked too.'

'The key is just here,' she says, gesturing towards it.

'From the outside,' he says, pulling the sheets up over his head.

*

As the lock clicks she feels the relief. At the same time, she's telling herself to trust her instinct, to believe that it hasn't left her entirely and that he's still there somewhere behind that sickening smile. Yes, he had fooled her over the years, but there's no way he could have done those things to those poor women, no way he could have walked all those miles to the nearest town to catch a bus to the nearest city, then hired a car, or jumped on a train for the long journey south. There's no way he could have piped chocolate icing onto their bodies so that she, and she alone, would know she had to see him. There's no way that those marks on his wrist were a sign of guilt, evidence of a struggle with internal demons, a struggle he had already lost. There's no way that, when she takes him to the crime scenes, she'll be taking him to places he's already been. *No way*, she thinks, bending back her fingers till the knuckles pop.

CHAPTER TEN

Nathan sits in the interview room in a pair of cuffs, sweating and twitching like the guiltiest man who's ever been invited in there. He's wearing a pair of corduroy trousers, a pale blue sweatshirt and Nike trainers. All are in need of a wash but fit him well. He'd watched Katie retrieve them from the bottom of her wardrobe, a wardrobe that most of her other clothes hadn't seemed to make it to. He'd wondered for a moment why she had men's clothes in there and had felt the tiniest flutter in his chest, although that was nothing in comparison to the swirling in the pit of his stomach once he'd found out where they were going. He'd wanted to protest, to demand that she agree to a few more promises, but it was clear from the look on her face that the time for negotiation was over.

She'd maintained that same look in the hour it took them to eat breakfast, get dressed, trim his beard to an acceptable length and drive to the police station, and she's wearing it still as she sits on the opposite side of the table from him. The one thing he had been able to insist upon was keeping the cuffs. On the way through the building several concerned-looking colleagues had pulled Katie to one side. He can't for the life of him imagine what explanation she could have offered.

Back when he was working as a criminal psychologist, he only ever came to the station when he had to. He remembers how increasingly hard it had become to look into a killer's eyes, knowing how close he was to being just the same as them. Worse even; most of them had motive, most had something to gain, most had limits to their imagination.

The room they're in is small and dark, with no windows and a very thick door. It reminds him of the psychiatric units he's helped to send so many people to, and of the times he'd considered finding a way to get himself locked up in there as well. What held him back was the thought of losing control, not of his freedom but of his story, and the one person who could never find out about his madness.

The man sitting next to Katie is in his late fifties, maybe older, well over six foot, with a broad nose, bad skin and a gut pushing his shirt to the limit. Nathan vaguely recognises him from the last time, but he can't put a name to the face even though Katie introduced him when he entered the room. She's leaning across the table towards him, and he can tell she's on the verge of clicking her fingers in front of his face to get his attention. As in the old days, she is the exact opposite of him: all focus and no distraction from the job at hand. The difference is that this time he has no idea what that job might be.

'Yesterday, a body was found in West Molesey,' says Katie. 'It was a thirty-eight-year-old mother of two, Sarah Cleve. I don't suppose that name means anything to you?'

He shakes his head and pushes out a long breath. During the long journey down, and the hours lying fully awake in Katie's flat, he's had time to work through the possibilities, to try and figure out why Katie might have felt the need to hold back, and he'd managed to convince himself there was a personal connection, that the victim was going to be someone he knew. Unfortunately, the relief he now feels at that not being the case slips out in the faintest smile.

But when he looks up at Katie the smile disappears.

'Her two little boys were with their father,' she spits through gritted teeth. 'And thank fuck they weren't there. Thank fuck the neighbour found her. Thank fuck they couldn't see her, because it was…' She looks away, at the same time revealing a face he'd almost forgotten, a face that betrays both anger and unbearable sadness. It's the face she would always adopt when standing over a body with him by her side, trying to figure out where they might go next. 'It wasn't pleasant,' she continues, calming slightly and running a hand through her hair, but he's already picturing the body of a thirty-eight-year-old mum, twisted and torn apart. He's already calling on all the other images of bodies, real and imagined, that he has stored in his brain to make a collage of the perfect murder, not one inch of the flesh untouched, the insides out and spread across the floor.

Katie is looking down at her notepad. 'We've just found the car. It was dumped at the Four Oaks Caravan Park on the outskirts of Henley.'

When she looks at him he can tell she's searching for a reaction to this information. He hadn't been expecting to have one, not now he knows the victim is a stranger, but the name triggers a memory which rushes into him without warning. Suddenly he can see all four members of his family squeezed inside a tiny CI Sprite caravan, their Volvo 240 Estate parked alongside. Bacon and eggs for breakfast, cooked on a stove outside. Long walks, early nights, games of chess and bedtime stories, barked orders, stifled giggles, secret pacts, a sense of security, a sense of eternity. Again, there's nothing he can do to stop the smile spreading. Then he hears the screech of a chair, and he's back in the room.

'You know the place?' asks Katie, leaning across the table so close he can smell the same soap he'd used to scrub his own skin earlier that morning. Distracted by this connection between them, he fails to respond immediately, and when he finally does, implored by Katie's wide-eyed stare, it's not the answer he'd intended to give.

'No.'

'You're sure you don't?' she asks.

'I'm sure.'

'And you don't know the woman?'

The images flash up again in his mind. He swallows hard, his feet shifting constantly under the table as he desperately tries to picture himself running circles round his house. But he feels so far away from there now.

'I thought you were going to help!'

'I'll help when I can.'

'Where were you the day before yesterday at around eight in the evening?'

Nathan can clearly see the truth of it now: she thinks he might be guilty. He realises it's probably all his fault; he had warned her not to trust him and he knows his behaviour is strange. There's also the way he was acting a year ago. He might never have shared his darkening thoughts and desires, but once he'd seen the body of Steven Fish, once he'd seen what losing control really looked like, he'd started to feel himself letting go. In that split second Katie spotted the change and saw him for what he really was. It was why she'd agreed to let him live in isolation, why she'd agreed to break off all contact without even saying goodbye. She'd probably believed him capable then, but hoped he might never act on his impulses. Now she's dragged him back, believing that's exactly what he's done. Nathan knows there's every reason for her to suspect him, and yet, despite it all, despite his behaviour, despite knowing himself and how close he has come to committing such a crime, he feels utterly betrayed that she's questioning him like this. That she of all people can think he would ever let the monster inside him win.

'I was at home,' he snaps, 'where I'm returning very soon.'

'I thought you came down to help us find this monster?' This time it's the other policeman speaking.

'So did I,' Nathan says quietly, pulling at his cuffs.

'Have you ever seen me naked?' asks Katie.

It's a question that takes him by surprise, and he can't quite look her in the eye.

'No,' he says. He wonders if this is for the record, something to set things straight with her boss and end the speculation that had started to grow the longer the two of them worked together.

'The man we're after has.' She presses a finger against the base of her left breast. He follows this movement out of the corner of his eye, feeling his cheeks blush. He looks across at the other policeman, wondering if he's feeling similarly embarrassed. Instead, he finds the older man staring at Katie with a look of confusion, as if this is news to him too.

'There are two marks on the second body that exactly match moles on my chest,' says Katie. 'They were made with dabs of chocolate icing.'

Nathan instantly thinks back to the chocolate he'd been given in the car: a test, no doubt, and another connection to the crime. Before he can stop himself, he licks his lips, thinking of that sweet taste, a taste that he'd frequently turned to when feeling stressed. It took him back to his childhood, when a chocolate bar had been waiting for him every day after his return from school. Then he thinks of the chocolate on Katie's body, and this time manages to keep his tongue under control, in part because he knows she's looking now, but also because his mouth has suddenly gone bone dry.

It was only a few months back, so he should have remembered straight away, but with all the distraction, with the running and the reading and the sleeping through the night, his mind can't call on memories the way that it used to. He's seeing it clearly now, though, every detail of the daydream that had risen as he'd stood stirring a pan of beans on the hob. It had been a frenzy, an ecstatic blur of blood and guts and, at the end, when everything was still, including the woman who had been at the centre of it, he'd marked the body with melted chocolate, following the path of the filthy streaks on the wall, spiralling round and round.

He shakes his head violently, wiggling his feet inside the slightly oversized trainers Katie had given him, feeling the hardened skin from all that running and reminding himself that he had evidence. Every single day he ran and drew a mark on the wall, proof that he was all the way up there in Scotland, waiting for both the year and his life to end, and never down here, killing people.

'We don't have any suspects yet,' says Katie, looking away.

It's clear that if that's what he is to her, she's not sharing this information with her team.

'But we do have another murder to talk about.'

He can hear her stand up and move towards the far wall, breathing out slowly.

'A week ago, another mother of two, this time with young girls, was killed in an almost identical way.'

Nathan can feel his forearms tighten and, for a second, fears he'll find a way to pop the cuffs open. 'With the same marks?'

Katie doesn't answer immediately, instead she shifts uneasily on her seat, the briefest of looks at the man sitting next to her.

'This is about you and me, Nathan,' she says, locking onto his gaze. 'It might be somebody we've come up against before. He knows about the work we've done. It's like he's taken elements from each of the crimes we've investigated together and sewn them into the crime scenes.'

'Each?' says Nathan, lifting his cuffed hands and bending back his fingers, unable to hide the tremor in his voice.

'Not that,' she says, making the connection. 'But many of the others.'

Nathan lowers his head and closes his eyes, wishing he could shut it all out, maybe take a sleeping pill as he'd done so many times to block the images he'd started seeing at night: bodies broken and ripped apart, elements from all of the crimes he'd ever investigated. But there's hope in the way Katie has started looking at him again, as if he's a partner, not a suspect. He doesn't know what's suddenly caused things to change back, and he's not about to ask, but it's made him more confident in his innocence, too, reminding him of the remarkable things he used to be able to do: the things he could see that he should never have been able to see; all the crimes he's acted out that he never committed; all the killers he's put away.

'Bollocks to this,' Katie says, standing up, the metal chair scraping across the floor, creating a high-pitched screech that causes him to flinch. 'I've not lost it completely. There's no point wasting what little time we have here. Nathan and I are going to go and do what we're good at.' She turns to the bigger policeman, who looks as uncomfortable with this idea as he had with her sudden outburst. 'Relax, Mike, this is entirely on me.'

The words take their time again, fighting their way from ear to understanding. When Nathan finally figures out what's happening he grips the table leg tightly and lets out a groan. He's already picturing the things they'll see. He's horribly vulnerable here without his routine, and he knows that as soon as they step outside the door, as soon as they step back into the world he had thought he'd left behind, it will only get worse.

CHAPTER ELEVEN

'What the *hell* has happened to you?'

It's a familiar question, one Katie has asked herself on a hundred occasions, staring into the mirror at a woman she barely recognises. This time, however, the words are coming from her boss. He's a big man, broad at the shoulders and fighting the spread, dressed as immaculately as ever in his tightly pressed uniform, his hat tucked under his arm.

'I think you're aware of the difficulties I've been having,' she says, maintaining the flat tone that she knows annoys him most.

'That's not what I'm talking about. You know full well we've given you more than enough support in that area.'

'You can name him, you know,' she says, moving in closer. 'He was a friend of yours.'

The big man coughs and inches back. 'All I'm saying is you could have taken some leave, should have...' He stops himself just in time, perhaps seeing her anger rising to dangerous levels. 'Instead you insisted on working.'

'And commitment to the job is a problem, is it?'

'The problem,' says Superintendent Taylor, seeming to gain another couple of inches in height, 'besides your general attitude, and the rumours I'm constantly hearing of inappropriate behaviour, is that your work is not even close to what it used to be. I could forgive almost anything if you were still bringing me the results.'

'My partner is back,' she says, nodding towards Nathan, who's standing at the end of the corridor outside the interview room, shuffling from foot to foot. 'We'll get you what you want.'

'There's plenty of questions to answer there, too,' says Taylor, not turning to look and lowering his voice to a whisper. 'Where has he been? I understand the work took its toll and he needed to get away, but I think you also know…' This time he does glance over his shoulder. 'Well, I've always felt he's the type that needs to be supervised.'

'I know what you felt, sir,' says Katie, placing just enough emphasis on the *sir* to let him know it hasn't come from respect. 'But you always trusted me, trusted my view on him. That view hasn't changed.' She struggles to hold her boss's gaze, and to keep it from Nathan, scared whatever doubt she might still be feeling could reveal itself on the surface. 'Or perhaps,' she adds, 'you just trusted in the results.'

'Your dad brought the results.' The superintendent pauses and the uncomfortable cough returns. 'He was the best detective I've ever worked with. Achieved so much without ever letting his standards slip, without ever crossing a single line.'

'Yes,' says Katie, with a sigh that she hopes disguises her discomfort. 'I've heard it from you and many others. What's your point?'

'My point,' says the superintendent, running a hand across his crown from a ruler-straight parting as he looks down at his shoes, the tips polished to a sharp reflection, 'is that he'd hate to see you this way.'

'And I hate to see him how he is now,' says Katie, lifting a hand to her knotted mess of hair. 'But I guess that's life.'

'You know what this case represents for you, don't you, detective? There have been more than enough warnings.'

'*More than enough*,' she says. 'Now, if you'll excuse me, I have things to do.'

Katie takes a step into the room. When she turns to urge Nathan to follow she finds his eyes are on everything but the body ahead of them, taking in every spotless corner and polished surface, blinding himself on the lights above. They're alone in the mortuary, the coroner making a swift exit for a cigarette break when he saw the cuffs on Nathan, so Katie grabs Nathan and pulls him up to her, waiting till his eyes finally settle on hers.

'Sarah Cleve,' she says, pointing towards the table in the centre of the room. 'Two days ago.'

'How do you know it's the same person responsible?'

'Come, and I'll show you.'

She pulls at the handcuffs again, but this time he resists. 'I can't.'

'Of course you can,' she says firmly. 'What are you afraid of?' She sees him glance across at a tray on the far side of the room filled with an array of objects for cutting bodies apart and wonders if she has her answer.

'Can you tell me what you're feeling?' she asks, tentatively.

'No,' he says, turning his eyes to the floor, where his feet are twisted awkwardly inwards.

She wonders if she even wants to know.

'You're the only one who can help us here, Nathan. We were a team. We did good together.'

'I'm not that man anymore,' he says, slowly shaking his head. He sneaks the briefest of looks at the body, but it's enough to send him stumbling backwards into a low table behind, his arm shielding his eyes and face. 'I can't.'

'Of course you can. You've seen far worse.' She's thinking of those bodies now, perfectly sliced from head to toe, decapitated, bottomless, burnt to a crisp, squashed to something resembling a pizza, a pool of ooze identifiable only by the smell.

She waits for him to look up at her. It takes a long time, but she stands there patiently. When he does finally catch her eye, she directs him downwards with her finger, towards the inner thigh of the corpse, then traces a shape in the air just above it.

'The first body had something here painted in chocolate icing,' she says. 'It matched the birthmark I saw on you the other night. I'd also caught a glimpse of it before, a long time ago…'

She feels the heat on her cheeks as she watches him reach back and grip the edge of the flimsy-looking table, forcing it to take so much of his weight it's a wonder the legs don't buckle like his.

'That's why I needed to come and get you. I haven't told the rest of my team everything yet, not until I know more, but this is about us. And I can't deal with it alone. I need you. I need the old you.'

She imagines he's tried to forget this part of himself over the last year, but he cannot have lost his special gift for reading the behaviour of the killers they hunted. He offers the briefest of glances; then, twisting his head, eyes widening, he takes a few tentative steps forward. He stops a stride short of the table, his shackled arms held out towards the stomach where the hundred tiny cuts spiral in towards the belly button.

'What the fuck is that!' he whispers, sliding slowly towards the floor, suddenly white as the room. 'He can't have…'

'Who can't have…? What have you found?' Her voice is rising as the questions return. Has he fooled her again? Has she fooled herself? She wants to ask him straight out, to take one of his fingers and bend it back until he talks, to use the case that had once ended his deceit to make him reveal the truth to her now. But she can't.

Instead, she leads him silently outside, watching him drawing in the cool morning air and doing the same herself. He doesn't speak for more than five minutes, but she gives him all the time he wants because this isn't so different from the old days. Back then he would stand over a crime scene as though he were asleep. Then would come the tiny twitches in his body, the twisting of his arms and balling of his fists. Sometimes he would even cry out, drawing the attention of those around him, before she learned to make them leave. It was the words that followed that would delight and frighten Katie in equal measure. It was as though she were listening to the killer recounting his crime, revealing his mistakes.

'It's impossible,' Nathan says, finally.

'What is? What did you see in there? Did you recognise those markings on the stomach?'

He lifts his forefinger then lowers it a few inches, as if drawing a line in the air. He repeats this action several times, before suddenly re-emerging from whatever trance he'd entered and vigorously shaking his head.

'No. No, it means nothing to me. I'd just forgotten… forgotten how bad…' His eyes snap across to hers, pleading. 'Take me back.'

Katie feels the anger rising, threatening to spill over. She won't be taken in by his acting this time. He's hiding things from her. He had recognised the pattern on the stomach of the victim. Even back at the station, when he claimed not to know the caravan park where they'd found the first victim's car, it had been a lie. She'd kept that from her colleagues; she'd kept all her suspicions to herself, holding on to two hopes. First, that her instinct hadn't failed her. Secondly, that solving this case might save them both. There will be no solution to any of this if he packs up his lies and heads back to Scotland.

'Sarah Cleve had two young boys,' she says, her voice shaking with emotion. 'Tate and Felix. One of them has long-standing health issues. He's small, and weak. Sarah was a nurse, caring for cancer patients, which is how she met her husband, someone she had helped to survive. She loved Pinot Noir, tending her roses, Philip Glass and the *Times* crossword.' Back in the day she would feed these details into Nathan so he could use them to populate his reimagining of the scene. This time, she wants him to choke on them. 'We can go and see all this if you want, we can see what you're walking away from.' She's almost shouting now, desperately fighting the urge to grab him by the collar and shake him, aware that she's being watched by the coroner as he stands leaning against a doorway with no cigarette, and no idea, she imagines, which of the two of them he ought to be scared of now. 'And what the fuck are you going back to? That wasn't a life. That certainly wasn't *your* life. And you're forgetting that I know you. Okay, so there were bits you manged to hide, but not everything. You were never satisfied, always pushing, always learning. How can you bear to lock yourself away up there—' She stops abruptly, aware that Nathan has lifted a hand. It's his right hand, several pale lines of scarring on his wrist evidence of those times when he really couldn't bear it.

'It's not my home I want to go back to,' he says.

He looks up and holds her stare, and she can see she's read it all wrong yet again.

CHAPTER TWELVE

The police cordon is still out the front of the first victim's house, as is a police car, the driver of which Katie recognises as a young PC she very nearly slept with on a drunken night out. The recognition is mutual and also useful, as she's able to shepherd Nathan by without a word. They'd come to the house of Sally Brooks, rather than the more recent victim, to avoid the crowds that she knew would still be there. She also wanted to take him to the place where the body had been marked as his had been marked; one at birth, the other at death.

The house is small. *Far too small for two children*, she thinks as she moves down the hallway, stepping over a floppy doll with no head. She doesn't remember seeing it before, but then there are plenty of toys scattered around. Nathan suddenly seems unsteady on his feet, and she has to take more of his weight as she guides him forward. Strands of his hair are stuck to his forehead, and his hands are balled against his cuffs.

They head towards the kitchen, passing a tiny living room with more toys scattered across the carpet and allowing a glance at a school photo on the wall. The sweet photo of the two girls seems to both strengthen and weaken Katie at the same time as she thinks of the ones she used to bring home to her dad every year, where she'd tried but always failed to follow the photographer's instructions. Like her, these girls will have trouble remembering the one person who will never get to see them grow up.

The forensics team have been and gone, but there's plenty of evidence of their work: dusted surfaces, measurement sticks and chalk footprints of items that have been taken away. One of those things was the knife; the other, the body, twisted into a pose, like the second victim, Sarah Cleve.

She watches Nathan carefully, remembering that little smile when she'd fed him beans last night. This time his face is pale, stretched in disbelief.

'Along with the chocolate mark,' he says, his hand hovering at his waist, 'was the stomach…?'

'Not lots of little cuts like the second victim,' she says, the image flashing up again, causing her to swallow hard. 'But the same circular pattern made with her intestines, which had been pulled out and carefully arranged into a spiral.'

He nods a couple of times, then goes through a sudden and familiar transformation. His face becomes expressionless and his shoulders sag forward as he releases a long breath. He remains frozen in this position for thirty seconds or more until his body starts to jolt and buckle. It would be easy to believe he were having a fit, were it not for his eyes darting around the room, taking in everything, then closing tightly.

She steps silently away, knowing better than to disturb him. She can hear a bird calling outside; it seems incongruous, as does the gentle ticking of a cat-shaped clock on the wall. It feels as though everything should have stopped.

For a moment, she wishes she *could* stop everything, to curl up in the corner of the room and give up, as she has so many times of late. Her stamina always came from her dad, but his, too, has now ebbed away, the Alzheimer's leaving him just a shell. She's picturing him now, wondering if she shouldn't have gone to visit, but she knows it wouldn't make any difference, beyond easing her guilty conscience.

Caught up in her own thoughts, she almost misses Nathan slowly moving forward. He knows what to avoid, what not to touch. He might have forgotten many things, but professionally it appears he is still intact. He walks over to the far side of the kitchen, arms outstretched. She wants to ask him what he's doing, but thinks better of it. He crouches down and touches the front of the fridge, close to where a tiny streak of blood can still be seen. Then he raises his finger a few inches and lightly taps the door. She had been the one to spot the blood in the swirls of colour of a child's painting, and it seems Nathan has also somehow spotted it, even with the picture no longer there. He stands and moves to the far corner of the kitchen, touching an already printed work surface, before tapping the top of a half-eaten bag of bread, twisted tight. Then, with the knuckle of a single finger for balance, he rises on tiptoes and leans over, peering down into a shiny toaster. He drops down and turns towards her with a nod. She joins him, her heart racing as she pulls on a pair of latex gloves. She follows his lead and leans over the toaster. At first she can't see it, it's clogged up with so many burnt crumbs, but finally she spots the pale corner of a piece of paper. Next to the toaster is a pair of wooden tongs, like an oversized pair of tweezers, used to pull out things that are too hot to touch. With effort, she manages to slip them down the nearest gap and grab the paper, drawing it slowly out. Strangely, ridiculously, she's reminded of the child's game, Operation, she would play as a kid and half-expects an electric buzz to sound as she brushes the sides. The paper finally comes free and she lifts it, holding it up in the air while she retrieves a small evidence bag.

'We need to read it,' says Nathan.

'We need to do this right.'

'I don't have time,' he says in a monotone, glancing up at the clock, a way to remind her there's just two days more.

'There could be fibres on here, some tiny clue.'

'That is the clue,' he says, gesturing at the paper. 'And it's far from tiny.'

Once more she senses this could all be part of his game: bring her back here to the scene of his crime and find a clue that nobody else has been able to, then push her into breaking the rules. 'You know who left it?'

'No,' he says, lowering his head. 'But it seems he knows me. Beans and sausage on toast is my favourite… I've been eating it up there.' Nathan points to the ceiling to signify the long journey north.

'So, he's been watching you in Scotland?'

He quickly shakes his head, and she can see what she takes to be a flash of frustration, annoyance that he might have just slipped up. 'I told you, nobody has been there other than you. Even if they had, they couldn't have seen what I was doing. I've never opened the shutters.'

'And you haven't been outside?' she says tentatively, thinking of the tracks around the house.

'Not to eat.'

He lifts his hands to cover his face, fingertips digging into his skin. Instinct is telling her he's holding back, pretending to be lost and confused. She finds herself looking across at the toaster, retracing the connection he had somehow made. 'How did you keep the bread fresh? Did you have a freezer up there?'

'I-I meant from before. I used to eat it before.'

'I don't remember that,' she says. She'd always been very careful about what she was eating: plenty of greens, plenty of raw, anything to try and gain an advantage in her work. Nathan had eaten whatever and whenever he'd liked, always ravenous after they'd visited a crime scene.

Their diet might have been different, but their commitment to the work had been the same. Late nights, weekends – it seemed to be all they were living for. Katie had even stopped visiting her dad regularly, choosing instead to go through old case notes with

Nathan, searching for clues. As a result, she'd missed the clues with her dad, and the very first signs of his decline.

Perhaps it's remembering this that causes her to push on, to touch upon a subject that she knows will upset him. 'Do you mean you ate them when you were a child?'

The look he gives her is one of shock. She'd agreed from the very start of their partnership that she wouldn't pry into the upbringing that had obviously troubled him. Even after he'd gone she'd resisted her natural urge to go digging around behind his back; wanting to forget him, scared she might find further evidence of how damaged he really was.

'You used to be good at keeping promises,' he snaps.

'And you used to be good at playing a part. Perhaps you still are.'

'I want what we've always wanted,' he says. 'What you've always *craved*.' He draws out that final word until she shifts her attention elsewhere. 'And if you want a win here then that should be our focus.' He jabs a finger at the paper she's still holding between the tongs. 'Not me.'

She pulls it back, hearing it crumple against her side, a sound that seems to have the same effect on her insides. 'I won't risk this sicko getting away on a technicality.'

'If we catch him in the next two days, then—' He cuts himself off, but she's seen enough already, seen that excitement sparkle in his eyes, certain that remarkable imagination of his is currently not being used to recreate a past crime, but a future one.

His gaze narrows the way hers had just a second before. 'You know it too. The rules don't count anymore, do they? It ends the way it has to end for us.'

Her thoughts turn to her dad again, picturing his face as it used to be, and as it is now. The difference is remarkable, shattering. As is the view she has of him as a person on those days when she believes what he said, when she accepts his confession. Might those three words he whispered to her have said something about her own potential to step over the line?

'No,' she says firmly. 'That's not me. Nor is contaminating evidence any more than I have to. You've heard me tearing into my guys at the slightest mistake.' She adds the last bit less for Nathan's benefit than her own. She opens the evidence bag and lays it on the work surface, before using the tongs to place the paper inside. It's a small piece with pale blue lines that run both vertically and horizontally. Leaning over and using the tip of the tongs she then carefully prizes the fold open. Nathan appears alongside her, bending over. He's standing close, and she can't help but notice the block of knives within his reach. But she finds her focus again, keeping her hand from shaking as she pushes open the paper and the words appear.

Home is where the heart is.

It's written in thick, hesitant strokes, as if by someone young, or very old. She glances across at Nathan and finds his eyes are wide and his face is white, just as when he'd heard about the caravan park, or seen the swirling cuts on the stomach of Sarah Cleve, or when he'd first spotted the beans on the floor behind them.

'You recognise the writing?'

Nathan stands straight and moves away, shaking his head several times, holding his cuffed hands down at his waist and avoiding her gaze. She's about to put the question to him again, once more convinced he's holding back valuable information, when she hears footsteps in the corridor behind, accompanied by a voice calling out: 'Please, sir, please, you really can't go in there!'

Katie moves quickly to the door and sees a tall man pushing past the duty PC and walking towards her. She instantly recognises him as the husband of Sally Brooks, having held him as he'd cried on her shoulder last week.

'My daughter needs her doll,' he snaps. 'And nothing is going to stop me getting it for her.' He's searching the floor and then looks up, finally noticing Katie.

'What are you doing here?'

'Just following a line of investigation, Mr Brooks.' She tries to make herself wider, turning to block his view through to the kitchen. As with the second killing, he'd been away with the children at his parents' house when the murder took place, and she remembers how, between sobs, he'd told her again and again that he should have been there to protect his wife. She'd wanted to assure him the man who committed the crime was both sick and ruthless and would not have thought twice about taking his and his children's lives too, but to provide evidence of this she would have had to have given him details of the crime, something she knew he wasn't ready to hear.

'How do I ever explain this?' he says, reaching down to pick up the doll he had come for, the same headless doll that Katie had spotted on the way in. 'How do I explain any of it to my daughters?' He reaches out and touches the wall, his hand falling between the two school photos. Tears fill his eyes, and when he speaks his words are so thick they barely leave his mouth. 'How are they ever going to cope?' And then, without waiting for the response that Katie is desperately trying to shape in her head, he switches back to anger. 'I need to see in there,' he says, pointing to the kitchen without looking across. 'I need to know.'

Mark Brooks is a big man, over six foot. If he wanted to barge past her there'd be nothing she could do, but she will do something if she has to. He shouldn't have to see even a trace of what she has seen.

The silent stand-off is interrupted by the sound of movement in the kitchen; the squeak of a shoe on the cheap vinyl floor. She hopes desperately that Nathan will stay out of sight and that Mr Brooks will simply assume it's another police officer, but she can see from the man's face, from the way it drops in shock, then tightens in horror, that Nathan has come into view. She turns to look for herself and finds Nathan standing there, head down, handcuffed hands held out in front like the accused standing in the dock at court.

Mark Brooks has clearly made a similar connection and charges forward, seeming not to see or care about Katie blocking his path. The impact knocks her off her feet before she can tell him he's making a mistake, sending her flying backwards into the kitchen door. Mark stumbles and falls partly on top of her, and they slide across the floor, coming to a stop close to the outline of the body and the word GUTTED spelt out in now heavily congealed beans. Mark stares for a second, unable to take it all in, then he returns his attention to Nathan, pushing down on Katie's face in his desperation to get to his feet. Straining to get a look, Katie can see Nathan hasn't moved, nor has he said a word.

When the first punch is thrown she could swear that he moves his head into it, taking the full force of the blow. He drops in an instant, slamming into the sideboard and slumping to the floor. Mark follows him, then reaches across the sideboard and draws a kitchen knife – the second to be taken from that block with intent.

Winded by her fall and unable to speak, Katie manages to get to her feet and fling herself forward, crashing into Mark's hip just as he's about to bring the knife down into Nathan's chest. The big man slams into the cupboards and lets out a groan that grows into a roar of rage. Katie knows he's about to try and sink the knife in again and that this time, even if she's in the way, he won't stop. He's blind to everything other than the need to inflict as much pain as he is feeling. She makes one last attempt to call out and fend him off with her arm. She can take a knife wound – she's done so before – but her lungs are still empty and her arm is twisted awkwardly under her. A quick look at Nathan tells her he's still not moving, he's not even trying to put up any kind of defence. The punch he took would have knocked many out, but his eyes are open, unblinkingly staring up at the man with the knife. And at the corner of his mouth, where she can see a thin streak of blood, she can also make out the tiniest trace of another smile. Is it madness? Is it guilt? She waits for the blur of movement, for a grunt of effort and the flash of the blade, for the warm spray of blood. But it never comes. Instead she hears a cry from behind her and looks up to see that the young PC who had been stationed outside the house has wrestled the knife away and subdued Mr Brooks.

With everything suddenly remarkably still, she untangles herself and rises to her feet, brushing the front of her top where she finds a streak of red marking the path of a single squashed bean.

'I'm sorry,' she says, fighting for breath as she moves to crouch down by Mr Brooks. 'This should never have been allowed to happen. But I swear this is not the man who killed Sally.' As she says the words she once again feels the doubt, but there's also her instinct, reassuring her that she's right. She's always been right, with every criminal she's put away, even with the ones the court has allowed to walk.

'What about the cuffs?' Mark Brooks spits back, a string of drool hanging from the corner of his mouth. 'Why is he wearing fucking cuffs?'

She already has her explanation prepared; it's the same one she's been using with her colleagues since Nathan's return, to keep them quiet, to keep them away. 'He's a profiler,' she says. 'The best in the business. What he does is put himself in the heads of those responsible. To do so, he has to be them. That's why he needs to be restrained, because he's scared he might lash out, act out the sick fantasies he's living. That's why he did nothing when you attacked him. You saw for yourself he didn't fight back.'

Mark blinks for the first time, and it's quickly followed by a swell of tears. Rather than holding him back, the PC is now holding him up, and Katie reaches out to help.

'Let's go through to the living room,' she says, cursing her unfortunate choice of words, as they both rise unsteadily. Her whole body aches from the fall, but she tries not to show any discomfort and gestures towards the door, letting go of Mark and turning back towards Nathan. She reaches down, holding out a hand for him, but he doesn't move, or even look at her. Not willing to leave him alone in the kitchen, she drags him up and stumbles towards where Mark is waiting, with Nathan leaning on her like a dead weight.

Moving down the hall she glances up again at the two school photos, hoping for strength but discovering something else. 'You find a way to fucking do this,' she whispers into Nathan's ear, before grabbing him by the chin and slowly turning his head towards the two smiling children. 'I don't care how, but you do it!'

*

'How?' asks Mark the moment they enter the room. Nathan is standing on his own now, as is Mark, pointing towards the kitchen, but looking at them. 'How could anyone…?' His arm and tear-filled gaze swings towards Nathan. 'Can you explain it to me?'

'I can't.' Nathan's voice is as small as the gap it emerges from. He falls heavily into a seat, then removes a small toy ambulance from under his thigh. He stares at the toy for a moment, then carefully places it on the cushion next to him. Katie can see he's avoiding eye contact, that his breathing is short and his throat constricted. His hands locked together, one kneading the other's palm, then scratching at it as if trying to remove a stain.

'Isn't that your job, to explain that sickness?' snaps Mark, taking a small step forward, closely shadowed by the PC.

'It was,' Nathan mumbles into his chest. He's almost folded over on the sofa, his head drooping towards his knees. 'But things just don't make sense to me anymore. I'm so sorry about your wife. She was a good woman.'

Both Mark and Katie's heads shoot across to look at Nathan at the same time.

'You knew her?' asks Mark.

'In a way,' says Nathan, without looking up. 'I've seen your home and I've…' He taps the side of his head. 'It's not just the bad minds I get inside. She loved you very much. And your children.'

Sam and Jess. Katie recalls the names. She can, in fact, summon up a hundred facts about Sally Brooks, seeing it not only important in her attempts to solve the case, but as her duty to the victim, to colour in and never forget the detail of a life that was so cruelly taken away. She looks across at the mantelpiece, at a wedding photo of Sally and Mark, both of them smiling broadly with the kind of love she has never felt. In a different life, in a different world, she could almost picture herself there on that day, as a friend of the woman who looks a little like her. But in this world, in this reality, it's work that has brought the two women together. And it's work she returns to now, searching for the strength to keep on hurting.

'You will have heard there's been another murder,' she says, looking at Mark.

'One of your colleagues informed me,' he says, lowering his head. His hands are moving down by his waist, and Katie can see, in addition to the red marks on his knuckles from where he hit Nathan, that he's found the headless doll again, the very reason for his visit, and is squeezing it tightly. 'Was it the same?'

'Similar,' she says.

'Will there be more?' On many occasions Katie has sat with those who could not see beyond their own suffering, or some who took comfort in discovering they were not alone, but she can see that Mr Brooks wants this to stop as much as she does. 'More children without a mother?' he continues, tears now flowing freely. 'More lives torn apart?'

'No,' says Nathan, standing suddenly, holding his cuffed hands in front of his chest. 'No more. I won't let that happen.'

'You swear?' says Mark, looking at him, childlike.

'On my life,' says Nathan.

Out of the corner of her eye Katie can see Nathan offer a clumsy bow, but her real focus remains on Mark's hands. She's sweating now, cursing her tiredness, cursing the madness that she's now certain has caused her to make a terrible mistake. 'Can I ask you to put that down, please?' she says, nodding at the headless doll.

'Why?' Mark asks, lifting the toy and seeming to consider it for the first time, as if he too had been blind to its significance. 'Christ, you don't think…?'

'I think it's best to investigate every possibility.' She reaches into her pocket, searching for a new pair of latex gloves, the others torn in the struggle, but all she finds is a condom wrapper and a crumpled cigarette.

'But you couldn't have missed this,' says Mark, carefully placing the headless doll on the mantelpiece and taking a step back.

'No,' says Katie, with a surge of defensive pride. 'We couldn't.'

It takes a moment, but she can see Mark getting there, his eyes jolting across to the door.

'So, you think he's been back?'

'I think we should leave,' she says, as calmly as she can manage. 'That way my colleagues can come in and check.'

Half an hour later, and she's driving the car. Mark Brooks has been escorted away, seemingly more reassured by Nathan's promise than anything she had said. Nathan, however, looks far from capable of solving any crime. He seems to have sunk back inside himself, as distant as he was on the journey down from Scotland. The only clue as to what he might be thinking about is in the anxious bending back of his fingers. Seeing this reminds her of her own increasing fear. Might the headless doll connect these murders to that same one last year? Or might that first murder simply have been the inspiration? She stares across at Nathan, knowing that whatever else he might be capable of, he is certainly capable of putting on an act. Had what she'd just seen been the big finale?

She's remembering the way he'd been unable to look at Mark Brooks. The way he'd apologised and flinched at hearing the children's names; the way he'd seemed happy to die in that kitchen, and the conviction with which he'd sworn to make it stop. She's thinking of the way these murders feel like a horrible amalgamation of all the cases they've previously investigated. And she's thinking of her dad, of those few words he'd said in a rare moment of clarity: words that have since forced her to question everything, including her instinct for identifying killers.

And what if her instinct is wrong? It was Nathan who had taught her to trust in it, to use her heart as well as her head, and convinced her to look beyond the evidence she'd so carefully collated. What if he knew the flaw all along, that she was blind to those she cared about? The world around her suddenly starts to spin, following the path of the wounds on the second victim. Fearing she's about to crash the car, she slows rapidly, pulling into a space she can barely make out through the swirl. She opens the window and starts to suck in the air, fighting the tiredness, the nausea, the doubt. When it's over, when the world has settled and clarity has returned, she turns to Nathan and finds him slumped against the door with his eyes closed.

'It can't be you,' she says softly, reaching out towards him, wanting to touch the side of his face, to at least feel a physical connection between them: the same connection she'd been searching for with all of those guys she'd slept with – guys like

Nathan – that she'd let in and then pushed out before they could hurt her. 'If it's you, then there's…' she pauses, feeling the truth before saying it out loud, 'nothing.'

CHAPTER THIRTEEN

Nathan hears the bedroom door lock. He's lying on Katie's bed, clothes on but loosened and handcuffs removed, having been half-carried all the way up from the car. He knows he shouldn't have put her through that – another deception, another lie – but he can't afford to have her asking questions, not until he's figured out what is going on.

He'd managed to grab the landline handset while she was manoeuvring him past the sofa, then tossed it at a pile of dirty washing in the corner of the room. There's a chance she'll come searching for the phone in a couple of minutes, but there's a better chance, given the state of the place, that she won't notice at all. He moves over to the far side of the room carrying a pillow to muffle his voice. The number comes to him instantly despite it having been more than a year since he last dialled it. He remembers every word of that call, in particular the end, when he'd asked the other man not to worry about him and not to try and track him down. It was for the best, he'd said, and he'd truly believed it. Now he's the one breaking the silence.

It rings several times before it's answered with a tentative 'hello?' It's only one word, but hearing it makes him want to cry. He responds with a choked-up 'hello', and then nothing more is said for at least a minute, just a silent acceptance that the connection has been made.

'How's Cornwall?' he says eventually, summoning up the images that have comforted him before.

'Sunny. How's… wherever you are?'

'The same.'

Another drawn-out silence, and then the conversation begins for real.

'Are you okay?' says the voice on the other end of the line.

'I am,' he says, trying to summon up a smile. From where he's sitting, and peering past the pillow, he can make out a full-length mirror. He stares at his reflection, at a face he hasn't confronted in more than a year, but it doesn't feel like he's looking at himself at all; it's the man on the other end of the line who he hasn't seen in… he starts to count back, seeing only swirling stripes, for so long his only way of keeping track of time.

'Six years,' comes the answer to the question he hadn't asked out loud.

'Almost exactly,' he says, reminded of the perfect symmetry, and of his need to get back to Scotland in less than two days.

'I was worried. I thought…'

'Don't,' he says, firmly. 'Don't you ever think that.'

'I took comfort in the fact that I would know if you had.'

'What do you mean?' Nathan breaks off and grabs at his wrist, nails scratching the hardened scar. He'd thought it was only him, another part of his madness that he'd never spoken about, never shared, never even dared to test these past few years for fear of being reminded of what he had lost.

'Don't you feel it too?'

'Feel what?' he says with a grimace, loathing the need to deny something so miraculous, so beautiful. But he has no choice, not now he knows the connection goes both ways. He needs to make the other doubt so that, when the two days are up and he is gone, there'll be nothing missed, no clue at all. He waits for an explanation, or perhaps just confirmation that the possibility has been dismissed, but there's silence at the other end of the line. Nathan speaks again, to break it before it breaks him. 'Just know that I could never do what she did.'

'That wasn't what I was worried about, Nathan. I take it you're still doing that stupid job?'

'It's not stupid,' he snaps, surprised at his anger, defending a job he isn't doing and has never done. 'You know I've found my purpose.'

'I don't know anything. You never talk. You won't even tell me why we can't talk.'

'It would put you at risk. I couldn't bear it if anything happened to you.'

'And yet, I have to live with that worry every single day?' The sound of a sigh, sad and familiar. 'Same old big bro.'

Nathan's surprised how much it shakes him to hear himself described as *brother*. He's tried for so long not to think of that word, to pretend that he doesn't feel torn in half. The memories surface from time to time – he could never erase them entirely – but the good ones, the ones he can stomach, are restricted solely to his youth. And it's to his youth he returns, to a phrase he'd said on a thousand occasions when something was wrong, something he didn't want to have to explain, something he didn't feel he needed to explain, not to his brother.

'You're supposed to understand.'

A momentary pause, followed by a deep inhalation, and he can picture that head dropping forward the way it had all those years ago when they'd both come to the realisation that this argument could not be won.

'I do, Nathan, of course I do. But for the very same reason I know you're not being true to yourself. This is not the life you want to lead.'

'We can't always do what we want.' Another look in the mirror, and Nathan silently mouths: 'Or be…'

'You are acting, of course,' says his brother.

Nathan feels a twist of panic, certain his brother has seen through his lies and read his intentions, that he understands it all.

'Only, it's not about good or bad reviews anymore,' his brother continues. 'This acting is life and death. Say the wrong thing, do the wrong thing, and it's over. Isn't that right?'

Nathan allows himself a shallow smile, content he'd been panicking for no reason before. His brother had not seen through his deception, just as he hadn't for all those years they'd lived together, when Nathan had pretended to be okay; to be normal, to be the same.

'I'm very careful,' he says, eventually.

'You were never that, big bro,' says the other voice, so softly and warmly that it feels like he's reached out and taken him in an embrace. 'I know I have to accept your decision.' He laughs, but it's a sad laugh, the sort of laugh that tries desperately to distract from the horror of an associated memory. 'I just thought we'd always be together.'

Nathan's lips start to shape the sentence, but before he's found the strength to share he hears it at the other end of the line.

'So sorry to have left you alone.'

These words have power: they rob him of strength and breath, they carry him back in time. In an instant he's picturing the kitchen table, broad, wooden and heavily scarred. In one corner is a photo of father and son; in the other a small sheet of paper with blue lines running horizontally and vertically. Soaking through the surface of that paper, written in the darkest, thickest ink, are the very words he's just heard.

He shakes off the image, dragging himself back to the present. 'You're not alone, though, are you?' he asks, while reaching out towards the mirror, fingers outstretched. They curl back towards him when he remembers the other reason for making this call. 'You still have your wife?'

'My wife?' He hears a snort at the other end of the line. 'Can you even remember her name?'

'Of course,' he says, desperately trawling through previous conversations, searching for descriptions of a life he's only ever heard about in telephone calls. Once or twice he'd wondered about looking for further evidence online, to confirm that at least one of them was getting it right, but he feared, despite how careful he'd been covering his tracks from the very beginning, that in doing so he might somehow inspire his brother to do the same.

'Your wife is called Karen,' he says, finally dragging her name up from the depths. 'And your son is Oliver. He must be two now, isn't he?'

'Almost three.' The sadness returns to the other voice, and Nathan can feel the weight of it right at his core. 'I'm afraid I still haven't told him about his uncle. It just seems too hard to explain.'

'I think one of us is more than enough for him,' he says, again adding a tentative laugh. This time there's no laughter back, and he curses himself for his clumsiness. Their conversations have grown increasingly awkward over the years. Sometimes it's seemed like a crime against nature, to have taken something so perfect and torn it apart, but when he pictures the scene in Cornwall – the sun, the beach, the wife, the child – it's enough to know such a life exists because of him, because he has been no part of it, because he made the choice to stay away.

'I take it there's no special person in your life, big bro?'

'Sadly, no,' he says. 'For the very reason you and I are talking like this, not sharing a beer, not staring out at the sea.'

'I thought maybe you could find yourself a nice policewoman, someone who understands that crazy world of yours?'

In wondering how his brother might know about Katie he arrives at a possibility far less troubling than the one that had inspired him to make the call. 'You've not been talking to anyone, have you, trying to find out what I'm up to?'

'You know I wouldn't put you at risk like that.'

'Not even an innocent conversation with a stranger, telling him about us, about what we've been through?'

'Jesus, Nathan, I haven't even dared speak to my wife about you!'

'I'm sorry,' says Nathan, reaching out towards the mirror again, imagining his hand resting on the other man's shoulder and giving it a gentle squeeze. 'If there was another way.'

'Of course there's another way! Trust me. Tell me where you are. Tell me *who* you are. Let me at least imagine your life.'

'I'm sorry,' Nathan says again. 'I can't yet.'

'Yet?' says his brother. 'So, this isn't for ever?'

'Of course not,' he says, staring down at the scars on his wrist. Wouldn't it be easier to give in? To go and see him and his family and be a part of their lives? He shakes his head with such force he loses balance and knocks the nearby table where Katie has left him a glass of water. It wobbles and clinks against the metal upright of the bed lamp. He peers over the corner of the bed at the door, waiting to see the handle move, but instead he can just pick out the faint murmur of a television. 'Listen, I've got to go now. But I need you to know—'

'The same,' says his brother. 'Always the same.'

He lets the handset fall to the floor and with the last ounce of energy he can muster he climbs to his feet and falls sideways on the bed, burying his head into the hastily drawn sheets. Now he realises the true reason he had to make the call. It had nothing to do with the case, with answering a doubt that had evaporated the moment he'd heard his brother's voice; the same way his agreeing to come down here with Katie has nothing to do with solving murders. He just needs to know that the people he cares about are going to be okay.

With Katie, he only needs to look around this room, a room that belongs to a completely different person to the one he left behind, to know that there's plenty of work to do. He'd felt such guilt for having tricked her into believing he was coping, for putting on an act, but isn't this proof she was doing the same? All those years he'd fed off her strength, off her control, off her order, and now…

He wakes in total darkness, unable to see a single thing around him, but he believes he can picture it: the closed blinds; the cracked ceiling above him; the swirling mural out on the stairway. The sheets under him certainly feel right, soaked in sweat and dragged up towards him from all directions. He rolls over, spreading out one arm to find the edge of the bed. He always likes to know how close he is to falling. Both of his wrists are sore, and his legs feel like they've run even further than usual. His head hurts, too, a dull pain on his jawline that sinks into his teeth. And he's hungry. He's often hungry, but this time he really does need to fill his stomach, and the exact meal has taken shape in his mind, a childhood favourite, straight out of the tin…

He sits up suddenly and throws himself at the edge he's just found, not knowing where he's going to land, just wanting to get into a corner, to get out of the way of a series of images that he desperately hopes are nothing more than the usual tricks of his mind. He falls against something hard, his forehead crashing into it, a flash of pain in the darkness. He dabs at the centre of that pain with his fingers, finding a wetness there. It could be sweat, but this feels thicker and warmer and it's running down past his eye and across his cheek. Suddenly a click and a square of blinding light appears ahead of him. He turns his head away and lifts his hands to cover his face, the pain on his forehead now coming in frequent waves. The light is everywhere, and there's a voice, distant but still far too close.

'What are you doing?' says a woman.

He has a name for that woman. He has a face, too, although he's still refusing to look at it. And the rest he's tried to push back, but it's all crashing in, forcing him further and further into the corner.

'What are you hiding from?' she says.

His arms are tucked behind his back, and he can feel a numbness in his fingertips, like they're no longer his, like he's losing control.

'The handcuffs,' he says. 'Please. Please I need them.'

'No,' she says firmly, refusing to move away.

If anything, she's moving closer, so close he can feel her breath on his closed eyelids.

'No more of this bullshit, Nathan. I think you heard me in the car yesterday. And I think you know it was the truth. If this doesn't work, if *we* don't work…'

He feels something being placed on his thighs, and when he opens his eyes his worst fear is confirmed. It's a carving knife. He tries to push back, to make it slip away, but she's pinning his legs down with her own and he can't move.

'We all have dark thoughts,' she says. 'I've had plenty of late. In fact, you only need to look around you,' she pauses, as if waiting for him to do so, but he's keeping his eyes shut tight. 'Well, you don't need to look, not you, not with your memory. You'll have absorbed the whole place the moment you entered, and you'll remember in impossible detail what my old place was like. Compare the two and you won't need to do that special thing you do to get inside people's minds. You'll see how I've slipped, almost at the very same moment you did.'

Leaning forward an inch he's managed to pull his arms free and they've fallen to his sides. He tells himself this is to ease the numbness in his fingers, which is getting worse. It's so bad that he almost doesn't feel those fingers being pulled back, but when he realises what she's doing and what she's referring to, he jerks his hand away and lets out a groan.

'What was it about that case in particular, eh, Nathan?'

He can hear a sudden intake of breath, and feel her shifting her weight on his legs.

'Not me,' he says, reading her discomfort. 'I would never… I could never…'

'Then what the fuck are we doing here?' she asks, this time shifting the position of the knife.

'Steven Fish's murder took me somewhere I hadn't been before,' he says, squeezing his eyes even more tightly shut. 'I had no control. No limits.' He's gasping for breath now and pressing his back into the wall. 'I only had a glimpse, but even so it was almost impossible to escape from that mind. And when I finally had, I knew I needed a way to escape from my own.'

'Have you lost control?' says Katie, moving forward again.

He shakes his head over and over.

'I want to believe you,' she says. 'I *need* to believe you. But you kept things from me before. And I know you're keeping things from me now.'

He opens his eyes wide, surprised by just how close she is. At least it gives him something to focus on, beyond the numbness in his hands and the position of that knife. 'I have nothing to do with these murders,' he says. 'I swear to you.'

'But you *are* keeping secrets,' she says, holding his gaze without blinking. 'Things we've seen have meant something to you.'

'I haven't killed anyone!' he says, matching her stare. 'You have to know that. Surely all you have to do is look into my eyes and you can tell? Jesus, Katie, you know me. What does your instinct say?'

'It's gone,' she says, softly. She blinks and turns away, and he follows her, taking in the cigarette burns and empty wine bottles on the floor beside him.

'How? What could make you doubt that gift, doubt all those years together, doubt who you are?'

'It's who you made me.'

'Rubbish. I just gave you belief. Who's taken it away?'

She opens her mouth and then closes it again, lifting the weight from his legs and snatching the knife.

'I'm not the only one with secrets, then,' he says. Now she's moved he can see the phone where he'd tossed it onto the floor after speaking to his brother. Katie stands with her back to it, and he tries to kick a pile of dirty washing over it, but she turns just before it disappears.

'You've called someone?'

'No,' he says, quickly. 'But I think I was about to. I haven't had a phone in more than a year, and for a long time before that I would never have had one by my bed because when I woke lost and confused in the night I would try and call home.'

He used to think he was smarter than this, smarter than the criminals who would ramble on to hide a lie only to give away another truth. Home has certainly been playing on his mind – not the one in Scotland; that's barely a home at all, just a place to hide away and wait – rather the place where he once had a family, where he wasn't alone.

He's tempted to tell her about his brother, to offer at least a little, but Katie's own lack of certainty holds him back. For so long he'd lived for her belief. Once he'd taught her how to look, she'd seen the good in him as clearly as she'd seen the bad in others. It was only when he'd stood over that headless corpse, its end drawn out in so many agony-filled ways, feeling like he was standing on the edge of a limitless black hole, that he'd lost the strength to even act like he was going to be okay. And yet… and yet, now that they're back together and she's joined him in his crisis, he's finding a different strength, ready to play another essential role.

'I'm sorry for not showing you who I really was,' he says. 'But I'd been pretending for so long before I met you, with everybody I met, even with…' His head drops, but he immediately lifts it back up, closing out the memories and moving on, just as this new, tougher version of himself he's created would. 'I thought it was the only way to hold on. Towards the end, though, I was starting to…' His hands are free and curled in front of his face, as if trying to shape the feeling that's taken hold of him: a feeling that can be described in a single, impossible-seeming word that he finally manages to push out. 'Trust.'

Katie turns back to him, and he can see the hurt in her eyes. 'We were so close,' she says, with an aggression that he fully understands.

'The closest I've ever been,' he says. 'But beyond all this superficial shit,' he grabs the front of his borrowed T-shirt and flicks his head towards the room around them, 'we do know the truth about ourselves. We will always have our own secrets. And we will always seek to uncover other people's.'

'Always?' says Katie.

'I don't know about the future,' he says, looking away. 'I guess that's been the problem all along. But I do know what I've done in the past. You don't need to trust me fully, you just need to trust me enough for us to make this work. One more time.'

*

Ten minutes later and he's sitting at the breakfast table finishing a second bowl of cornflakes. He looks around the tiny flat, watching Katie as she stands at the sink washing up dishes that have clearly been there for days. He notices the number of wine glasses too, several in pairs, dotted around the room.

'Do you have friends over much?'

She spins quickly, almost dropping the dish she's holding, wearing an expression that he takes to be guilt. 'Why?'

'It's none of my business,' he says, holding up his hands by way of apology. He lowers them and drags a well-chewed fingernail over the surface of the table, following a snaking groove, amazed at how personal this has suddenly become. 'And given it's only a couple of days, it's probably best that we don't—'

'You weren't the only one trying to forget about things,' she says, cutting him off. 'I just chose a more sociable route.'

He's surprised to find his cheeks flush as she lowers her head and drags down her white shirt, the front of which has been splashed with soapy water. He wants to move on, to move away from this awkward situation, and so turns back to the small talk. 'How's your dad?'

Her shoulders slump, and this time she lets go of the plate in her hands. He hears it sink to the bottom of the water. Once again he knows he's got it horribly wrong, making a mistake he would never have made before, back when he was switched on and tuned in, when he knew that stepping beyond the professional world was guaranteed to bring them both pain.

'He's been sick for a long time, long before you left, but it was one more thing I was blind to. This last year…' Her shoulders drop further. 'The deterioration has been so rapid, faster than the doctors could ever have imagined, like he's given up. You remind me of him. When you've gone off to wherever it is you go. That's why I can't stand it. I can't have you living on the other side of that wall. Not if we really do only have a couple of days.'

He instinctively looks at his wrist. It could almost be mistaken for a glance at his watch, to check the time, and in a way, that's exactly what it is: a reminder that it's running out. He flips the wrist over and stretches his arm across the table. He wants her to turn round, he wants her to take his hand, he wants to offer comfort, to convince her that she's going to be okay, he wants to have some strength to share but, in the end, all he has is regret and the same old words that have haunted him for so long. *So sorry to have left you alone.*

'I should have recognised his Alzheimer's far earlier,' says Katie. 'At least then I could have said what I needed to while he still understood. I could have eased my conscience, made it easier for myself.' She laughs again and shakes her head. 'Easier.'

'Is there anything I can do to help?'

On this occasion, he can tell he has said the right thing because she turns towards him with half a smile, not seeming to care about the water dripping from her gloves.

'Don't go.'

He should have seen it coming. Perhaps he had, perhaps he'd wanted to hear her say it; although now that she has he wishes she hadn't.

'It's not just faith in my instinct that faded while you were away.' She stands in front of him, pushing her shoulders back and brushing a stray strand of hair away from her face, tucking it behind her ear. She had always been beautiful. The rumours of a romance between them had spread quickly, an obvious way to explain the closeness between them, and on weaker days, on days when for just a moment he forgot himself, Nathan had started to imagine it too.

'It's only since you've come back,' Katie continues, 'that I've started to remember there might have been more.' The two of them stare at each other for a moment, neither blinking, neither seeming to breathe. Then Katie turns away. For a moment he thinks she's going to reach for a bottle of wine, perhaps even finish the dregs of one of the old ones on the side, but her hand darts to the right at the last second, picking up a glass which she then fills with water. She takes a big swig and then returns to him, peeling off her marigolds and offering an enthusiastic nod. 'Right,' she says, clapping her hands together, as she would always do to silence the room back at work. 'It's time to hear your insight.'

'It was never insight,' he says, spreading his hands out on the tabletop and slowly pushing them away, trying to knead out the tension he can feel building again. 'Just a dark imagination.'

'A gift.'

A nail catches on a groove in the table and he continues to pull, enjoying the tug of flesh. 'A curse.'

'You could see somebody,' she says hesitantly. 'I have. It helped, for a while.'

'You gave up?'

She runs a hand down either side of her trousers as if ironing out non-existent creases. 'I made a mistake.'

Nathan spots the tiniest look across at the bedroom door, and he thinks he understands. A silence settles over the room. In the distance he can hear the steady stream of traffic, and he's reminded that it's not just him and Katie: there's a whole city out there, millions of lives, all with their own complications, secrets and desires.

'I'm not sure I can go to the station again,' he says, gripping the edge of the table, his bare feet pressed firmly to the floor. 'But I need to see everything we have on this case.'

'Fine.' She gestures for him to move towards the kitchen door and he does so, passing very close to where she's standing.

Joining him in the living room, she points to another door that he'd somehow missed before, part hidden behind a colourful drape. She moves across and pulls it back, drawing out a key from behind a stack of paperbacks on an overcrowded bookcase. They're adult books, thrillers by the looks of it, and he finds himself giving them a wide berth, even though he suspects that what's beyond the now-open door, in the darkness that's been revealed, will be far more dangerous.

CHAPTER FOURTEEN

Katie lifts a finger towards the light switch, before quickly withdrawing it, suddenly convinced she's made a terrible mistake.

'On second thoughts, I'll bring the stuff out to you,' she says, trying to block him with her arm.

But he's already moving past, stepping through the doorway into the darkness. She reaches out to pull him back, as if this black hole might absorb him for ever, but he slips through her grasp. He flicks the switch and the room ahead is flooded with the blinding light of a naked bulb. She lifts a hand to shield her eyes, then lowers it to cover the whole of her face.

She doesn't need to see the room; she can place every item in it in her head. Unlike the rest of her flat, everything is exactly where it should be. In the centre is a swivel chair, lopsided and broken, discarded from someone's office at the station. The floor is bare wood, sanded down and painted white. The walls are also white, but there are only occasional glimpses of it. Floor-to-ceiling – and parts of the ceiling – are covered in photos, printouts of data, maps and reports. There are many flashes of colour, with little bits of tape and string, and plenty of red on the images. Tucked in the corner is a metal filing cabinet, another reject from the office, from a time before computers took over, back when she was new to the job and she believed she would solve every case. The room is so tiny that when she stands in the middle and spreads her arms she can practically reach each wall. She remembers the day she first looked around the flat, how the letting agent had tried to hurry her on, waving her past what seemed to him little more than a walk-in cupboard, saying a few words about storage space. But the windowless room had struck a chord with Katie, and she'd pushed her way past the agent, standing with the light off, picturing how it might eventually be.

She feels as if she ought to offer an explanation to Nathan, something to make her feel a little less exposed, but when she removes her hand from her face and turns to him, she realises he's likely suffering far more than she is. He's looking at the forensics from a case that fills almost half a wall: lab reports; phone logs; witness statements; handwritten notes and, at the centre of it all, the photos. Some show the head. Some show the body and the curls of peeled skin. And one colour image shows a hand, the wedding-ring finger of which has been snapped back.

'You never caught anyone?' he says, without looking across.

She realises now that he hasn't asked before, even though the Steven Fish murder must have been on his mind from the very moment they met. One more thing he's been holding back.

'I tried,' she says. 'Everything.' For all the unsolved cases in this room, this had seemed the most important because it represented the start of her decline. She'd thought if she could solve it that the others would follow; that her confidence, and her instinct, would return.

'What are all these?' asks Nathan. He continues staring, unblinkingly, at the photos.

'Cases from the past year,' she says, before adding quietly, 'unsolved.' She points at the nearest, hoping to pull Nathan's attention away. 'This was a man in his seventies who had his throat slit on the way back from visiting his wife's grave.' He was the first of the year's failures, and she remembers clearly the frustration at having to move on, and how even then she'd felt like something inside of her was slipping, like she was losing control of something fundamental. 'This,' she continues, stepping to her right and jabbing a finger noisily against another image, 'was a teenage boy who was shot in the stomach. We were close to an arrest, but I…' She lowers her head again, shaking it slowly.

'Throat and stomach.'

Katie looks across at Nathan and can see he has finally left the image of the hand and is staring at the latest additions, photos and documents that have covered up others. The light above almost seems to have been angled in on them, bringing out the vivid red of the blood. Nathan leans towards a photo of the body of Sally Brooks.

'I've made the connection, of course,' she says. 'But I don't think it was the same man.'

'It can't be,' he says, vigorously shaking his head. 'But I do think he is mocking you for these failures.'

She shoots Nathan a look, unable to suppress her anger. 'You think you could have done better?'

'I think *we* could, yes.' He turns back to the image of the teenage boy lying on the filthy floor of an alley, still clutching his stomach as he'd watched his life spilling out of him.

'It's not too late,' says Katie.

'This case,' says Nathan, lining himself up with Sally Brooks again. 'One final case, like we agreed.'

'Fine,' says Katie, with another flash of anger. 'But to solve it we can't afford to shut ourselves off from the others. What if he's doing this because of something we were involved in years ago?'

'You mean a relative?' says Nathan, a suggestion he seems to instantly regret.

'Perhaps of someone we put away, yes,' says Katie. She's already worked her way through that lengthy list, but she knows there might have been something she missed.

'I don't think so,' says Nathan, his voice suddenly sounding distant. 'I believe it goes further back than us.'

'What makes you say that?' she asks, although she already has a suggestion, taking her back to a place she'd sworn she wouldn't go. 'The clue in the toaster? The toast? Are you talking about your childhood?'

Nathan doesn't say a word. He's within reach; he couldn't be anything else in this room. Katie has to fight the urge to grab his shoulder and reverse him, to look into his eyes and demand he do what she's far from willing to do herself – to talk about the distant past.

'I'm sorry,' he says, eventually. 'I had a thought. But I was wrong.'

'Don't you fucking dare!' she says, leaning in. 'I brought you here, I showed you my failings, showed you how I couldn't fucking cope without you. Why?' She doesn't wait for the answer, although he might well be able to give it, knowing her as well as he does. 'Because nothing else matters.' She moves in close so they're both just inches from the picture of Sally Brooks. 'Nothing matters but making him stop.'

'Exactly,' he says quietly as he turns and walks out of the room. 'Which is why we need to go.'

'Where?'

'The last place in the world I ever wanted to return to.'

Staring at the back of his head, she's again reminded of how little she knows about this man. While she's always been thorough in researching her work, considering every last detail in an attempt to understand the whole, with personal matters she's barely scratched the surface. She doesn't need a professional to tell her why, although the one she'd been casually speaking to at her dad's care home had made it nice and clear. And it's in considering that man's words, the source of her own pain, and the places to which she would least like to return, that the answer comes to her, accompanied by the image of six words scribbled in thick ink on a scrap of square-lined paper: *Home is where the heart is.*

CHAPTER FIFTEEN

Perhaps it was inevitable that he would come back to this place; it might have been his plan all along to return one last time before his three days were up. Or perhaps he's answering a genuine concern that someone else has been here, raking through his past to use it as a weapon against him, making him think unthinkable things, to believe he might have committed these crimes. And then to start imagining something far worse.

The house is a huge Georgian property on top of Richmond Hill, not more than two minutes' walk from the park. Nothing seems to have changed since he was last here. He's amazed and in a way disappointed to see the front door hasn't been caved in and all the contents taken. It would have been obvious to any burglar scouting potential targets that the car in the front drive, an ageing Citroën, hadn't moved in a long time, and peering through cracks in the dusty curtains would have revealed that the house had been unoccupied for just as long. Maybe it was the garden that had saved the place, the immaculate lawn and carefully maintained flowerbeds giving the impression that someone was still around to care. Perhaps the old guy they'd employed to come once a week had been mistaken for the owner. He had, from Nathan's memory, looked like the sort of eccentric who might live in squalor on the inside while maintaining a kind of splendour on the outside. Whatever the reason, the house looks untouched and so, realising he still needs a key, he lifts a plant pot containing a recently deadheaded rose and slips one out from underneath.

Even after the door is unlocked he needs to use his shoulder to barge it open, such is the mountain of post behind it. There must be menus for every restaurant in the area, many of which will be long out of business; there are local papers, for which he imagines the same is true; there are bills, letters, postcards, presents, even leaves blown through the letterbox on the windiest of days; and there are large white squares, often lying in twos: one for him, one for his brother. He swallows hard as he steps over a pair by the far wall, seeing a number 20 handwritten in the corner of an unopened card: a reminder not of the birthday that hadn't been celebrated, but of the twenty years since he last entered the house. Yet more evidence of the perfect symmetry of it all.

As they move to the base of a small set of stairs, confronted by clouds of dust and a damp and musty smell, he looks across at Katie and wonders if she's surprised by this place he's brought her to. He has no idea how much she knows about his family. Before, he could almost have guaranteed it was nothing, but he knew she was more than capable of finding things out behind his back and the last year had given her every reason. His own particular skill for reading people assured him she would respect his wishes, as did the similar request for privacy she'd made in return.

'What are we looking for?' she asks.

'I don't know,' he says, although as he stands there, barely inside the house, he feels like he's seeing everything. To his right is the corner where he would fling his school bag and kick off his shoes. To his left is the place he stood punching the air on the day he got his acceptance to RADA. Ahead, at the base of the stairs, he can see the rug he'd tripped over while doing some acting a few years before the RADA letter, running around pretending to be a policeman, a fall that had resulted in a deep cut to his chin. He lifts a hand to feel for a scar, then realises there'll be nothing there. Not because it has long since healed, but because it was never there in the first place – he wasn't the one who got hurt. The mistake is not surprising: the line between him and his brother was always so blurred that he has difficulty remembering who did what; although he does now recall that he wasn't the policeman. He was never the policeman.

As they reach the top of the steps and enter the hall he looks to his left, seeing the kitchen door still closed. He reaches for the edge of a cabinet to balance himself and when he pulls his hand back he can see he's left a sweaty palm print. He moves hurriedly ahead, not sure where he's going, just wanting to be away from that room.

The lounge seems even larger than it did when he was a child. The ceiling is high, with ornate plasterwork and a huge chandelier. The walls are lined with hundreds of books, many of them leather-bound and dating back centuries. Tucked in the corner, on an antique table, is the huge family telly. Huge in depth, that is, with a screen that seems ridiculously small compared to modern sets. The ornate rug that covers two thirds of the dark wood floorboards is old and starting to fray at the edges. It's the same rug Nathan and his brother had lain on as children; most likely it was the same rug they'd been put on as babies, staring up at the ceiling, understanding nothing of the world. Were it not for Katie, he would lie there now.

The huge windows at the far end of the room have the curtains drawn and only a narrow strip of sunlight has made it through. Nathan moves over and readies himself to pull them back. His dad had never allowed them to do so, preferring to sit in darkness with only a lamp by which to read his books. It's therefore with a sense of rebellion that Nathan grabs the curtains and throws them open.

The face is up against the window, so close that its features are pressed against the glass, squashed, deformed, hideous. A flash of something out of the corner of Nathan's eye draws his attention down, and he can see a hand holding an object, long, polished and coming to a point.

'Get away!' screams Katie, as she rushes forward.

Nathan doesn't move, but the figure on the other side of the glass does, jumping back and almost tumbling down the rickety wooden stairs that lead up from the garden, revealing the object in his hand to be a pair of garden shears. The fear and tension instantly flood out of Nathan, a change so dramatic and so sudden that he very nearly drops to his knees. In its place is something unexpected, and equally strong. Disappointment. He knows that this could so easily have been the end, for him or for the case. Either way it would have been fine. Just a day ago he'd have wanted to wait for the perfect moment. Now it would be enough to know his worst nightmare hasn't come true.

He reaches forward and unlocks the glass door, pulling it open.

'Are you okay, Mr Markham?'

Nathan had remained on the pavement the last time they'd met, peering over the low white wall at the front of the garden, resisting all requests to step onto the property. The old man doesn't seem to have changed at all in the five years since. He has the same close-cropped grey hair receding to the crown, the same small, dark eyes hidden behind thick-rimmed glasses, the same narrow lips, topped by a straggly grey moustache, the same hollow cheeks, tanned and weathered. Even his clothes are as Nathan remembers them: a blue checked shirt, rolled up to the elbows and a pair of pale brown corduroys, for ever dirty on the knees.

'I'm so sorry, sir,' he says in a strong Northern accent – Yorkshire, from what Nathan recalls of their rare and brief conversations. 'I didn't mean to startle you. I was down the other end of the garden, and I thought I saw movement inside. Then the light came on and... well, I were going to call the police.'

'No need,' says Nathan, managing a smile and directing an arm towards Katie. 'This is Detective Inspector Rhodes.'

'Nice to meet you, lassie,' says Mr Markham, holding a hand out towards Katie, before spotting the dirt coating his fingers and withdrawing it quickly. 'Detective, you say?' The gardener hesitates and looks down at his shoes, old brown brogues as filthy as his hands. 'Of course, it's none of my business.'

'Nathan and I are friends,' says Katie with a smile.

The comment causes Nathan to smile too, albeit briefly.

'Have you had any trouble with people trying to break in?' she adds casually, looking out at the huge walled garden, a square of immaculate lawn surrounded by roses, hydrangeas and various other plants the names of which slipped Nathan's mind the very moment his mum taught them to him.

'No, ma'am. I'm only here once a week, mind, but I do keep an eye out and check all windows and doors are locked.' He glances across at Nathan, seeming a little embarrassed. 'I know it's not my role to pry, but I thought…'

'Thank you,' says Nathan. 'You've been doing a brilliant job. Mum was so passionate about this garden, and would have loved what you've done. In fact, I haven't increased your wages while I've been away, have I?' He taps his pockets as if his wallet might be in there. There's no cash. No wallet. Nothing in his trousers. They're not even his trousers. 'I'll make sure to do that as soon as I get the chance.'

Another look of embarrassment crosses Mr Markham's face, and he lifts his hand to rub the back of his head. 'Thank you, sir. But that really isn't necessary. You and your brother—' He cuts himself off, a filthy hand part-rising to his mouth. 'You've always been very kind.'

Nathan shoots a quick look at Katie, and her surprise alongside a flash of anger confirms that she hasn't done her research and knows nothing of his family.

'You deserve it,' he says. 'I'm only sorry I haven't been able to appreciate the garden myself.' He smiles and hopes the man in front of him will relax, but if anything his discomfort appears to be growing. 'Is there something wrong?'

'No, sir,' he answers quickly. 'No. It's just…' He starts to rub the top of his head.

'You can tell me. Do please tell me.'

'It is Nathan, isn't it?' he says, finally managing a smile. 'Not Christian?'

Another look across at Katie, and this time her confusion is expected. 'Of course.'

'Then I must have got it round the wrong way. Or misheard. My wife always used to say I'd had too much sun. I guess it's why I chose gardening and not driving a bus or the like.' He smiles again, a broad smile, but still with a trace of discomfort.

'Have I said the wrong thing?' he asks, desperately trying to run through what he has said in search of his mistake.

'Not the wrong thing, sir,' says the gardener, lowering his head again, both hands now fumbling with the shears down by his waist. 'The same thing.'

Nathan's heartbeat starts to rise, his fears already well ahead of his thoughts, thoughts he's so desperately trying to restrain. 'I'm sorry?'

'About the garden. And your mother. And about raising my salary. Which is very kind, and I'm not trying to be rude, sir, and I wouldn't have mentioned it at all, but…'

Nathan takes a small step back, as if the space might give him room to breathe. It's true he hasn't done much talking, and there's no chance he could recount word for word what he's said in the last few minutes, but he knows he's only said it once. And then there's that fear, growing, sharpening, slicing through his defences. He turns to Katie, as if she might be able to protect him, to offer an explanation other than the one he can no longer avoid. 'Did you catch any of our conversation?'

'Enough,' she snaps, clearly angry at the information he'd failed to share.

Nathan turns back to the gardener, taking in his age, the potential for confusion. He'd always put him at around seventy, but he has one of those faces that could easily belong to someone ten years older.

'The lassie weren't in the house before, was she?' asks Mr Markham, leaning in through the window to get a better look.

'Right over there,' says Nathan, aware that the curtains must have blocked his view of her a few minutes earlier.

'Oh, right,' he nods. 'Only, you said you couldn't bear to go in there. I guess I just assumed nobody was. That's why I wasn't expecting to see anyone in there today. Why I came rushing across.'

Now it's Katie's turn to do the same; she appears at Nathan's shoulder, almost barging him out of the way. '*Today?* You mean somebody was here before? Somebody who looks like Nathan?'

'Exactly like him,' says Mr Markham, directing the shears at Nathan. 'I guess it must have been Christian, then, but I'm sure he said he was you. And the funny thing is…' His hand comes up to his chin, drawing down his fingers to suggest the length of beard. Then it moves behind his neck to show the length of the hair.

'You're wrong,' says Nathan. 'He wouldn't have come here. He's just like me.' He wipes his hands down the sides of his trousers, as if suddenly finding they're as dirty as the gardener's, adding a barely audible, 'Not like me.' He remembers the phone call, remembers the doubt so swiftly answered, remembers the vision of sunshine and beaches and the nephew he's never met. 'You're wrong,' he says again, this time with a little more force. 'Christian is down in Cornwall. I spoke to him only yester—' He cuts himself off a second too late, and doesn't need to look at Katie to know that she's staring. He returns to the phone call, carefully working through the conversation. Had Christian specifically said he was in Cornwall? No. He'd simply said it was sunny there.

Might he have been worried by the call, sensed something in his voice and come to London looking for his brother, starting in the most obvious place? The timings don't work, even Nathan with his loose grasp of time can see that. But he can also see that it doesn't matter, because his brother might not have needed a phone call to sense something was wrong; it might have been in the connection he'd described, the one that Nathan had tried to deny, the one that might also explain how he'd grown the same hair and a beard.

'I think you must have misheard,' he says, a calmness in his voice to reflect his growing satisfaction with the explanation. 'He probably said he was *looking for Nathan.*'

Markham nods. 'I imagine you're right. My ears are not what they used to be. And maybe he thought I were answering that question when I told him I hadn't seen either of you in years.'

'Did he say where he was going?'

'No. He left quickly. I think he got a bit upset about...' He looks over Nathan's shoulder into the house.

'But did he seem okay in general?' Nathan asks, a different concern growing this time. If his brother looked exactly like him in his current state then he couldn't be doing very well at all. It's a far cry from how he'd pictured him on the days he'd allowed himself to do so: the perfect life, the perfect family, playing on the beach or quietly pottering around his legal practice in a pinstriped suit.

'If I'm honest,' says Markham, 'he seemed a bit...' He tips his head back, as if the word he's searching for might be somewhere up in the clear blue sky, or in the tangles of clematis trained to the wall above the door. Several possibilities present themselves to Nathan, although none matches the answer that finally emerges, '... scared.'

'You mean, worried?'

'No, it was definitely more scared. He was constantly moving and kept looking around, peering down the side of the house.'

'Like he'd seen something, or someone?'

'Kind of,' says Markham, and now it's the gardener's turn to be shifting nervously from foot to foot.

'What do you mean?' says Katie, cutting in.

'Well... it don't make sense, because it's your house and everything, even if you couldn't ever bring yourself to...' He readjusts both his feet and his line of conversation, before returning to Nathan. 'The point is, although I haven't seen you and your brother that often, I know you two. I know you're good people, and so...'

'So...?' Katie jumps in again with increasing impatience.

'It was like he didn't want to be seen. I mean, when he first spotted me I think he were surprised. I'm not supposed to be here on a Wednesday, you see. Today is my normal day, but the work were getting on top of me a bit so I came in yesterday as well. Plus...' Markham looks directly at Nathan as if waiting for permission to proceed, which he eventually gives with a reluctant nod, eyes closing in anticipation, expecting the worst. 'He told me not to tell anyone he'd been around. And I wouldn't have done if it hadn't been you, or rather if I hadn't believed you were him come back.' The gardener glances nervously across at Katie. 'Have I done something wrong?'

Katie answers for Nathan, a tightened excitement in her voice. 'Absolutely not. You've helped a great deal. Now I need to have a quick word in private with my friend, and then we're going to have a look around the house. I hope you don't mind, but it's probably best if...'

Nathan is aware of her looking across at him, despite the tears blurring his eyes, despite the whole world seeming to tilt and sway.

Markham offers a little bow and starts to retreat. 'I understand, ma'am,' he says. 'I'll pack up my things and be off. I'd done most of what I needed to anyway.' He catches Nathan's eye and offers a hesitant smile. 'I hope you and your brother are okay.'

'So do I,' says Nathan, weakly.

CHAPTER SIXTEEN

Katie stands facing Nathan, not knowing which emotion to turn to. There's the fizzing excitement of a breakthrough in the case, a suspect she's never met before but whose face could not be any more familiar. There's also the doubt; how long had Nathan suspected his brother? Long enough to have cost someone their life?

'I need everything,' she snaps. 'Now!'

'It's not him,' Nathan snaps back.

'I will be the judge of that.'

'Says a detective who can't solve a case.'

The words strike her with a physical force and she steps back, taking a moment. 'Well, this one seems clear enough, even to me. Food from your childhood, references to home, knowledge of intimate marks on your body—'

'And on yours.' His body has straightened, stiffened, set firm. He looks ready to attack. 'Is my brother one of the many men you've fucked recently?'

'You think I'd go anywhere near someone who looks like you?' she shoots back.

His hand leaves his side and she's ready for him, but it's only to grab the shirt she lent him. 'The clothes certainly fit.'

'It's what's on the inside that counts. And you're not fooling me about that anymore.'

'You still think *I* am capable of killing someone?' he says, the anger suddenly leaving his eyes.

'I think you would let someone else die to protect your brother.'

'And what about your dad? What secrets are you keeping to protect him?'

Her mouth falls open. How could he possibly know? But it's the same question she always asks about Nathan. The question she'd asked right back at the beginning, after she'd first taken the young profiler to a crime scene and watched him perform his magic. Although this is different. No good can come from this. She shouldn't have trusted him; shouldn't have allowed her desperation to cloud her already questionable judgement. She shouldn't have invited him into her home.

She's looking at the ground now, fighting the urge to sink towards it, but aware he's moving closer.

'I'm sorry,' he says. 'Your family has nothing to do with this. And this is what we agreed to focus on. Nothing else.'

She lifts her head and meets his gaze, seeing the sadness she'd thought she'd heard. 'You need to help us find your brother,' she says, pulling out her phone, trying to remember what she'd already found out from the gardener, Markham. 'It was Christian, wasn't it?'

Nathan pushes out a long breath before answering, as if even this is some kind of betrayal. 'Yes.'

'And do you have an address?'

'I have a telephone number.'

She remembers the phone in her bedroom, and Nathan's attempt to cover it with the dirty washing. 'Did you call him last night?'

'To check he was all right.'

'And to check he was innocent,' she says, shaking her head as she punches DS Peters' number into her phone.

'He is innocent,' Nathan insists. 'He couldn't have committed those crimes.'

'How can you be so certain?' she asks.

His eyes open even wider and seem to draw her in. 'I know how killers think, remember. That's what you always used me for.'

Used. She could hardly argue with that.

A voice answers at the other end of the line. She gives the name and the telephone number Nathan reluctantly shares. She also gives the address they're at, along with instructions for a team to get here ASAP. Her discomfort grows with her own sense of urgency. She hadn't considered that the brother might still be here, in the house with them now. She's about to ask Nathan for a description to share with the team, already knowing there must be a strong resemblance given Markham's confusion between the two, but over his shoulder she spots a selection of family photos. She pushes past him and picks up a small silver frame tucked away at the back. It shows two teenage boys standing side by side; their clothes, their height, their faces identical.

'You're twins!' she says, turning to face the grown-up version of one of those boys.

'But we're not the same,' is all he says in response, not looking at the photo.

She hangs up on DS Peters. Placing the frame carefully back on the table, she returns to the centre of the room, never once turning her back on the door through which a second Nathan might pounce at any moment. She dials the mobile number she's just been given for Christian, half-expecting to hear it ringing behind her. She spins round, but the line is dead.

'He must have been to Scotland,' she says, working through what she already knows. 'To check on you. How else would he know what you look like now?'

'Because we have a connection. Because we've always done things like that – chosen the same cars, clothes, haircuts – without having spoken to each other.'

'You recognised the caravan park I mentioned. You recognised the writing at the first victim's house, and the reference to your favourite childhood meal, a meal you both enjoyed, perhaps? I think you also recognised the pattern carved into the victim's chest, possibly something related to your life in Scotland. You swore to me that nobody had been up there to see you, that they couldn't have seen you. So, either you were wrong about that, or you're right about this connection to your brother.' She hates herself for carrying on, for ignoring his pleading look, his open hands in front of his face, the scars on his wrist, but she knows there's still fight in him.

'I think what we're doing here is exactly what the real killer wants us to do. To doubt each other. To doubt our own flesh and blood.'

For a moment Katie's thoughts turn to her dad, but she cannot allow the distraction.

'I need to know everything about your family,' she says. 'Perhaps it's best you tell me before the others get here. Let's start with your brother.'

Nathan looks as if he's about to protest, his arms now folded, his chin low, but he offers a reluctant nod. 'I don't know much,' he says, 'not anymore. We've been apart for the last few years, for the past…' He tilts his head, as if searching for a number, but Katie doesn't doubt he could give her the very day. 'It was just before you and I started working together. It's not that Christian and I don't get along, it's… well, it's complicated, so complicated I couldn't even explain it to him.' A plane passes low overhead. 'I decided in the end to tell him a lie. I convinced him I was living undercover, that I'd changed my name and my appearance and that if we got in contact beyond the occasional phone call it might put his life at risk. Perhaps he sensed that there was something wrong, or perhaps it's because…' He casts another look over at the family photos and then at the grandfather clock in the corner of the room. 'This is a significant time for us. And it would make sense for him to think I might do something…' He reaches for his wrist, running a shaking finger across the scar. 'Whatever the reason, he's come back, and here is the most obvious place to start trying to find me. He's probably worried how I will react because I made him swear that he would never come for me.' Nathan pauses and waits for Katie to nod in acceptance of her own failure to respect this same request. 'He's probably trying to check on me without me knowing, to see for himself that I'm doing okay. That's probably why he lied to me about where he was and why he was worried about bumping into Markham. If he looked scared it's likely he's worried he's blown my cover, that he's put me and his family at risk.'

'Family?' says Katie, cutting him off. 'Your brother has a family?'

'A wife and a kid.' As he says it, she can see the fear grip him as suddenly as it had gripped her.

'Are you sure you don't have an address for them?' she asks, pulling out her mobile again.

'I've never been there.'

'Okay,' she says, placing a gentle hand on his arm. 'Let's go outside. Some air will do us good. And my team will be here soon.' It seems strange to refer to them as her team when for so long they had been his too. Although they had never quite accepted him and his unusual ways. Most were scared of his talent, despite the successes it won them. Nathan looks scared now, too: scared of what they might have already uncovered, scared of what it might mean for him. He holds out his hands, and she's happy to slip the cuffs back on, wishing she could be doing the same to his twin.

Ten minutes later and Katie is standing at the top of the stairs leading up to the front door, watching her colleagues arrive. They've pulled up into the drive, tucking the black BMW up alongside the rusty old Citroën. She waves them in, walking down the steps to meet them and keeping a close eye on Nathan.

'Watch the front,' she says to DS Mike Peters. She can tell he wants to ask a hundred questions, but instead he slowly rubs his balding head. Alongside him is DC Alice Jones, a newbie who looks far calmer than her colleague.

'You take the back, but watch from there,' says Katie, pointing over at the barred gate on the side of the house. 'We're keeping this low-key for now, but shout as loud as you can if you see anything. When the others get here, double up. There's no reason to believe anyone is still here, but I'm not taking any risks.' Trying to look casual for the benefit of neighbours, and working through the best course of action, she only notices DC Jones' confused stare at the very last moment. She follows her gaze over to Nathan, sitting on the steps, his hands hidden by his legs but clearly in cuffs to anyone with a trained eye.

'Good spot, Alice! That's exactly who you're looking for. Another one of him.'

'But...?'

'Identical twins,' explains Katie. 'This one works with us. Nathan is going to stay with me at all times. And... Can I?' She points at DS Peters' fluorescent bib and, understanding immediately, he takes it off. She holds it up in front of them. 'Make sure to let the others know that Nathan has this on.'

They nod in agreement and move to their positions while Katie walks over to Nathan, draping the oversized bib across his shoulders. 'One day we'll get you some clothes of your own. But to avoid confusion...'

'Christian is not hiding here,' he snaps. 'At least give me credit for knowing that much.'

'Okay,' she says calmly. 'But keep it on anyway, just to be safe. Now, there's definitely no other way to get out?' She points towards the small door down the side that they'd walked past on the way to the garden. 'Just the conservatory where we bumped into Markham, and the front?'

'That's all,' says Nathan, pulling against her restraint.

She can feel him jump at the sound of a car door slamming and turns to see five more men clambering out. They couldn't look more like police officers if they tried, and she can almost feel the curtains twitch around her. The Internet will be alight with gossip in no time, but she'll have to deal with that later. Right now her priority is finding Christian.

'You two, outside,' she says, pointing at those she knows to be the least experienced. 'You three, with us.' She steps inside the house and somehow it feels colder. She stares down at the pile of mail, making a mental note to get someone to look through it later. Then she addresses the three policemen who've followed close behind.

'We stay together at all times,' she says. 'If you hear a sound you say so and we all go and have a look. Let me be one hundred per cent clear: you do not go wandering off to investigate. If you think you've found something of interest, you say, "I think I've found something of interest", and you leave it there for me to come and have a look. I'm sorry if it sounds like I'm stealing all the fun, but that's just the way it is. If you see anybody in here then you run and let the whole fucking world know what's going on. Am I understood?'

'Yes, ma'am.'

She can see it in the eyes of the men in front of her: they know it, and she knows it. It's been a while, but she's beginning to sound like her old self again.

CHAPTER SEVENTEEN

Nathan sits perfectly still while his thoughts continue to surge and swirl. If his brother is guilty, it changes everything. It takes what he had imagined as a perfect life, walking on sunny beaches with a wife and son, and drapes it in a darkness even deeper than his own. He tells himself it can't be true, that Christian can't have kept his true nature hidden from him all these years. But then, hadn't he been confident he'd done exactly that himself?

He lifts the cuffs in front of his face, watching as they slide down and reveal the lines of scarring on his wrist, realising that he was mistaken before and that not everything will change if Christian is guilty. He still needs to carry out his plan. He doesn't have to worry about his brother finding out anymore, though. In fact, perhaps he ought to make sure he does so that Christian understands this has to stop, one way or another. It's a thought that takes him back twenty years, to a kitchen table a short distance from where he's standing and a note written on squared paper, a note he's always been convinced spoke of a similar madness.

'I could be wrong,' he mumbles to himself as he, Katie and the three officers enter through the front door, the mail spread out ahead of them. 'Wrong about it all.' He moves tentatively. Old catalogues and letters are slipping left and right under him, and he's certain he's soon going to come crashing down.

They move quietly into the hallway. His dad's study is directly to their left. Nobody else was ever allowed in there; even after he died Nathan had never dared as he does now. It's smaller than he'd remembered it, filled from floor to ceiling with dusty books, stacks of newspapers and files of his legal case notes. It's obvious there's nobody else in here, but he does double-check under the desk to be sure. As boys, Christian had always been the best at hiding, often staying in his chosen spot for half an hour or more, while Nathan had searched and shouted, growing increasingly angry. Whenever he finally revealed himself, Nathan often seeking out their mum to insist that he do so, Christian always emerged from the strangest places with a broad smile. It's that smile that Nathan is picturing now as he turns back towards the hall, back towards further possibilities. As he approaches Katie, who has been directing things outside the study while clearly keeping an eye on him, his attention is drawn to a series of books on a shelf above the door, and his blood runs cold. They're out of reach, even on tiptoe, and he has to drag a chair across to pull the first one down. The cover is black with tiny red slits circling round and round towards the centre.

'You know these books?' asks Katie, stepping forward. 'Of course you do,' she corrects herself. 'Everyone does.'

Nathan doesn't say a word; he's slipping back more than twenty-five years to when he was fifteen years old and standing in a bookshop, holding the same book, somehow knowing before he'd even turned a page that the author would speak to him directly.

'Did you like his books?' Katie asks again, standing in the doorway, not crossing the threshold.

'His?' says Nathan, finally looking over.

'J.M. Priest. I read them when I was younger, under my duvet at night, desperately hoping I wasn't caught.' She pauses, running a hand through her hair, clearly uncomfortable at opening up about her own past. 'Bizarrely, it was one of the things that first got me thinking about police work,' she continues, 'maybe even more than following in Dad's footsteps. I couldn't bear the mystery of not knowing who Priest was; I needed to find out so

I could thank him for all those dark and twisted stories, and so I could find out why he suddenly stopped. Actually, there's no mystery in that last part. He'll have been too busy spending his fortune to write.'

Nathan finds himself looking upwards again, not at the shelf of books, but as if seeing up through the walls to the full extent of the house on Richmond Hill that he's never sold, that he's never had to sell. Distracted, he misses Katie reaching forward and snatching the book from his hand. He's about to protest when he realises that she's looking at the swirling pattern on the cover.

'Of course!' she says, holding the book up. 'How could I have forgotten?'

'My brother never read that sort of thing,' says Nathan, 'if that's what you're thinking.'

'But he did know about them?'

'You said it yourself,' he says, pushing past her to get out of the room and away from the conversation. 'Everybody does.'

The next room is the kitchen, but he's not ready yet. He might never be ready to go back in there. He stands just outside with his head lowered, listening for sounds of a struggle or retching, but instead the policemen are out a minute later. He's relieved. If there had been anything to find, he'd felt certain that would have been the place to make the discovery. The kitchen was where his family would get together, enjoying meals at the large table in front of the window. The kitchen was where his family was ripped apart.

He stumbles towards the stairs. He knows the way Katie's mind works, knows she wants to be methodical, but she's also always been willing to follow his lead. He climbs the stairs slowly, amazed and not a little disconcerted by the breadth of them, so different to those in his tiny Scottish cottage. On the walls hang a series of oil paintings depicting previous generations of his family going back hundreds of years. They had fascinated him as a child and bored him as a teenager; now, at the age of forty, he finds he's looking again. In particular, at the general in full uniform rising majestically on his muscular steed, wondering what elements of his and now perhaps even his brother's personality could be blamed on this man.

Before reaching the top of the stairs he stops and ducks sideways to shoot a look round the corner. Again he's remembering all the places his brother would hide as a child, often leaping out and startling him. Of course, they'd soon learned to stifle their screams and giggles for fear their dad would come; heavy footsteps on the stairs and the promise of a smack with whatever book he'd been distracted from reading.

Katie is ahead, and Nathan hurries after her with the other three policemen close behind him. The first room they pass is the guest bedroom. He allows the three policemen to go in and can hear them searching cupboards and finding nothing. His focus is on the two rooms at the end of the corridor: his room, then his brother's room. His room is exactly as he'd remembered: an eighteen-year-old's hideaway, with the dark blue paint he'd fought for barely visible beneath the posters of depressing bands and flyers for the various theatrical shows he'd become involved in. Around the age of sixteen, when dramatic changes were taking place in body and mind, acting seemed a far simpler and more productive way of avoiding the thoughts that were troubling him. He remembers the release of getting lost in the parts, often to the point where he didn't want to come back.

Framed and hung high on the far side of the room is his acceptance letter from RADA. His proudest day: the day he'd started to believe he could build a successful life out of pretending to be anyone but himself.

The bed is made and, save for the layer of dust and the moth-eaten curtains, the room looks tidy in a way that it never would have back when there was life in this house. He never kept his things in order, clothes and books and CDs strewn across the floor to his mother's despair and his father's rage. A mess to reflect the chaos in his head. Crumpled trousers, unruly hair, T-shirts adorned with skulls and troubled lyrics. Everyone thought he would grow out of it, but it only ever got worse.

He's so wrapped up in the memories this room has stirred that he only notices Katie behind him when she accidentally knocks a lone trophy from a shelf. It would normally have been holding up a row of books, but those books were the only thing from the house he'd taken with him to Scotland, boxed up and put in the back of Katie's car. How he wishes he could escape into one of those childish tales right now…

'You never told me you were good at rugby,' says Katie, looking at the trophy and carefully placing it back on the shelf. She seems to have relaxed now they've reached the final rooms and it's clear they are alone.

He remembers his teammates had called him a madman while offering congratulatory slaps on the back. His only focus has been on winning, no concern for the welfare of himself or others.

'We need to find something that shouldn't be here,' he says, returning his focus to the room.

Katie's previous calmness disappears in an instant. 'Why?'

'Something doesn't feel right.'

'What sort of thing?' says Katie, talking in that soft, persuasive voice she always used when he was slipping away into the thought process of their suspect.

He stares at the wall ahead, thinking about who used to sleep on the other side, and tucks his hands down by his sides so Katie can't see how badly they've started to shake.

'What if I was wrong about Christian?'

'You think he's guilty?' says Katie.

'No,' he says sharply. 'What if I was wrong about why he looked scared? What if he was being followed? What if the killer thought *he* was *me*?'

'Even you don't look like you anymore,' she says, and he's aware that she's pointing at a long mirror in the corner of the room. 'I could easily have walked past you in the street. So unless this killer saw you in Scotland…?'

He can picture her face, one eyebrow raised, waiting for his response. In the end, all he does is hover his cuffed hands above his stomach and move them slowly round, following the path of dirty marks he remembers so clearly from his other home.

'He must have done.'

'Unless that was from the J.M. Priest book.'

He looks down at the floor again, the place he's always looked for inspiration, and another terrible possibility presents itself.

'What if it wasn't a mistake? What if he was targeting Christian?' He twists the fluorescent top he's been given, as if that might help wring out the tension in him. 'Maybe he knows it's the best way to hurt me. The only way.' He glances down at his wrist, then back up at Katie, recalling his brother's words in their phone call: *I take it there's no special person in your life… I thought maybe you could find yourself a nice policewoman, someone who understands that world, who could protect themselves.*

'It's possible, I suppose, but it doesn't seem likely.'

He nods his acceptance, returning his attention to the room, wondering if he should check the drawers or behind the curtains but, at the same time, knowing there will be no need. The clue will be obvious, like the beans and sausage on toast, like the birthmark at the top of the thigh, like the words that had brought them to this place. He turns and brushes past Katie. She doesn't say a word, just follows close behind as he enters the next doorway along the hall, into the room that belonged to his brother.

The room is brighter than his, with white walls, colourful pop music posters, blue sheets and curtains and a thick white carpet that has somehow remained spotless despite the dust. The furniture in the room is all arranged in the exact same way as his own, but Nathan finds he's far more comfortable considering the differences. He runs his fingertips along the unbroken spines of a number of difficult literary novels, and turns to find Katie holding one of Christian's trophies.

'Christian was into golf then?'

'Yes,' he says tentatively, knowing there must be meaning in her question. 'He likes less aggressive sports. He wasn't like me. He isn't like me.' Every time he says it he knows he sounds less certain, but he has to keep saying it until all hope is gone.

'Sarah Cleve was twisted into the pose of a golf swing,' says Katie. 'Holding the same knife that had…'

Nathan looks away; she doesn't need to finish.

The last time he stood in the centre of this room the whole world seemed to be vibrating with the possibilities the future presented. He was off to RADA, and his brother had a place to study law at Cambridge. Both were so overwhelmed, bouncing around like young boys again, turning their music up loud because their dad was out of the house. Those weeks for Nathan were the best of his life, the cresting of a wave he didn't even know he was riding. At last, he and his brother knew who they were, and where they were heading.

Katie puts the trophy down and moves towards the door, and Nathan reluctantly follows. Out in the hall, shifting his weight from side to side, to try and compensate for the way the whole world seems to be moving, he becomes aware of the other police officers continuing with their work; doors being opened and closed and the occasional thump as they lower themselves to the floor to peer under a bed. He remembers the flutter of excitement he would get knowing that his thoughts, his insights, his curse, had brought his team to the verge of making an arrest. He also remembers the sense of hypocrisy he felt when they celebrated taking another 'sick bastard' off the streets. The truth is, he'd always felt closer to the criminals, perhaps even from the days when he would play the robber and his brother the policeman. Always the policeman.

At the end of the corridor is another staircase, smaller, narrower, leading up to the third floor. Nathan could never sleep while his parents were downstairs, always waiting to hear his mother creeping by. He recalls the times he would sneak upstairs in the middle of the night, whispering for his mum to come out of the bedroom. Somehow she always managed to hear him, like she'd been lying there, waiting. They'd sit on the top step and talk quietly about his latest nightmare. Christian was never troubled by such things; always smiling, always happy and joking about. In their teenage years he started calling Nathan 'big bro', not because he was older but because he'd always seemed so aged by all those dark thoughts.

Nathan finally steps over the threshold of his parents' bedroom. He breathes in deeply and is convinced he can smell his mum's perfume, but he knows there's nothing left here but memories and dust. The beds are made tightly, the way his dad had liked it, and pushed close together. Nathan realises his mum must have done this in the days leading up to their dad's death. On the final day she had telephoned both boys to share the news, told them she loved them and to take care getting home. She'd then tidied the house from top to bottom, scrubbed every surface till it was gleaming. She'd prepared a meal, not for her, but dished up on two plates and placed on the kitchen table. It was the boys' favourite, a comfort food from when they were children: a tin of beans and sausage on toast. By the time Nathan got home, and he was the first home, travelling from central London rather than Cambridge, the food was stone cold. Their mum was not, but she was well on the way, sitting at the kitchen table with a half-empty bottle of wine and an entirely empty bottle of sleeping pills.

Standing in the middle of his parents' bedroom, Nathan's eyes are locked on those same two things tucked away at the back of his mum's dresser. He might have missed them had he not so vividly remembered the room from the last time he was here, having travelled home to see his bedridden dad and to hold the hand that no longer had the strength to smack him. Nathan has always had a remarkable ability to take in his surroundings, to notice the details that others miss. Many times, like that last day spent with his dad, he's wished he didn't have that gift, but it's served him well in previous cases and it's serving him well now. He approaches slowly, not quite believing his eyes, looking back over his shoulder and half-expecting to see his dad's twisted, pale body stretched out on the bed, a scene he had never actually witnessed but that he's imagined a thousand times. When he does finally touch the surface of the wine bottle he strikes it so hard, half-expecting his fingers to pass straight through, that he nearly knocks it over. It rocks and then straightens, his body following a similar path. He reaches out again but Katie grabs his shoulder.

'If you think it's something, then don't!' she says sharply. 'Not without gloves.'

'Prints.' He says the word out loud while looking down at his fingertips, at the one part of his body that isn't identical to his brother.

Katie pulls on her gloves and carefully lifts the bottle, revealing a label that Nathan instantly recognises. It was one of his dad's favourites, a case he would select from when they were celebrating: the last time being the evening the boys had got their places at Cambridge and RADA. He'd looked proud, smiled even, but they could never have known what was going on inside his body. Nathan turns and looks at a box of tissues on the bedside table and remembers his dad hacking away so loudly he'd woken them downstairs, wondering when was the first time he felt that strange metallic taste.

Nathan turns back to the bottle, wishing he could take a swig, but he can see from the light streaming in through a gap in the curtains that it's empty of wine. Instead, there appears to be a white square of paper curled up in the neck. Katie has spotted it, too, because she's started to stick a single finger inside to try and draw it out. It's a slow process, but somehow Nathan knows it'll be the same squared paper he found in the toaster at the Brooks' house, with the same thick ink soaking through. He also knows what will be written on it, the words carefully shaped on his lips, just as they had been during his phone call with Christian. *So sorry to have left you alone.*

CHAPTER EIGHTEEN

'What do you think it means?' Katie asks, moving the paper closer to Nathan's face, hoping to break his glazed expression.

Nathan slumps to the floor, grabbing a handful of the thick rug beneath them.

'Is there another body here?' she asks, urgently.

'I don't know,' he says, eventually. 'I don't know anything.'

She can't help but notice the two sides of the bed don't match. One is a pale pink, the other white. It looks like they've been pushed together at some point; a sign, perhaps, of marital issues. She sits down on the floor next to Nathan and lightly places a hand on his arm.

'Is it his handwriting?' she says. 'Have they *all* been his handwriting?'

He shakes his head, but she can see the truth in the way he's sitting, part folded over, every slow breath seeming to squeeze a little more life out of him. She's trying to think of something she can do when he suddenly sits up straight and pushes back his shoulders. She can't help but be impressed by this act of strength, one final fight against the truth. But then she feels something else building inside. She's thinking of school photos in a narrow corridor; she's thinking of a boy's little shoe; she's thinking of an anniversary and of a kitchen that cannot be entered; she's thinking of a house that has not been used for a very long time. She's also thinking of what Nathan intends to do in less than two days' time.

'It's the anniversary of the death of your mother.' She speaks quietly so she can't be overheard by the other policeman on the landing outside.

He shoots her a look, a mix of surprise and anger.

'Might that explain your brother's choice of victims?'

There's no reaction, this time, beyond a slow exhalation; a pressure finally released.

'Give us a few minutes,' she calls out to the men by the door. 'Maybe check the other floors again. And again, if you find anything, or *anyone*, don't play the hero.'

When they've gone, she turns back to Nathan. He seems, as she had feared, to be drifting away, but he squeezes his eyes shut and forces the words out.

'I'm not stupid.'

'You're the least stupid person I've ever known.'

'And yet I might have missed this.' A sweep of the arms seems an attempt to take in everything, as if everything is what he's missed. Then he lifts his cuffed hands in front of his face. 'I could see it in myself, but not in him. He even told me on the phone yesterday that we were the same, and that was how he knew I wasn't living the life I wanted to. I thought he meant…' His head sinks further into his chest, and his words become muffled. 'I don't know what he meant.'

'You think he was trying to confess to you?'

Nathan pauses before replying. 'It hadn't sounded like a confession. Maybe he was trying to recruit me?'

'Then *he* is stupid.' She reaches out and takes his arm, holding it just firm enough to stop him retreating. She can feel his heartbeat jumping under his skin. 'I may not know this.' She nods towards the room. 'But I know *you*. I know what you are and aren't capable of…' She hesitates, remembering the doubts.

He pulls his hand away. 'Family,' he says, 'family shows you what you can't see on your own.' He glances across at the empty pot of pills on the dresser, and presses his back into the pink side of the bed. 'I thought it was just me that had these awful thoughts, for such a long time, right up until…' He reaches out to the carpet with both hands and with his two forefingers starts to draw circles in the rug, spiralling inwards towards the centre.

'You knew when you saw the second victim?'

'No,' he says, his voice growing distant again. 'I knew from the moment I saw my mum's book.'

Katie stares at his spiralling fingers, feeling almost hypnotised by the movement until something finally clicks at the back of her mind, a connection that could only have been made sitting here, in this expensive house with a dark story. Flawed police, likeable villains, unthinkable crimes committed by both. It's all there in the case they're working now, and in the dark imagination of the man sitting next to her.

'Jesus!' she says, far too loud, before lowering her voice to a whisper. 'Your mum was J.M. Priest?'

He doesn't answer; he doesn't need to. Just like in those gruesome books she would so hungrily read, she can see a story opening up in front of her that both horrifies and fascinates in equal part.

'How did your mum die?' she asks, more bluntly than her training would have allowed. 'It's important,' she adds, as if to reassure herself and justify the coldness.

Nathan eventually points across at the pot of pills on the dresser. 'The day cancer took my dad,' he says weakly, 'she called us home, and I found her in the kitchen with a note: the same note…' This time he nods towards the scrap of paper she's carefully folded up and placed inside an evidence bag. 'I thought for a long time that she simply couldn't live without Dad, and I guess in a way I was right, because he had always been there to keep her in line, to keep us all in line.' He closes his eyes, flinching slightly as the images come to him. 'Our family solicitor called me into his office not long after they were gone, and I remember the look on his face was like he was the one that had lost his parents. He handed me a book by J.M. Priest, and within its pages, between the words I knew so well, was the will of the woman I suddenly realised I hadn't known at all.'

'So, you think she was just like…?'

'Yes.' His answer is far firmer than her tentative question. 'I may not have known her, but I knew the person that had written those novels, and I knew the darkness that was inside of me. She had the same desires; she knew without Dad beside her that she was going to take a life and, in the end, I guess she only had one choice.' He's looking at his wrist, the faintest smile on his lips.

She reaches out and grabs that wrist, pinching it just below the cuff. 'You can be different.'

'I started to take comfort in her words,' he says, as if he hasn't heard her. '"So sorry to have left you alone". It meant she believed it was she and I that were afflicted, that Christian only looked like me.' She feels his forearm tense under her grip. 'That's why this…'
He tips his head back and lets out a breath so long it could be his last. 'It doesn't make sense. I know him. I *knew* him. He was the one without complications, the one who dealt with everything that had happened and moved on. That's why I was happy that we were seeing less and less of each other. Why I was delighted when he moved to Cornwall. I thought the distance would keep me from contaminating him.'

Suddenly Nathan whips his arm away, jumps to his feet and draws back the carefully made sheets on the bed. In the centre of the pink sheet is a small copper key, and it's in his hand before Katie can say the word 'gloves'.

'How did you know?' she finds herself asking again.

He stares at the key, twisting it slowly in his fingers. 'When we misbehaved,' he nods towards the bed, 'that was where we were told to sit. It was our version of the naughty step.'

She nods as if it makes sense, but the leap in logic still worries her. 'But how did you *know*?'

The key remains held in front of his face, and she can see it start to shake.

'I just thought about what I would have done.' She struggles to hear the next whispered words, and doubts she was ever intended to. 'We are the same.'

'What's it for?'

'The basement,' he says, looking down at the floor as if he can see straight through it.

She feels that familiar tightening in her gut, just like she felt when DS Peters had called her yesterday, knowing that they'll soon be standing over another body. 'What are we going to find down there?'

'I guess it's time to stop imagining,' says Nathan, pushing past her and heading for the door.

CHAPTER NINETEEN

The door down to the basement is well hidden. Nathan remembers the first time he and his brother had stumbled across it, tucked away behind an old dresser. The key had been in the lock back then, and they'd turned it with a sense of almost unbearable excitement. There's no excitement this time as the lock pops and the door swings open. Katie drags Nathan back, insisting she go first, but he surges on as they both squeeze into the narrow entrance.

Katie pushes ahead holding a torch out in front, so he doesn't bother reaching for the well-hidden switch, imagining how much worse the scene will look if he sees it all at once. He follows Katie down the stone stairs into the darkness, shifting sideways with both cuffed hands on the rickety banister.

The other policemen are close behind, and he can tell they want him out of the way, but still where they can see him. He's caught them staring. He wonders how much they've been told, perhaps that he's the twin of a monster, perhaps that he's the biggest fool on earth. Of course, it's not so different from before, when they used to look at him as a fraud, a guy who just got lucky on a few cases, or a practitioner of the black arts.

He follows Katie's torch beam as it pans quickly from left to right. He can see the shelves stocked with his dad's favourite wine – a bottle of which is clearly missing. On the other side of the room are boxes of old toys piled high, and two little bikes, one black, one white, leaning against each other. Katie is shuffling forward, barking orders for the others to hold back and leave the door open for extra light. Her beam strikes the far wall and finds nothing, drops to the floor and reveals only dirt. When she lifts the torch again, this time to the far-right corner of the room, there's a flash of white and the beam returns, moving swiftly up and down. A human skeleton floats in mid-air. It's only as they move tentatively forward that Nathan can see it's held together by a wire frame.

'Is this what you were expecting?' asks a breathless Katie.

Nathan shakes his head before realising he needs to speak. 'There will be words.'

Katie finds them instantly, spelt out on the floor at their feet, each letter carefully arranged in baked beans.

I Mark Them So You Know

Katie's beam returns to the skeleton, picking out the skull and following a long trail of brown piped along the jawbone. Katie steps closer, but Nathan doesn't move. He knows what this is – it's exactly as he had predicted up in the bedroom – a discovery that at once confirms his suspicions about his brother and solidifies the fears he has about himself. This is not the latest victim. It's the first. He knows this for a fact. He knows because it's the very first murder that he would have committed, had he lost control.

'You think he took it from a hospital?' Katie asks.

His lips feel as numb as the rest of him as he mumbles the words. 'From a doctor.'

'How could you possibly know that?'

He realises she's misunderstood. 'From under a doctor's skin.'

Now she turns to look at him, and he feels himself sinking back into the darkness.

'Who is it?'

'The man who failed to spot Dad's cancer.'

Katie turns back towards the skeleton. 'And what's the significance of the chocolate icing mark?'

Nathan can feel his fist bunch by his side as it had more than twenty years earlier, just a month before his father's death. 'It's where I split the doctor's jaw after I realised what he'd done. Or, what he hadn't done.'

'The other marks weren't related to the victim bearing them,' she says. 'They were marks on you and me. How can you be certain there's a genuine victim here, and not just a skeleton stolen from a school or hospital?'

The answer again comes to him far too quickly, as if a message is being transmitted through the darkness from an outside source. It's cold in the basement, but not as cold as his shivering suggests.

'Look inside.'

'What?'

Nathan is staring down at his feet, or what little he can see of them, trying desperately to see nothing other than the faint outline of someone else's shoes.

'Look inside the skeleton,' he says, lowering his head.

It's the policeman over his shoulder who tells him he's right with a horrified gasp. Nathan starts to retreat, back towards the stairs, and he can see the other policeman stepping out of the way, giving him far too much room to pass. When he reaches the unsteady banister he grips so hard he feels it almost give way under him. Or perhaps that was his balance; the weakness in his legs; or the sense that everything is shifting again, moving under him like the pile of post in the hall, or spinning like the marks in the dirt, on the wall, on a book, on a body. As he rises towards the door, he reaches out and flicks the switch, filling the room behind him with light. He doesn't turn back.

CHAPTER TWENTY

'You want one?' Katie asks, holding out a packet of cigarettes towards Nathan. He doesn't react. She crumples up the packet and slips them in her pocket, feeling foolish. They're sitting on the front steps, tucked to one side, allowing the forensics team to move in and out. Any chance of keeping things secret from the neighbours, and therefore from the rest of the world, has gone. The first two murders have already become big news; the media have even snappily named the killer 'The Cartoonist'.

'Do you want me to take you somewhere to try and get some sleep?'

'I must have been asleep all my life,' he says softly, casting a glance back at the house.

Katie looks at him, knowing she has to find a way to keep him here, for his sake and for hers.

'I'm going back to Scotland,' says Nathan, as if reading her mind. 'I'll make my own way.'

'You'd leave before we've found your brother?'

He's staring out at a clear blue sky. 'What makes you think I want to find him?'

'What makes you think you have a choice?' she says, feeling her anger starting to build, remembering the other man she can't get through to, the other man she couldn't stop slipping away. 'He wanted you down here. He wanted you to find out the truth.'

'And now that I have, I don't give a fuck what he wants.'

'So, you'd just walk away? He's killed three innocent people!'

'You think the doctor was innocent?' Nathan snaps back.

'He didn't deserve to die. Nor did those two mothers. Jesus, if you're willing to let him get away with this and carry on killing, then you're as guilty as he is!'

'Don't worry,' he says, looking away, 'I won't be getting away with it.'

'*That* is not fucking happening either!' she says, reaching to take hold of his cuffs, only to remember that she'd insisted on him taking them off before they left the house, not wanting the press to get a shot of him in them.

He moves close, pressing his face up to hers. 'Unless you arrest me, I'm gone.'

'Fine,' she says, reaching for the cuffs again, certain she'll have no trouble convincing her bosses that Nathan could have been involved, or was at least aware of what his brother was doing. When she thinks about it, clearly, professionally, she can see that possibility herself. Back in the day she would always make sure to look those she was arresting in the eye, either searching for more evidence that she'd got it right, or conveying through an unblinking stare that justice had and would always win. But when she looks at Nathan, the truth is there, as clear as it has ever been. He's not acting this time. The pain she's seeing is very real. How could this be justice, to take the freedom away from the man she has dragged back into this nightmare? And why has she dragged him back? If this is a moment for honesty, then she also has to accept that it wasn't just work.

'Okay,' she says, finally, blinking back the tears. The words she turns to in the end are the very same words she had spoken to her dad: 'I will let you go.' They stand in silence, holding each other's stare, feeling the connection again after more than a year; stronger than ever, perhaps.

The spell is broken by the slamming of a car door. She turns to see that a new vehicle has arrived on the other side of the street; black and shiny and not at all out of place in such a prosperous area.

'Shit,' she says, shifting herself and preparing for the verbal onslaught she knows is coming.

The man shoving the gate open at the end of the path ahead of them is tall and broad, with a shock of white hair swept back tight. He's removed his hat and tucked it under his arm, but the medals and the silver braid and the perfect shine on his shoes tell her he's rushed from an official engagement. He waits until he's just a few feet away before he speaks, but she's felt herself flinch with his every approaching step.

'No more fucking lies from you!' he says, pointing at Nathan. 'This ends right now.'

'Don't you dare,' Katie says, surprised that the first blow was aimed at Nathan, and moving across in front of Superintendent Taylor. 'Do you have any idea what he's going through?'

'Do *you*?' says the superintendent. 'I don't think we know a single thing about this man.'

'What are you talking about?' she says, lowering her voice. 'This is the man whose successes you've been taking the credit for, for *years*.'

Superintendent Taylor leans out to get a view of Nathan, who has slumped down on the steps behind. 'And why do you think he was always so keen not to take the credit himself? Why do you think he would never allow his name or photo to make it to the papers? Why do you think he always sneaked away from crime scenes, hiding away in the shadows when anyone arrived who might be asking questions?'

Katie believes she knows, but she's not about to share. 'Because we're not all after the celebrity,' she says, holding her boss's glare. She's waiting for the satisfaction of seeing that vein throbbing in his temple, but instead his face splits into a smile.

'You really don't know the first thing about this man, do you?'

'Nathan,' she says. 'His name is *Nathan*.'

'That much I'll give you,' he says. 'That much he didn't steal. As for everything else…' He broadens his stance. 'I had a bit of time on my journey over here, got some people to do a bit of digging around based on new information that has come to light,' he gestures towards the house, 'and I suspect Nathan, here,' his face twists as he uses the word, 'is not the man he told us he was when he took on the role. Indeed, he hasn't been himself for the last twenty years, which, coincidentally or not, is the same number of years ago that Nathan Marks, a highly educated but highly troubled young man, disappeared from the streets of Bristol.'

She turns to look at Nathan in utter shock, and having to think fast about how much she wants and needs to defend him, her head telling her this could damage her career beyond repair, her heart telling her that that career is as fucked as the rest of her life and there's only one thing that matters anymore. 'Fine,' she says, holding up a hand. 'So now you know. I didn't want to say anything for the very same reason that Nathan didn't, because he wanted to protect his brother from knowing what he did. Because he didn't want him following a similar path. One,' she stops and gestures towards Nathan, 'that has clearly taken its toll.'

The superintendent tips his head back and barks a laugh that echoes off the walls of the buildings around them. 'You expect me to believe that he didn't know?'

'I expect you to prove that he did,' she says, inching further across and blocking the path to Nathan. 'And before that, I think we should be trying to find his brother, Christian, to determine if he really is the man behind all this.'

There's no laugh this time. 'We? Why the hell would I keep you on this case? I would have retired you a long time ago if it hadn't been for your father.' For the first time Superintendent Taylor stumbles over his words, readjusting his hat under his arm and noisily clearing his throat before continuing. 'And then there was the whole fuck-up with Mark Brooks and you rolling around on the floor where his wife had been murdered.' He squeezes his eyes shut and shakes off a grimace. 'I had to phone him personally to ask forgiveness for the unforgiveable.' He looks up at the house, drawing in a deep breath. 'Finally, there's this. Evidence, as if any were needed, that you're far too trusting. No, DI Rhodes, you're the last person in the world I want working on this.'

'*Want* has got nothing to do with it,' says Katie. She'd been losing energy – thinking through the possible reasons for yet another deception from Nathan, wondering what happened to a poor homeless man twenty years ago, doubting her own assessment of more recent events – but the mention of her dad has given her impetus, and the burning desire to see this through to the end, no matter the cost.

'You know full well that you need me and Nathan, otherwise you are going to be paying your respects to many more families and looking even more incompetent to the press.' She slows to wave a finger at his full dress uniform, guessing where he's just been. 'And summoned many more times to explain your failures to your superiors.'

The vein is throbbing on his temple now, more fiercely than she's ever seen it before, but in his eyes she can see an equally fierce intelligence weighing up the truth in what she's just said.

'But his own brother—'

'Is a wanted man,' she cuts him off. 'And who better to find him?'

'Which is why we need to take Nathan in for questioning again. I've half a mind to—'

'Arrest him, and I walk away,' she says. 'From this. From everything.'

'Were you not listening just a minute ago? You're hardly irreplaceable now.'

'Together,' she says, taking a step towards Nathan, who remains seated behind her, not joining in the conversation but clearly listening. 'Together: that's exactly what we are. And I'll make you a promise. If we don't get you a result in…' She looks up at the sky as if searching for a figure, but she already has one in mind. 'Two days. If we don't have a killer behind bars in two days, then you can take me off the case. In fact, you can have the very thing you've been craving these last six months – you can have my resignation.'

He stands motionless, weighing up the offer, no doubt remembering all the times this past year that he's called her into his office and told her to shut the door. But he'll also be remembering the years before, when she and Nathan had delivered, time and again. She knows how badly he's wanted that back, almost as badly as she has herself, and although it's far too late for Nathan, he might just take the risk for her.

Through gritted teeth he eventually speaks. 'DS Peters takes the lead, you advise and that's all, and you keep him,' he jabs a finger over her shoulder, 'by your side at *all* times. One step out of line and he's behind bars. If I find out he knew what his brother was doing, if I find he was involved in any way, if I find you had the slightest inkling…' A flash of doubt crosses the superintendent's face, and Katie fears she's about to have the offer withdrawn, so she shoots a quick look down to the end of the street where the press is gathering behind a line of officers. Following her gaze, the Super suddenly rises and the doubt is replaced by an expression of calm, even if the words that accompany his departure are anything but. 'You find your fucking brother, Nathan Radley!'

Katie stands and watches him go, her lips shaping a new surname for a man she had thought she knew. Although now that she's heard the surname, she realises she's seen it before, just a few minutes earlier, on the acceptance letter to RADA hanging high on the wall in his bedroom. Somehow she'd managed to shut out that fact, to be blind to its significance, just as she's been blind to so many things about this man. She wants to spin round and confront Nathan Radley, but she's certain she'll only be wasting her time. Which is why she's so surprised when she hears him speak: a single word delivered with feeling.

'Thanks.'

She can't decide what to say in response. She wants to ask him the extent of his lie and demand that he tell her everything. She wants to take him by the throat and squeeze the information out of him, to hear all the apologies she believes she deserves. But she doesn't speak, and she doesn't move; she stares at the man she had, up until a year ago, trusted more than any other.

'Just this case,' he says, eyes wide and unblinking. 'That's all that matters.'

She continues to look at him and she knows that he's right. She holds out a hand, waiting till his skinny fingers grip hers and she can drag him to his feet.

'You give me everything you've got,' she says, no question, no doubt. 'For the next day and a half.'

'I promise.'

'Do you have any idea where Christian might be now?'

He shakes his head as DS Peters appears behind her, looking nervous at interrupting, while slipping his mobile into his pocket.

'Sorry,' he says. 'But I thought you ought to know.' The tone is a familiar one; it's the way he'd spoken to her on the phone back at the very beginning when he'd been scared to share the news of another murder. And she's certain that's what he's come to share now.

'Another mother?' she asks, picturing the photos and Tate's little shoes.

'No,' says DS Peters. He glances over at Nathan and, lightly taking Katie's arm, tries to pull her away.

'He's with me,' she says, resisting. 'You can tell us, whatever it is.'

'Is he dead?' says Nathan, before shaking his head, dismissing the possibility.

'It's the doll,' says DS Peters. 'The headless one from the Brooks' house you asked me to have checked.'

'Go on.'

He breathes out slowly, glancing over at the press in the distance as if they might be able to hear. 'We have photos,' he says. 'We have proof that it wasn't there on the day of the murder. Nor was it there when the team went back yesterday morning. Which means—'

'The killer has been back,' says Katie, turning quickly to Nathan, reminding herself with a brief but powerful sense of relief that he was with her for the whole of the day.

'Yes,' says DS Peters. 'But there's more. Something forensics discovered stuffed inside the doll that…' He opens his mouth then closes it again. He still has his hand on her arm and she's still resisting, but now she places her hand on top of his, trying to calm him, fearing that the old detective is looking faint.

'Blood?' she asks.

'A piece of skin.'

'Whose?' she asks, trying to piece things together. 'The victim in there?' She gestures towards the house. To her right, she's aware of Nathan rising from the steps. Then her eyes move to his hands, where one hand is pulling against the other, dragging the ring finger back.

'No!' she says, turning back to DS Peters. But she can see from the twist of his face that it's true.

CHAPTER TWENTY-ONE

Katie parks the car around the corner as arranged and waits for the PC to appear. Further up the road she can see a car she suspects belongs to a journalist and, as she pops open the door and climbs out, she thinks she can make out the flash of sunlight reflecting on a lens. She closes the door behind her and nods as the PC approaches. She only vaguely recognises him, but he clearly knows her.

'He's not going anywhere,' she says, flicking her eyes across at the car. It's less an instruction than a statement of fact. Nathan hasn't moved for the whole of the twenty minutes it took to drive over, and there's no sign he's about to now.

'I won't be long,' she says, moving away, not looking back to check but certain the PC will remain outside the car.

Fifty yards up the road, she comes to the address she'd been given. She'd known in advance that it wouldn't be a big house, but seeing the tiny bungalow very nearly breaks her heart. As does the sight of Mark Brooks appearing at the door. He couldn't have known she was coming, so he must have been standing by the window staring out into the street. He looks like he hasn't slept since the last time they met.

'Is he with you?' he shouts. 'Is that bastard here?'

She holds up a hand to slow him, all the time aware of that blasted camera lens in the distance.

'Let's go inside,' she says, firmly. 'We need to talk.'

The house is even smaller than it had looked from the outside, with a narrow hallway leading down to a small conservatory that the builder's son might have constructed himself. Everything about the place screams ageing parents: the faded pictures on the wall; the ornaments carefully arranged on a table; the umbrella stand; the pale brown wallpaper. The exception is the small pile of shoes in the corner, one of which has escaped to the middle of the floor. It's bright pink with Velcro fastenings, and it reminds her in an instant of Tate's shoe alongside the squashed toy tractor. It also reminds her why she's here.

'Did you know?' asks Mark, standing far too close. His face is flushed and his hands are balled into fists, but there's control there, too, his voice lowered to a whisper. 'Because *he* knew. That's how he was able to make that promise. That's how I was able to believe him. That's why he wanted the cuffs. It's why he let me…' He runs his fingers across the back of his other hand where a large bruise has formed on his knuckles.

'Who told you?' she asks, knowing he might have seen it on the television, with speculation bound to be growing, but also sensing she's been betrayed.

'What does it matter?'

'I just wondered,' she says, carefully. 'Because I'd wanted to tell you myself, face-to-face, so we could talk through the possibilities.'

'What possibilities?'

'We are working on a number of theories,' Katie says, maintaining her calm this time as she gestures towards a small book-lined room to their left. 'I also understand your doubts about Nathan, but if you'd seen how this development has affected him you'd know—'

'Guilt,' snaps Mark, rubbing his hand again. 'That's all it is. Guilt at the secret he kept. You're just blind to it.'

'Not blind at all,' she says, holding his stare, before moving into the small room and hoping he'll follow. When he has, and she's convinced him to take a seat on a neat, blanket-covered chair in the corner, she perches herself on the edge of the desk upon which sits a computer that ought to be in a museum.

'I need to know about the doll,' she says, at the same time scanning the spines on the bookcase for the name J.M. Priest. She's not surprised to find *she* is not there.

'What about it?' asks Mark. His feet are jumping around, mirroring the movement of his hands.

'Why did you come and get it?'

'Because…' He lifts a hand to his hair. It's thinning on top and in need of a wash. All of him is: she can smell that from where she's sitting. Not that she's any better. 'Because my daughter Ellie insisted. She got incredibly upset.' He looks down, pulling at that hair. 'Of course she did. She's only four but she's not stupid. She knows what happened.'

Katie's attention is drawn again to something she'd heard when she first stepped into the house, something she'd not quite believed. Now there can be no doubt. It's the sound of a child laughing.

'Is that her I can hear?' asks Katie.

'Yeah,' says Mark. 'It must be the shock, but they're both like that. They have seemed okay ever since I returned the doll, or since I stopped at a shop and bought Ellie one that didn't…' He holds his hand up in front of his face, as if considering the doll's decapitation. 'I suppose I could have stitched it back on, but I could never do that sort of thing, that was always…' He looks to his left, and following his gaze Katie spots a series of small photo frames on a shelf in the corner filled with pictures of the family. They're far smaller and cleaner than the ones she'd seen at Nathan's home, but even with the curtains pulled and the light low Katie can make out all the fingerprints on the glass.

'So he's been in my house again,' says Mark. 'Is that what that doll proves?'

'Yes,' says Katie, not yet ready to share what else it proves. 'Does your daughter believe it's the same one?'

'I think so. It wasn't that old anyway. And to be honest, it wasn't that precious to her before, which is why she'd left it behind when I brought the two of them here.'

'Can I speak to Ellie?'

'Why?'

'It might be important.'

'You're not going to upset her, are you? I mean, it might be shock but I prefer to hear them laughing.'

It doesn't matter, because a young girl has appeared at the entrance to the study clutching a floppy doll to her chest, the head still intact. Behind her is a man who must be in his seventies looking as worn down as the son he resembles so closely.

'Everything okay?' says the older Mr Brooks, with an expression that makes it clear nothing will ever be okay again. 'I'm sorry about...' He nods towards the girl in front of him. 'I tried to stop her, but you know what she's like.'

'You can leave her with us, Dad,' says Mark, opening his arms for the young girl to run into.

'Hello,' says Katie, matching the smile now spread across the girl's face. 'Are you Ellie?'

The girl nods, a blonde ponytail bouncing at the back of her neck.

'And what is your doll called?'

The girl looks down, twisting her head as if confused by the question. 'I don't...'

'That's okay. It's obvious she's very important to you, though.'

Again the girl nods, this time even more enthusiastically.

'Can you tell me why?' It seems a strange thing to ask a child, to wonder why they might like one toy more than another, but Katie's fear is starting to grow.

'It's a secret,' she says, looking down at her feet.

'I love secrets,' says Katie, trying to avoid Mark's glare over his daughter's shoulder. 'I also love sharing them with people I trust.'

The young girl looks back at her dad, asking the question without saying a word. He nods, to let her know that Katie can indeed be trusted, even though his eyes are saying something very different.

'Will it still happen, though?' asks Ellie, squeezing the doll. 'I mean, do you promise?'

Katie sees Mark's mouth open, sees his desperation to find out where this is heading, to make that promise. But Katie knows how this works, knows the grudge that even a young child can carry for years if a promise so important is not kept, so she cuts him off. Ellie runs out of the room and is back with them minutes later. In one hand is the doll, in the other something so small she's managed to hide it.

'You are special,' she says, looking at Katie with the sort of absolute trust and admiration that only a child could offer so quickly. 'You are the one that will make it happen.' And then, with an even broader smile, Ellie opens her hand.

The paper is folded over and over, but there's no mistaking the presence of both horizontal and vertical lines. Katie reaches out for it, then stops. She'd been so wrapped up in the horror of it all that for once she had forgotten the process. At the same time she knows that putting on the gloves might upset Ellie, might even make her snatch it back. And it's already been handled by the child. Nevertheless, she will stick to the rules.

'I don't want to damage something so precious,' she says, reaching into her pocket and pulling out a pair of blue latex gloves. Instead of worrying her, seeing them seems to excite Ellie even more. As, it seems, does the sight of Katie's whole arm shaking as she takes the paper off her and carefully opens it up.

HA HA, YOUR MUM IS DEAD

Mark is standing by Katie's shoulder, his breathing short, his eyes wide.

'What is this?' he spits.

'What do *you* think it is?' asks Katie, crouching down to Ellie's level.

'It's what he told me.'

'Who told you?'

'The wizard in the garden. He pushed the paper through a hole in the fence. He said it was a magic piece of paper and that whatever was written on it would come true.' Ellie looks a little embarrassed at her next confession. 'I can't read yet, so he told me what it said. It said I needed to get this back.' She holds up the doll triumphantly. 'If I did, and if I keep our secret, then Mummy will come back too.'

Mark pushes past Katie, knocking her onto her knees, and takes his daughter in his arms. He's sobbing uncontrollably, and Ellie looks up at Katie, the first sign of worry on her face.

'Are you not here to help bring her back? Did I do something wrong? Was it because I told my sister Ava about the wizard?'

'You've done nothing wrong,' says Katie, her own voice breaking, unable to find the strength to rise. She knows it won't be long before this little girl learns the truth – the same truth she had learned at a very young age. There is no magic in this world.

Finally standing, she wants to leave, to walk away and never come back, but there's work still to be done. She places a hand on Mark's back, and he turns to her with a look that's a mix of hatred and desperation.

'Why?' he says. 'Why would he do this?'

The answer had been there from the moment she'd discovered the significance of the doll to a killer who delights in drawing out pain. She had known that in pursuing the link she would somehow be a part of inflicting that pain and yet, as always, she couldn't stop herself. The truth would come at any cost.

'I will need to get a team here,' she says softly, and Mark's eyes close in resignation. This had been a place of escape, somewhere to hide from the hideous events. And yet now it will be trampled all over in the search for clues that she knows will not be there, not unless the killer has left them intentionally. It's all part of the game: it's a game that she knows, as she looks at Mark, then at his dad, who has appeared in the doorway with an even smaller girl alongside, she is losing.

Twenty minutes later, and Katie is walking back to her car. She glances at where the suspected journalist had been. He or she has been moved on by one of the team that has arrived. She hears the sound of a car window being lowered and looks down at a black saloon that's pulled up next to her. Dr Miles Parker is staring up at her with a twisted grin.

'What's your partner got caught up in now? Always had my suspicions about him. Surprised you didn't. But then I guess it's true what they say about love being blind.'

Katie bends over and leans heavily on the sill.

'You told Mark Brooks about Nathan's brother.'

'I merely kept him informed of developments. In the same way you ought to have.'

She should have seen this coming. She should have heeded DS Peters' warnings. She had created an enemy. Or rather she had followed her instinct from the first time they'd met, looking into the doctor's eyes and seeing the sort of person he was.

'You undermine my investigation again and I will ruin you.'

'Don't think you carry that weight anymore,' Miles says with a sneer. 'Rumour has it you're on the way out. Not even Daddy's reputation can save you this time.'

'That's right,' she says. 'The bosses think I'm losing it, that I'm reckless and dangerous.' She leans in closer, so close she has to fight the urge to use her forehead to spread his nose across his face. 'What do you think?'

He leans back, face paling. 'I think you're as crazy as your boyfriend.'

'Quite possibly,' she says, noisily dragging her nails across the door trim. 'And imagine the damage the two of us could do.'

Back at her own car, she finds the PC has kept watch the entire time, and she thanks him with a nod. He doesn't say a word, looking relieved to be able to move away. Falling into the driver's seat and starting up the Rover's engine, she searches for something to say to the man slumped against the passenger door, wishing he could tell her what to do next, wishing he could be her partner again.

And, as if he's sensed her need, he struggles to push himself up and to find his focus.

'I don't know what happened with the family in there,' he says, thumping his forehead. 'But I can imagine… I can imagine. And I'm sorry, so sorry for everything he's doing.' He opens his eyes wider and settles his stare. 'I will do whatever it takes to make this stop.'

'Does that mean…?' She can't bring herself to complete the question, knowing what it would represent for Nathan: risking his control, his sanity, his very identity.

'Whatever it takes,' he says, closing his eyes.

CHAPTER TWENTY-TWO

Nathan is sitting staring at Katie's kitchen table, lost in his most vivid and most difficult memory. He'd thought his mum was asleep when he'd found her, drained by the exertions of looking after his dad, but it hadn't taken long to realise the terrible truth that both of his parents had gone in a single day. Even though he'd known she was dead, he'd rocked her gently, as she would have done him when he was at the very start of his life, until she'd started to slump towards the floor. He'd reached out to grab her, falling himself and remaining on the floor, holding her tightly. He didn't move for nearly two hours. When he'd heard his brother walking up the drive he'd jumped to his feet to block him off at the door, then turned back towards the table, removing the one thing he knew would hurt Christian even more than the sight of their mum's body.

He's thinking of that item now, rapidly rewriting the past the same way he had after he'd been given his mum's book and wondered if she somehow knew about him – reading between the lines of his terrible nightmares and perhaps identifying the very same dark vision that had shaped her writing, and possibly her life. Might she also have spotted the same affliction – and that's the only way he's ever been able to think of it – in Christian? Might that have been the reason she couldn't carry on, heartbroken, envisioning a life without her husband, but also terrified of what she had passed on to both her sons?

He snaps back into the present, aware that Katie is pacing around in the living room, impatient for them to begin.

'What did he do to those little girls?' says Nathan. He hadn't wanted to ask, but he knows he can use this.

'He gave them hope,' she replies. 'Made them believe their mum might come back.'

Nathan nods, thinking of his own mum again, thinking of the desperate prayers he'd said on the day that he found her.

'Okay,' he says, pushing himself up and heading for the small door behind the curtains.

'I'll just be outside.'

'No!' he says sharply, before breathing out slowly to make himself clear. 'I need to know there's no other option, nowhere I can go, nobody I can shout out to. No escape.'

'You're kidding. There's no way I'm leaving you here on your own. You heard what the Super said. I'm amazed he hasn't already got you locked up.'

'And that's exactly what I will be,' he says, nodding at the room again. 'I want you to take the key with you.'

'Even so…' She shakes her head.

He pauses before speaking. 'Do you want me to do this, or not?'

She stands in front of him with her arms crossed, but already he can see her features soften.

'No,' she says, clearly. 'I don't.'

'Of course you do,' he says, with an unsteady laugh. 'Think of those mothers. Think of those children. Think of what might still be to come.'

'I didn't think I'd ever have a limit,' Katie says, eyes wide in revelation. 'I've been stabbed, shot at, thrown myself down a flight of stairs…' She lowers her head. 'And I've done far worse to others to get a result. But this… You… I guess I'm just realising how important you are.' She drags at her hair. 'And I don't just mean the work.' She waves an arm at her surroundings: the dirty flat filled with dirty clothes, cigarette ends and empty bottles. 'This mess isn't just because I can't do the work.'

A new fear starts to spread through Nathan, something stronger than the anticipation of what he might find in that tiny room behind him. The only thing more terrifying to him than his constant fight with the darkness is what might happen to him if he ever let in a little light. He searches Katie's face.

'We need to go ahead with the plan,' he says finally, through clenched teeth. 'If I can make it through this, then maybe…'

'It's too much,' says Katie. 'I mean, look at you.' She fails to do so herself, gesturing, instead, at somewhere near his feet. 'You've been away too long.'

'I only have one more day.'

Without warning, she reaches out and grabs him by the wrist, her fingers pressed against his scars. 'That's enough! I know you feel like you need to take back control over all this madness. But that is not the way.'

'And I know you don't want me to walk away from this case.'

'That's the last thing I want.' She lets go and knocks past him on her way towards the tiny room. She disappears into the darkness, flicks on the light and he can soon hear paper being torn from the wall. When she emerges, he already knows what she's holding before she shows him: details of the murder that he has never been able to face. The crime scene that he knew for certain would push him over the edge. The body that proved to him that his darkest desires were possible and sent him running for the hills.

'I shouldn't have been such a coward,' he says, realising he's started bending his fingers back, testing the resistance. 'I should have tried to solve that a long time ago.' He points at the papers in her arms. 'Unless I always knew, deep down, that it was Christian.'

'We don't know for sure it was the same person. Steven Fish's murder was very different.'

'How else could Christian have got hold of the skin he left inside the doll?'

'Well, then maybe it was different because it was his first.'

'The doctor was the first.'

'Maybe Steven Fish was when he really lost control, killed a stranger, tortured a stranger. There are no signs he's tortured anyone else.'

'Only the families of his victims.'

'That does seem to be the point.'

'I think maybe I'm the point,' says Nathan. 'It's twenty years since Mum took her own life…' He pauses to squeeze his eyes shut. '"So sorry to have left you alone", that's what she said, written on the same squared paper. And I think Christian does feel alone. I think he's doing this in the hope that I'll join him, that I'll be his twin again.'

Katie wraps her arms even more tightly round the papers held to her chest. 'And maybe that's why he's given us this link to the Steven Fish murder. He thinks it will be the trigger for you.'

Nathan takes a step back, recognising the sense in her words and the danger in what she's holding.

'But what was Christian's trigger? The doctor wasn't killed when I wanted to kill him, more than twenty years ago. The autopsy will likely prove it happened in the past year. So why did Christian wait so long after my dad died?'

'Maybe something else happened in his life to send him insane. He could have lost that wife he told you about. He could have lost the child.' Katie takes the papers from her chest and slips them into a discarded supermarket bag, tying the top as if to hold in a stench. 'Or maybe there's been nobody. Nobody to keep him in line.'

'I should have been there for him,' says Nathan with a grimace, remembering what his brother had said on the phone: *I thought maybe you could find yourself a nice policewoman, someone who understands that crazy world of yours.*

'So how long do you need?' says Katie, nodding back at the little room.

'A couple of hours. I'll also need something to drink – something strong – to get past myself. Because this will be different to the other times. I'm not imagining a stranger.' He nods towards an almost full bottle of wine next to the television. 'That'll do,' he says. 'All of it. In something unbreakable.'

'How will I know when it's over?'

'Come back in two hours. Go to the station, or something.'

'Not the best idea. I'm meant to be with you at all times, remember? But I think I might know somewhere I can pay a visit.'

Katie heads towards the kitchen, pulling open a cupboard and locating a red plastic mixing bowl which she holds up for approval.

'Two hours.'

She reaches out and grabs his hand, and he feels a jolt. He pulls away but continues to look her in the eye and, despite the tightening he can feel in every inch of his body, he somehow forces a faint smile.

Nathan stands in the tiny room with his head pressed against the door. Fifty minutes have passed since he heard Katie turn the key in the lock and then the sound of the front door closing. Since then, he's been working his way through the evidence from the Brooks case, reading every report and every forensic note, stopping every now and again to make sure she hasn't returned. If he's going to commit to this he needs to know she's not nearby.

When he's finally happy he's on his own and that he's read all he can about the killing of Sally Brooks, he reaches down and picks up the mixing bowl, watching the contents swish around – red bowl, red wine, red visions already starting to appear. It takes several gulps to finish it all and no little effort to keep it down. He's never been a drinker – always so afraid of letting go.

The room starts to swim as he finally turns towards the images and forces himself to look, pressing his nose right up against the bloody scenes until it feels like there's no air left in the room and he is forced to sit down on the spinning chair in the centre. Gripping the arm with one hand, he lets his eyes follow a path around the walls, taking in a series of photographs pinned to the wall of the victims Katie has failed to find justice for in the year he's been away, and noticing the blank space where the papers about the torture and murder of Steven Fish have been removed. Round and round he goes, running laps around the room with his eyes and tiring out his brain just like he did in Scotland. Suddenly he stops, lining himself up with an enlargement of the chocolate copy of his birthmark on Sally Brooks. He hadn't considered his birthmark had looked like a skull until he was in his teens. Before then it had always been an animal's head, a monkey or pig, but as his thoughts grew darker the skull seemed the perfect fit. He'd once wanted to take a knife to it, desperate to break free from the curse, but as he'd sat on the side of the bath with a shaking hand he worried it would achieve the very opposite: that the blood would represent the beginning, and not the end.

He closes his eyes, knowing he's seen more than enough. Now he has to let go. He leans forward and stares down at the floor, a tiny drop of sweat landing between his shoes. He tucks an imaginary strand of hair behind his ear, picturing his brother's hair as it had been; tidier and shorter than his own, parted on one side. His head lowers further, his chin almost touching his chest, and he can feel himself slipping, starting with the tiniest twitch at the tip of his fingers, then spreading like a poison down his arms and into his chest, ice cold and unrelenting.

He was only eight or nine years old when he first discovered he could think so convincingly as someone else, putting himself in the place of a sportsman, or adventurer, or musician, or sometimes just a son impressing his father. The longer he did it the better he got, to the point where his imagined train of thought felt so perfectly real he could almost be living it. All he needed were details and room in his head to truly believe. It had made him a formidable actor, until he started losing control.

Today will be his greatest challenge yet, since the person's mind he is attempting to occupy is a killer he knows almost as well as he knows himself. Here he can see out through eyes that are the same, down the bridge of a nose the same, past a fringe the same. Part of him wants to stop, but the other part of him has already taken its first step…

He's standing, tucked into the hedge with a rose bush behind him and thorns digging into his legs. He should feel pain, but he doesn't feel anything but excitement and anticipation. He stares at a tiny window in the distance. There's a woman there – beautiful, black hair, pale skin – washing plates in yellow gloves. He looks down at his own hands, a long knife with a serrated edge in one, a tiny tremor in the other. He looks up at the window; the woman is still there. The faintest whisper in his heart is wishing she'd disappear, that she'd see him and he'd run, but he knows he won't be going anywhere. She's smiling. He can't believe he didn't notice before, because it's so broad, so beautiful and so strangely familiar. He starts to walk forward, tingling with desire, telling himself to stop.

He crouches down by the side of the window, still unseen. He can hear music, an old song from the fifties or sixties, but it's one he knows well. He looks down at his feet, a pair of unremarkable black shoes, unpolished, size 10…

Things are suddenly cloudier than they were before. Part of him is relieved, part of him enormously frustrated. He stares harder and finally the image sharpens. He can see his trousers are blue jeans, dirty on the knees. His sweater is black and frayed at the sleeves. The whole outfit strikes him as cheap – the sort of thing he wouldn't mind getting dirty; the sort of thing he'd be happy to throw away. He's caught a tiny strand of the sweater on the rose bush. He stares at it, but doesn't remove it, knowing he needs it, needs it for this… He can see his feet in the soil below, can see the depth of the mark he's left, and the longer he looks the more rounded his stomach seems. He follows the line of it with his free hand and it disappears. Although now it's the hands that don't look right: dirty and lined, rough on the knuckles. He twists them and bunches them and they slowly return to what he'd seen before. He tries to look for a reflection in the window ahead of him, but there's nothing there: he's invisible, even to himself.

He moves confidently round the side of the house, past a well-tended lawn and carefully weeded flowerbeds. Flattening flowers as he goes, sometimes bending to slash at them with his knife. Open flower heads litter the floor. And there are more footprints. Still too deep.

On the patio behind the back door is a brightly coloured bike, a hula hoop and a tiny plastic hedgehog. The door is partly open, just an inch or two; he reaches out, pulling to make the gap large enough to squeeze through. The music has stopped. There are no birds, no wind, no cars in the distance, no sound of singing, no sound of his heart.

He's in the house; more toys spread out on the living room floor. There's a soft, floppy doll ahead of him, and he stops to pick it up, tucking it into his pocket. As he moves forward his boot makes contact with a Lego brick, sending it spinning away. Again, there's no sound. Although when he looks up towards the kitchen it's clear that there should be. The woman at the end of the hallway is staring straight at him; her mouth is stretched wide in a scream, the rest of her body completely frozen.

He's moving quickly now, although not as fast as Nathan wants, not as fast as Nathan would himself. The knife leads the way. As he continues down the hall he allows himself time to consider the photos on the wall, images of two small girls smiling out at the camera. The woman in the kitchen has turned for the door; she's slipping and stumbling and crashes into the cupboards. He rushes forward as if trying to catch her, but his movement is clumsy and surprisingly slow, and his own feet slip twice on the mud still caked to the soles. The woman turns to look at him, her eyes wide, her open mouth now twisting hideously as the blade enters her neck. An arc of blood sprays across the floor, onto his shoes and his trousers and onto a painting pinned by a magnet to the fridge door. He stares at the child's brightly coloured work of art, seeing his addition, before turning back to the woman. Her mouth is full of blood and her body is motionless, twisted unnaturally down on the tiles, although the mouth is still moving, still trying to shape sounds. But it's in her eyes he sees the truth, the reflection that hadn't been there before, badly blurred but unmistakable. The man there is nothing like him, or his brother.

Nathan rises at such speed he almost topples backwards off the chair, tearing down a few of the photos as he tries to steady himself. He drops into a crouch, elbows pressed against the wall behind, his eyes darting left and right, his breath short, sharp and wild like an animal's. He wishes he could have stayed there for ever in the blood, but there's something important he needs to do. He reaches for the door handle, only to find it locked and that he is trapped in a devastating space between reality and fantasy. He rests his head against the door as an unspeakable feeling of loss and helplessness washes over him. Outside, he knows someone's life is in terrible danger.

CHAPTER TWENTY-THREE

Katie stands staring up at a window, one of many in a large building ahead of where she's parked. She knows the exact one to look at because she's been here before, sitting in this very spot, looking up and wondering if she has the courage to go in.

She has another question troubling her today. Did she do the right thing in leaving Nathan alone in her flat? Might it change him, as he had always feared? Might it lead him to hurt others? Or make him even more likely to hurt himself? She might have removed details of the murder that she thought would be the most damaging, but was that just a selfish act to ease her conscience if he can't cope? She fights the panic, remembering the way he'd looked at her when he'd said goodbye. She knows what it sounds like when that goodbye is for ever: she'd heard it in her dad's voice once before.

She pops open the door of the car, feeling the cool of the late evening air. At the main door to the building she's met with a smile as broad as you would hope for with all the money she's paying, although it slips when the woman behind the desk hears what she wants.

'I'm so sorry,' she says, turning towards the clock on the wall behind her, 'but the visiting hours are—'

'I know what they are.' Katie cuts her off. She reaches into her pocket with a sigh and brings out her warrant card.

'Really?' says the woman, her concern growing. 'Is everything okay?'

'Just a case I'm working on,' says Katie. 'It's become… personal. And I wanted to check…' She points upwards.

'I can assure you that the security here is of the highest level,' says the woman, gesturing towards a camera in the corner of the room, then down the corridor ahead at a shut door with a keypad entry system.

'Nevertheless,' says Katie, moving towards that door as she slips her warrant card away.

Having convinced the woman to go back to her desk after letting her through, Katie has climbed two flights of stairs and is standing in the doorway of a room she hasn't visited in several weeks. Nevertheless, it all still seems horribly familiar; even the figure in the armchair close to the window is exactly as she remembered him.

'Hello, Dad,' she says, placing a hand on the back of the chair as she moves alongside. His head is slumped against the high back and his mouth is partly open, as are his eyes, which, rather than looking at the beautiful sunset out of the window, seem to be focused on nothing. She wonders if he's ever noticed this view. Even when she'd first moved him into this care home he was deteriorating so rapidly that she was certain she was spending all the money on nothing. Nothing other than her guilt.

'I should have said these things to you before, a long time ago,' she starts, her hand slipping from the back of the chair to his shoulder. There's no response. 'But I couldn't…' She creates a fist and twists her face, as if struggling even now to say what should be the simplest thing for a daughter to say to a dad who has given her everything. 'I love you. I've always loved you. And it doesn't matter what you've done.' She leans in closer and lowers her voice to a whisper. 'If you killed him, I know there was a reason.'

She's distracted by a sound behind and spins round to find a man standing in the doorway. Instantly she can feel her cheeks flush. She'd almost forgotten how unattractive he is. He's over-weight, his hair is thinning and his features somehow look like they don't fit the overall shape of his face. Yet when he smiles she finds herself smiling back, feeling a warmth spread through her that she's only ever felt with Nathan.

'Is everything okay?'

On his chest is a badge bearing the name 'Martin Coates', and below that the word 'carer'. She remembers staring at that tag and, in particular, that word on the floor of the hotel she'd taken him to, her eyes struggling to focus from all the drink, her regret overwhelming.

'I just wanted to see him.'

'I thought that would be it. Barbara at the door,' Martin gestures down, 'told me it was police business. But I knew it would be something far more important.'

'Listen, I need to speak to you,' she says.

'And me to you.' Martin's voice has always been very quiet, his words slow and measured. 'I want to apologise, Katie, I'm appalled at what I did.'

She very nearly laughs at the suggestion that he had been the one to blame. 'Why?'

'Because of the job I do; because it's clear I abused my connec-tion with…' Martin looks across at Katie's dad, who is oblivious, she's certain, to the conversation they're having. 'Otherwise you would never have…' He turns his attention back to her, his rounded face starting to redden as he removes thick glasses and rubs his eyes. 'Not with someone like me.'

'That's not true. It's not your job. It's who you are. It's who you've proven you are with all the help you've given Dad.'

He smiles and puts his glasses back on. 'I'm glad you think that.'

'I haven't been here for him myself,' she says, the words catch-ing in her throat.

'We've spoken about this before,' says Martin, taking a step forward and lightly resting a hand on the top of her arm. 'There is no blame here. It's a natural reaction, an understandable fear.'

'Maybe,' Katie says, squeezing the bridge of her nose as if that might stop the tears. Her phone starts to ring and she pulls it out quickly, wondering if it's Nathan, before reminding herself that he had been left a prisoner in her home.

She raises an apologetic hand to Martin and then turns away, answering the call. 'Hi, Mike. What's up?'

'Sorry to disturb you, boss, I just wanted to check you were doing okay.'

She wipes the tears from her cheeks. 'I'm fine, thanks.'

'And what about Nathan?'

'He's okay,' she says, taking another step away from Martin, before looking back over her shoulder and finding that he's gone. 'Again, thanks for asking. You're the only one that has.'

'You know about my brother,' he says, lowering his voice to a whisper. 'You know what I've been through with him.'

Katie remembers the day from just a few months ago, when she'd been taken out to a run-down estate to visit a drug addict that looked so much like the sergeant that no explanation had been needed. It was proof of his trust that he was willing to show her. It was also, she can see now, a warning about the effect all the drinking and the sleeping around might have on her own life.

'You remember what Nathan used to be like.' She pauses as the images come into focus. 'When he was doing his thing, it was like he travelled somewhere else, but you could see he was finding it harder and harder to come back. It's the same with…' She reaches out and places a hand on her dad's shoulder. He hasn't moved in the chair. 'I'm sorry,' she says, having drawn in a deep breath.

'Don't be,' says DS Peters. 'Your dad was a good man.'

'And you're too good a detective, Mike,' she says, acknowledging his understanding. She finds herself straightening, muscles firming, barriers rising. 'Now, what more do we know? Anything on the phone number for Christian?'

'Nothing yet.'

'What about CCTV of the house?'

'Again, nothing. A couple of the neighbours have cameras, but we haven't had a chance to run through it all.'

'And the family doctor that Nathan spoke of? Any joy with him?'

'Some. We know he was living in Spain until a little over four years ago. Then he was marked coming back through Heathrow. Nothing after that.'

'Nobody reported him missing?'

'As far as we can tell there's no family or friends. He was living out there as a recluse, pretty much. We're still working on tracking down former colleagues to see why he left, and to find out what sort of guy he was.'

'If Nathan's experience with his dad is anything to go by, not great at his job. What about his medical or dental records? We might not have to wait for the lab if they can get back to us with something first.'

'If you're in a hurry for forensics it might be best not to piss off the doctor,' says DS Peters. 'I hear you had another clash. He says you threatened him.'

'Absolutely,' she says. 'After he'd told Mark Brooks about Christian.'

'As you probably should have done yourself.'

'I was choosing the right time.'

'For him, or for Nathan?'

She feels a flash of temper; the rarest of things with DS Peters. 'Nathan wants what I want.' The knot in her stomach tightens. 'Jesus, if you only knew what he was putting himself through right now.'

'What do you mean? Is he not with you?'

She hesitates for a moment, weighing up the need to lie. 'No. But he's not leaving my flat, I can promise you that.'

'So where are you?'

'I came to visit my dad.'

'Then I'm sorry I disturbed you.'

'Don't be. I was just leaving.'

'Don't suppose you have time for a detour on your way home?'

Katie looks at her watch. She has more than an hour before she's due back at her flat. 'What do you need?'

'PC Smith and I went to talk to Markham, but he wouldn't let us in. He's obviously badly shaken after discovering what Christian had done. He said he would only speak to you. Now, I don't mind driving over there as well. I can stay in the car.'

'I'm better on my own, thanks, Mike. You know what I get like at times like these.'

'I'm counting on it,' he says, with a laugh.

'What about the super? Is he going to be all right with me doing this?'

'He doesn't need to know.'

'I don't want you getting in trouble.'

'I'm far too old to worry about that. Between you and me, I think this might be one of my last.'

'I doubt I'll have that choice.'

'Well, as long as I'm around you'll have my support. And as far as I'm concerned this case is still yours to lead and solve.'

'I won't let you down, Mike,' she says, hanging up. She stands for a moment, staring out of the window at the setting sun. Then she crouches down and takes her dad's hand. It's horribly thin and pale and offers no resistance when she picks it up, but she squeezes it tightly and leans in close with an awkward smile. 'I'm sorry, but I need to go to work.' As she says it, she remembers all those occasions when he'd said the same to her. And just like she did back then, he says nothing in return.

*

She starts up the engine of the Rover and almost reverses into the car of one of the care home workers turning into a neighbouring slot. Waving a half-hearted apology, she pulls away in a big cloud of smoke. It's getting dark, so she flicks on the lights and heads down the long tree-lined road leading to the exit, before forcing her way out into a stream of traffic, ignoring the honked horns and the mouthed expletives from other drivers.

As she considers her new destination, she starts to wonder if she's made a terrible mistake in waiting so long to interview Markham. The old gardener is the only witness; the only person to have seen and spoken to Christian. What if he's unwittingly in possession of a key piece of evidence? What if she's not the only one to have realised this? What if the real reason Markham had so adamantly told DS Peters to go away was because he wasn't alone? The longer the journey goes on, the greater the concern builds inside her.

By the time she arrives her fingers are aching from how tightly they've gripped the wheel. She half-runs up the pathway to the front door. It's a small house in a terrace, with a narrow strip of garden that isn't as well kept as she might have expected from a gardener. Before reaching for the doorbell she looks in through the window; the light is on and the curtains are only partly drawn. There's a big TV and shelves full of books in a living room that doesn't appear to have changed much since the 1970s: the carpet flowery and losing colour, the black leather sofa worn bare on the arms. There's nobody in sight, nor is there any sign of a struggle. Crouching down to carefully raise the letterbox, she can just make out a small kitchen at the back. Everything is as it should be, dishes washed and left on the side to dry and several pairs of boots under the stairs. Taking a step back she can see the frosted glass of a bathroom window upstairs. It is closed, and there's no sign of anyone moving inside. She reaches quickly for the bell, picturing the old man lying on his bedroom floor with blood seeping out of him, desperately hoping that someone will come and help; only it's not Markham she pictures at all, it's her dad. A man of much the same age whose life is also seeping out of him, one memory at a time.

The bell rings and again she takes a step back, out of range of an arm and a knife. It's not 'The Cartoonist's' MO, but she's not taking any chances. There's no response. There are no cars in the neighbours' drives and no twitching curtains around her to investigate. Perhaps Markham is not at home. She considers getting back in the car and going to see Nathan, but a glance at her watch tells her there's still an hour to wait. Thinking of Nathan has also reminded her of something else: of standing on his doorstep up in Scotland and not giving up. So she gives the door one last, frustrated thump. It pops open a couple of inches.

She swallows hard, gives the door an extra push and watches as the hallway appears ahead of her. There's fresh mud on the doormat and another pair of muddy boots, cast untidily at the base of the stairs. Then she notices the blood. A tiny pool of it previously disguised in the rose pattern on the carpet. Instantly aware of a blind spot inside the door to her left, she jumps to her right and stumbles as one foot slips off the path and into a flowerbed of bright red roses identical to the one she had seen at the second victim's house.

She is unarmed, but she can see a block of knives on the side in the kitchen. To reach them she will have to make a mad sprint and hope there's no one hiding behind the door. She lightly pats an empty pocket, cursing herself for having left her phone in the car. She'd taken it out to check the traffic en route.

She has no choice but to move forward, her head darting left to right, her eyes taking everything in, anticipating every potential threat. As she passes the bloody stain, she notices several other drips leading through to the kitchen. At the entrance, she holds her breath and leaps forward, crouching down at the same time to throw an attacker off. As she jumps she spots some vegetables on the side; a few of the carrots are in the process of being prepared, and a large kitchen knife lies next to the chopping board. She reaches for it, swinging the tip between the back door and the hallway from where she's just come. She reaches with her left hand to try the back door. It's locked.

She'd spotted a landline in the hallway. She should make the call and ask for help. She's about to reach for it when she hears a floorboard groan upstairs. Someone is here. She lifts the knife and turns towards the stairs. Someone is coming.

The first thing she sees is a pair of socks, blue, pulled up high. Followed by a pair of bare legs, muscled, hairy. Next come boxer shorts, also blue. Then the weapon. It's a black-headed hammer, gripped tight in a fist. Katie steadies her shaking hand.

'Is he here?'

The words take a moment to translate, as does the face that's appeared above a body she now realises is far too old to belong to Christian.

'Jesus. I thought you were dead!'

'Why?' Markham's eyes focus on the knife in her hand. 'Oh God, he's here?'

She shakes her head and points down at the carpet. 'The blood!'

He lifts his empty hand up towards her by way of explanation. It's wrapped in white fabric, a small streak of red pooling through.

'I was trying to make something to eat. Although God knows how I'd stomach it. My hands were shaking so much I missed a carrot and got me palm. The result was…' He seems suddenly to become aware of his lack of clothes and crosses his arms in front. 'You're sure he's not here?'

'Was it you that left the door open?'

A moment of silence, and his face twists as he searches for an answer.

'I'd been to my allotment, to get summit for dinner and to try and clear me thoughts. I guess I must have cleared them a bit too much.' He looks over at the door and shakes his head. 'Right bloody stupid. But, you see, I haven't ever been in a state like this before.' He holds out the trembling hand gripping the hammer. 'I mean, you think you know somebody, or at least take them to be kind and generous and friendly, only…' He looks over his shoulder again up the stairs and comes down another step closer to Katie. 'That's why I've kept this nearby.' He gives the hammer a twist. 'Just in case he comes back.'

'We're okay now,' says Katie, gesturing for him to lower it.

'Is it just you?' asks Markham. 'I didn't rightly trust nobody else, but now…' He glances behind him again.

'I'll call in for a couple more officers. I've just got to pop out to my car to get my phone.'

'You won't be long?' says Markham, reaching out towards her with his bandaged hand. He looks terrified.

'By the time you've been upstairs and put the rest of your clothes on,' says Katie, with her most reassuring smile, 'I'll be back and have the kettle on.'

He offers a nervous nod and retreats up the stairs, still holding the hammer. She nips through to the kitchen to replace the knife she'd taken and suddenly notices the smear of blood on the tip and more of it close to the carrots. She's breathing easier now and greedily draws in the late evening air as she fetches her phone while the kettle is boiling.

When she's back in the house and the tea is made, retrieving milk from the fridge and a couple of sugars she wouldn't normally bother with, she sits down in the living room and waits for Markham. He reappears in a grey sweater and a pair of jeans, looking slightly embarrassed. He's also still holding the hammer, which he places next to him as he sits down on the edge of the old leather sofa.

Katie's perched on a small wooden chair with a high back and slightly bowing legs. She's sitting as lightly as she can manage, most of the weight kept on her toes.

'How's the hand?'

'I'll survive,' he says, all the time looking around, seemingly unconvinced.

Katie has one eye on the hallway, certain she'd heard Markham bolt the front door as he'd come down the stairs. She makes a face and gets up, holding her tea.

'Mind if I put a couple of sugars in here?'

''Course, lassie. China pot next to the kettle.'

She leaves the room. From where Markham is sitting he can't see if she goes left or right, so she quickly does both: first heading to the front door, where she draws the bolt silently back, and then through to the kitchen where she makes plenty of noise but adds no sugar.

'How are you doing?' she says on her return, offering a concerned smile.

'Are your colleagues coming?'

'I think we'll be okay,' she says with a smile. 'And I'm going to need you to accompany me to the station to make an official statement, anyway.'

'Now?' he asks, part-rising.

'In a minute,' she says, gesturing for him to sit back down. She takes a sip of tea. She'd wanted to take him away immediately, but the other part of her, the part that insisted she go and pull back the bolt on the door, wants to risk everything if there's a chance of catching Christian. Something in her gut is telling her the killer is close, watching, waiting. All around her are weapons – a vase to smash, a poker by the fire, even a pair of secateurs on the mantelpiece. 'I thought we might have a more informal chat about yesterday before we go.' She glances across at the TV, small and covered in a layer of dust. 'You will have heard about the body at Nathan and Christian's house. We don't know whose it is yet, and we don't know when it was put there.'

'They were talking about a connection to some other killings?' he says, nervously picking at the edge of the bandage on his hand. 'Were those Christian, too?'

'We're not sure at present,' she says. 'But it's something we're looking into.'

'It's unbelievable,' he says. 'Those boys were always so polite and kind and...' He stops to nod at the TV. 'They're saying Nathan works with you people, that he's some kind of criminal psychologist. Did he not recognise what was going on with his own brother?'

'Sometimes people are just too close, or too good at hiding who they are,' says Katie, as she considers her own willingness to put the old man at risk – to use him as bait.

'We should go,' she says, standing up.

'Okay,' says Markham, doing the same. 'Just let me get a jumper. I know it's not cold, but...'

'No problem,' says Katie. 'I'll be waiting here.'

Markham heads slowly upstairs again, and she can hear cupboard doors being opened. She stands in the doorway to the living room with a good view of both the front and back doors. Markham took the hammer with him, so she'll have to make do with the poker she's lifted from the fireplace. She stands perfectly still, listening to every little noise. She jumps at the sound of her phone ringing. She slips the poker under her arm while she retrieves the mobile from her pocket, before peering down at a number she could hardly fail to recognise.

'Are you all right?' she whispers, taking a step back into the living room.

'Where are you?' asks Nathan breathlessly. 'Are you okay?'

'Are *you?*' she asks again, searching for clues in his voice. 'How did you get out of the room?'

'I had to break the door down.'

She can hear the slur in his words, and she remembers. 'Did you drink it all?'

'Yes,' he says, as if suddenly remembering himself. 'But that's not the point – the point is I've been there, and...' He pauses, and she can hear him swallow.

'Did you see something?' she says, although she's not sure *see* is the right word.

'It's not my brother.'

'What isn't?'

'None of it. None of the killings. It wasn't him.'

'What makes you say that?'

'Because it wasn't right, it didn't feel like him,' he says, the slur seeming to get worse. 'You know how it works.'

She doesn't, she never has, but now is not the time to try and understand.

'He wasn't moving like my brother. You remember the footprints in the flowerbed, the thread on the rose bush, the scuff marks on the floor, the way the victim didn't die instantly like you said, but had time to lift her arms, to slip, to fall. He was slow. He was clumsy. He made mistakes.'

'People make mistakes.'

'Christian wouldn't,' says Nathan, and a moment of silence follows.

'Come on, Nathan,' she says eventually, moving away from the door and laying down the poker so she can shield her words with her other hand. 'I'm sorry, but...' She tips her head back, with no desire to go through it again; he's drunk, he's desperate, there's no need for her to spell it out, and yet her disappointment in his failure to help with this last case pushes her on. 'He was seen at your house, looking suspicious. The victim found there was somebody known to you and your brother, somebody you both had reason to want to hurt. The other victims might have been strangers, they might not, we don't know yet, but there were personal markings, clues specific to you. If it were anybody else we wouldn't be having this conversation – there'd be no doubt. I mean, it's natural that you aren't quite ready to accept what's happened, but…'

She stops and listens to the silence, digging a nail deep into her thigh as she curses her directness. There had been that moment back in her flat when she'd been sure she felt the walls finally coming down. But now, as always, work is getting in the way.

'What if my brother never went to my parents' home?'

'What?' It takes her a moment to digest. 'But we know that he did,' she whispers. 'We have a witness.'

'And you believe him more than you believe me?'

'It's not a question of believing. It's about following the evidence.' She tells herself that's exactly what she's doing; weighing it up, shutting out the emotion. She knows what it's like when there's family involved, how easily it can interfere with reason.

'Where are you?' says Nathan. The rising panic in his voice sets her heart racing.

'I'm with Markham.'

'Is he in the room with you?'

'He's upstairs.'

'Then get out!'

'Why?'

'What if he was lying?'

'Why would he lie?' She asks the question, but she's already reached the answer herself. 'No,' she says, remembering the old man's face when she'd arrived. 'No, that's not possible.' She shakes her head, and raises her voice beyond the previous whisper. 'You're wrong.'

'Leave anyway.'

'Not without Markham.'

'Then take him with you. But get a weapon first. Don't turn your back, and take him out in the street. Stand where people can see you. I'll get someone to you as quick as I can.'

Before Katie can open her mouth to reluctantly agree, she hears a noise – the creak of a floorboard – and she knows it's already too late. She's been distracted. She's been a fool. Someone has crept up behind her. Before she even has a chance to turn, there's a thud and a blinding light behind her eyes as she tumbles forward. Sprawled out on the floor, she stares at the poker on the other side of the room, curling her fingers as if she might be able to pick it up. To her left is the phone that has slipped from her hand, and either side of it a muddy boot below the frayed seam of a pair of jeans. She's often stood over victims, wondering what was going through their mind at the time of their death, beyond the physical pain and fear. For her it's a moment of revelation, not about the work – for once that has been pushed to one side – but about the man who had come so close to breaking down her defences. And it's only now, at the very end, with nothing more to lose, that the brilliant truth about Nathan shines through.

CHAPTER TWENTY-FOUR

Nathan lets the phone fall from his ear. He's tried three more times to call Katie's number, without success. Images of her body being twisted and stretched as his own birthmark is carefully copied on her thigh flash through his mind, but he can't allow himself to believe that it has happened for real. He needs to get to her. And he needs help.

He's connected to her office in less than a minute, his memory somehow dragging up the number, along with the name of the colleague she'd often talked about and clearly trusted. He won't explain everything – it would complicate matters and slow things down, the same way it had with Katie. If he'd told her to get out instantly, if she'd trusted him instantly, the way she always used to, if he hadn't had so much to drink, then perhaps he wouldn't need to be making this call.

'DS Peters?'

'Speaking.'

'Katie's in danger,' he says, glad that the terror rather than the alcohol is registering in his voice. 'At Markham's house. You need to get there!' He hangs up, desperate to do the same himself, but is suddenly confronted by the practicalities; the house is far out to the west, the width of the city from where he is now. He doesn't have money for a taxi, bus, or train, and there's no cash he can see around the house. He thinks of her expression as she'd pulled the door closed on the little room, and realises a new frenzy building inside of him; a desperation not to take a life, but to save one.

He snatches a knife out of the block on the side in the kitchen and feeds it up the sleeve of his top so he can feel the coldness of the blade on his skin as he rushes out the door.

Out on the street he's spinning round and round, searching for a solution. There are so many forms of transport in front of him, above him, below him, and yet nothing can get him there quickly enough. He could run, he could run for miles – his body has been craving it ever since he got back – but he knows it wouldn't save her. He tries to slow his breathing, give himself room to think. The traffic is moving freely, some cars travelling at speed. When he sees a gap he steps out into it then turns to face a car racing towards him. He holds up a hand and hears the brakes scream. He closes his eyes and prepares himself for impact, wondering if he was being brave or reaching for a way out.

He only looks when he hears a door opening and the shouting start. The man is not as big as his voice, and the closer Nathan gets the more his words lose their strength.

'Are you fucking mad?'

'Yes,' he hears himself say, and he means it as his fingers grab the man by the front of his hooded top and fling him towards the pavement. For a terrible moment, he wonders if he might stay to finish the job – take a random life while his desire is this high. But there's still a part of him holding on, telling him there's no time, telling him to think of Katie and only Katie.

He sinks into the driver's seat and closes the door, and before he knows it the lights of the city are flashing by. It's been a while, and the gear changes are far from smooth and the alcohol is still flooding his senses. A part of him hopes a police car might stop him so he doesn't have to turn up alone, but all he sees are angry faces and the occasional scared-looking pedestrian.

*

As he pulls into the street where Markham lives he realises what a miracle it is he'd remembered the way. He'd barely even looked at the signs. It wasn't a route he remembered driving, certainly not from Katie's house, and yet again he's been able to drag up bits of information he hadn't known were there.

He bumps up the kerb and skids to a halt, flicking off the engine and leaving the keys in the ignition. He rushes for the gate, flinging it open and almost tripping and falling flat on his face. He doesn't care who might be waiting for him on the other side; he just wants to be there, as he should have been, to try and help, or face the consequences.

The front door is open a couple of inches and the hallway is dark but there's a light on in the kitchen at the end. Rushing forward, he slips on something and nearly falls, righting himself as he approaches. As his focus sharpens, he thinks he can make out a hand poking out from behind the door. The tightness in his chest is unbearable as he feels for the knife up his sleeve.

The first thing he sees is her face. Her eyes are closed, and he can see no expression, and her skin is horribly pale. Her body is laid out in the shape of a cross: legs together, arms stretched wide. There's blood on her neck and on her temple, and far more above her head. A great pool of it, still spreading as the rest of her remains deathly still. Her fingers are flat, unbent, unbroken, and this, at least, brings a moment of relief.

He looks across and sees a small plastic shopping bag, not dissimilar to the one Katie had filled with the Steven Fish papers. Poking out of the top is something dark and hairy with eyes wide and a mouth stretched in agony. He takes a closer look. It's far easier to look at this than to look at her. Up close he can see it's the rigid remains of a black cat, fur sticky and matted with blood.

He turns back to Katie and reaches out to touch her face. There are things he wants to tell her, things that might have made a difference to them both. He draws a finger down her cheek, desperately trying not to look at the neck and see the very point where her life was ended. Even on the periphery of his already tear-stained vision he can tell that it isn't as bad as his imagination would have him believe. He dares to look closer and sees that he was right; the line is too thin, no white of the windpipe, no tear of the skin at all. It's also too dark, like congealed blood, like… He touches the line with the point of his finger and then slips it into his mouth. In his fantasies he's gone this far, drunk the blood that he's been so desperate to spill and found it wonderful, found it sweet – but this is too sweet. Chocolate. He lets out a triumphant cry, lowering himself towards her mouth, tilting his ear to listen, one arm lightly resting on her chest, the other holding the knife behind him. Then, as he searches for her breath, a blow to his ribs takes all his away.

A split second later something strikes him across the back of his neck, sending him tumbling off Katie and into the side of the cupboards. It had been a trap. He was the target all along. The thought fills him with a sudden strength and a murderous rage. He tries to get up, but he's kicked again and this time there's screaming, a man's voice he half-recognises, repeating the very desires that are lighting a fire in his own mind: 'I'm going to tear you apart, dig your eyes from your sockets, rip your head from your shoulders.' He feels for the knife, but it's no longer in his hand. Just as he's thinking about punching his way out, his arm has been flipped over and squeezed against the floor, his other tucked underneath him and his face pressed against the tiles. In front of him, all he can see is something that looks bizarrely like the tip of a carrot.

He tries to roll, but there's a boot pinning him down and that voice again, shouting words in a wall of rage that he can't translate, or even separate. He realises he's outmatched and it terrifies him.

Nathan feels his muscles slacken, certain that this is where it ends for him. He'd wanted it to be tomorrow, to disappear in his own, quiet way, but now he knows he'll soon be carefully arranged on this very floor, turned into another cartoon for people to photograph and investigate.

He's slipping away, drifting somewhere he hopes will be more bearable, when a woman's voice cuts through everything.

'Don't kill him!'

It's Katie. He wants to tell her to stop. He wants to tell her to run. But now she's screaming. He hopes she's somehow found his knife and will be able to defend herself. But he can't hear her moving above the sound of his attacker panting and waiting to land another blow. Then, suddenly, he is released and Katie's voice floats above him.

'It might be Nathan,' she says. 'It might be Nathan.'

CHAPTER TWENTY-FIVE

'What an all-fucking-mighty mess,' Superintendent Taylor barks as he climbs into the front passenger seat of the police car and tosses his hat on the dashboard.

Katie is slumped against the door in the back. She doesn't respond. She's not sure she can. Her head is throbbing, but she's not telling anyone that, either. She knows something terrible has happened, something that should have marked the end of her life, but she can't come to terms with it yet. The problem is, if she's going to use it to her advantage, she needs to find a way to talk. She pictures the moment she'd found Nathan standing on the doorstep of his house in Scotland; she pictures the moment she'd found her dad standing on the doorstep of their family home, both distant, silent, lost; both so removed from the person she knew was trapped inside.

Her still-throbbing head starts to tip forward, and she desperately wants to fall to the floor, to curl up and search for somewhere, anywhere, where she doesn't have to do anything, to think of anything ever again. Then, just as she's convinced it's going to happen, she hears Nathan's voice beside her, strong and alive.

'Have you got Markham's description out to the press?'

'We've done what's necessary,' says the superintendent. 'His and Christian Radley's images are being circulated.' He reaches for his hat, picking it off the dashboard, dusting it down.

'Why the hell are you involving my brother in this?' says Nathan, pushing himself between the two front seats. 'We know it wasn't him.'

'Do we?'

'I worked the evidence and played it through in my mind. The killer is older, less able, overweight—'

'Like Markham, yes,' the superintendent cuts him off. 'I've never failed to be amazed by your imagination.'

'That imagination has built your fucking career!' screams Nathan.

'And it's going to end it,' Superintendent Taylor says calmly, 'if I don't recognise the conflict of interests here.'

'What about what Katie saw? The boots. His trousers.'

'That doesn't prove anything.'

Nathan hesitates. 'Christian was always pristine.'

'Detective Inspector Rhodes,' says Superintendent Taylor, twisting the rear-view mirror to catch her eye in the fast-fading evening light, 'has passed on what you were able to tell us about Christian.' He twists the mirror back, lining it up with Nathan. 'Your brother appears to have pulled the same trick as you: changing his name and vanishing from our systems twenty years ago.'

Nathan opens his mouth as if keen to dismiss this as impossible, then closes it again, brow furrowing. 'You couldn't find his wife or child, either?'

'No trace at all, of him or his family.'

'I'm not surprised,' says Nathan, with the faintest smile. 'I guess the three of us were always the same.'

'Three?' says the superintendent, twisting in his seat to look directly at Nathan for the first time. 'Please don't tell me you have another brother?'

'My mum,' says Nathan, all trace of the smile gone.

'And she hid her identity from the authorities too?'

'From the world.'

The superintendent now twists to try and see Katie, but she's slipped back down in her seat.

'I changed my identity to protect my brother,' Nathan continues, 'so that he didn't follow me into this. I lied to him. I said I was using my acting skills to work undercover and as a result had taken on another life. I said the people I was up against would think nothing of taking out whole families if my cover was blown. I told him it was enough for us to stop seeing each other. He obviously decided to do more.'

'Don't tell me you believe this?' says the superintendent, stretching further to try and see Katie, the strain registering on his face.

She rubs the back of her head, pretending not to have heard the question. She's still not ready to reveal Nathan's true motivation for ending contact with his brother, to reveal the darkness that – she reminds herself of the poor homeless man whose identity Nathan had taken – had maybe already led him to take a life. She fears she's going to be asked again, to be forced to take sides as she was when she first started working with Nathan and so many of her colleagues expressed their doubts about his unusual methods. However, in keeping his secret, hadn't she already chosen a side?

'When has he ever let us down?' she asks, pushing herself up, her leg pressing against Nathan's.

'How about the day he ran off without any explanation?'

'Only because he pushed himself to the brink of madness for us,' she snaps back, causing her head to throb.

'The brink?' the superintendent replies, raising one eyebrow.

Katie forms a fist and opens her mouth.

'I'm going to forgive you your previous outburst,' says the superintendent, getting in ahead of what would have been another. 'Because of what you've just been through. But I'm sick to death of us having this conversation. What the hell happened to the model detective who followed the process and always had everything in line, who was just like her dad?'

'You know nothing about my dad,' she says, then wishes she hadn't, remembering that she too might not know him as well as she'd once believed.

A knock at the window, and DS Peters leans in. She can just make out a mobile phone in his hand. 'Sorry for interrupting, sir,' he says. 'But we've done an initial background check and Markham is who he says he is.'

'Hallelujah!' says the superintendent, slapping the dashboard. 'Finally, somebody is telling the truth.'

'The truth about who he is,' says Nathan, still leaning between the two front seats. 'But it's what he's done you should be worried about.'

Superintendent Taylor gives a dismissive grunt. 'There are things he couldn't have known.'

'And things my brother couldn't have known, either,' says Nathan, lifting a hand to slap the left side of his chest.

Katie flushes as she makes the connection, her fingers twitching as she fights the urge to touch the location of the two moles.

'I imagine that's becoming increasingly common knowledge,' says the superintendent, and Katie's flush deepens.

The two men lock eyes, and Katie wonders if she's going to need to intervene. She can see that DS Peters has already pulled back a little.

'We need to find a way to work together,' she says, resting her hand lightly on Nathan's shoulder.

'What I need,' says the superintendent, 'is people who can follow orders. I told you not to leave him alone.'

'I left him locked in my flat.'

'And yet, here he is. How is that, exactly?' He looks at Nathan again.

Katie follows Nathan's gaze over the superintendent's shoulder to a row of cars, one of which is parked half up on the kerb.

'How did Nathan's brother get here?' asks Katie, suddenly seeking to shift her boss's attention. 'If it was him. We should check for CCTV.'

'We already are.'

'And where has Markham gone?' says Nathan. 'If it wasn't him. He must have put up a struggle. There must be evidence.'

Katie looks out the window at other members of the team moving in and out of the house, wearing the same white paper suits that she and Nathan have been given to replace clothes that have already gone off for analysis. Cringing, she wonders what they might find on Nathan's borrowed clothes besides evidence of her shame.

'Neither of you are part of this anymore,' says Superintendent Taylor, popping open the door, the light flicking on above them again. Suddenly DC Alice Jones, the youngest member of Katie's team, or what she's slowly starting to accept is not her team, appears at the window.

'We found some kind of journal on the bed upstairs,' she says, lifting up a large bagged object to show the superintendent, before adding a belated, 'sir.'

'Wait there,' he says, grabbing his hat and climbing out of the car.

He's gone for several minutes, time in which the light in the car goes out and Katie and Nathan say nothing, both focused on the window to see what's going on outside. DC Jones, DS Peters and Superintendent Taylor are huddled together at the back of the forensics van, deep in conversation. When the superintendent returns he's holding the same evidence bag and is wearing a glove on one hand. This time he climbs into the driver's seat.

'You'd better look at this,' he says, pulling open the bag. It looks like it originally had a red cover, but is now covered in hundreds of doodles, all in black ink, all with jagged edges and with the nib digging deep into the card. Katie has pushed herself ahead of Nathan this time, squeezing between the front seats, and so it's only when she turns to ask him if he has any idea what the book is, that she sees he's fallen back and covered his face with his hands.

'Mine,' he says, his voice muffled by more than just his fingers. 'It's my book. I wrote it when I couldn't cope, when it all got too much.' He lowers his hands and stares at Katie. 'Please don't let anyone else read it.'

'It's evidence,' she says, softly. 'There's nothing I can do.'

'No,' says Nathan, in weak acceptance, eyes closing as though trying to shut out the world. When they open a couple of seconds later, they're stretched wide and he's moving forward, finger jabbing. 'Evidence! That's exactly what it is! It's evidence of how Markham knew all the things he couldn't have known! I talk about the doctor in there, about how he failed us. I talk about Mum, about the drink, about the pills, about what she said in her note. I talk about Christian, about the difference, the birthmark. I talk about beans and sausage; I talk about swirls; I draw a load of fucking swirls!' He traces one more in the air ahead of him, round and round towards the centre. 'I talk about my fears, my desires, my fantasies…' He's not holding back now, everything is coming out, and Katie suddenly wants to slow him down, or shut him up in case he says too much. Perhaps spotting the concern on her face he appears to realise this himself, visibly paling and wrapping his arms across his front, holding his confession in. 'Nightmares, as well,' he adds, and Katie's wondering if he's written about imagined murders, possibly even murders similar to those they're investigating now.

'Where did you leave the book?' she asks.

'I don't remember,' he says, his face twisting in confusion. 'Why the hell can't I remember?'

'I have an idea why,' says Superintendent Taylor quietly, and Katie shoots him a look.

Nathan appears not to have heard, gripping the back of his neck and drawing in a long breath. 'After my parents died... I filled up all the pages in a hurry.' He recovers and looks straight at Katie. 'It was probably at my parents' home, though. Markham could have found it and used it to frame Christian.'

Superintendent Taylor closes the bag and opens the car door again. 'It's a line of enquiry. But for now, our focus remains the same and we need to find both Markham and Christian, as quickly as possible.' He turns to look in the back. 'Go home. Get some rest. And come to the station to make your statement in the morning.' He directs his stare at Nathan, who seems not to be looking at anything at all. 'Keep out of trouble. And stay out of the way. I don't want a load of false sightings when the photo gets out.'

Katie watches her boss walk away, passing the evidence bag to DC Jones before pulling off his latex glove and retrieving his hat from the back of the forensics van. When he walks past the van and out of view there's a flash of lights in the distance; the press, eager to get the very latest on 'The Cartoonist', desperate to find out if there's been another victim. She looks down at the paper suit they've dressed her in and considers how close she came to being one. She can see from her reflection in the window that she still has a line of chocolate icing drawn across her neck. She wants to wipe it off, she wants to scrub every inch of her body, but for now she doesn't seem able to move. She slumps down in the seat and draws in a long breath. One hand is squeezed inside the other, and her knuckles start to whiten.

'Give me the keys to your car,' says Nathan. 'I'll drive us back.'

'Yeah, right!' she says. 'You've broken enough laws already.'

'I have,' says Nathan, distractedly. 'I *have*.' He seems childlike and excited, the discovery of the journal convincing him of his brother's innocence and lightening his burden.

Katie turns for the door before her unsteady smile slips away completely. She doesn't want to spoil his moment. She knows it may not last.

CHAPTER TWENTY-SIX

The journey back to Katie's flat is silent. He'd like to talk to her about the journal, about how it all makes sense to him now, but at the same time he's fearful of the questions she and the others will ask once they've read it, once they've shared his most intimate thoughts. He risks a glance across and wonders if he shouldn't be saying something to check she's okay, although it's clear that she isn't. Her driving is unusually reckless and aggressive. Back at Markham's he'd witnessed her retreat, slipping back into the place he's been so many times himself, unable and unwilling to process emotion, but now that she's re-emerged, one emotion seems to be dominating all others.

'That fucking idiot!' she shouts out as onrushing headlights flash their own complaint.

The glare of lights, alongside the horns, the swearing and the scream of the Rover's engine has given Nathan an appalling headache.

'Stop!' he shouts as they race towards a pedestrian stepping out into the road.

'Relax,' says Katie, as a dab of the brakes and a twitch of the steering wheel guides them by.

'We have to go back,' says Nathan. 'I did that – I stepped out like that so I could steal somebody's car. I left it at Markham's.'

'I guessed as much,' says Katie. 'There will be a report. The guys will probably put two and two together.'

'You mean, they'll think it was my brother? I can't let that happen.'

'I'll let DS Peters know,' says Katie. 'Hopefully he still won't need you until the morning, by which time some of that alcohol might have left your system.'

Suddenly the world around Nathan swims, a little reminder of what he'd somehow forgotten. 'It worked,' he says. 'The drink. It allowed me to see what I was too controlled to see when I was sober. My brother is innocent.' He sinks lower into his seat and his voice weakens as the truth hits home. 'I betrayed him. I thought he was like me.' He presses his head back. 'And you'll know what I'm truly like when you've read that journal. I'm a monster.'

She turns to look at him now, her face occasionally lit up by flashes of passing streetlights.

'Just words,' she says softly.

'Words that represent feelings.'

'But not actions.'

'Not yet.'

Katie squeezes the steering wheel and stares straight ahead. 'Recent events,' she says, a hand coming up to her throat, then dropping down again, 'have opened my eyes to a few truths. And you're not the only one feeling guilty for blaming someone, someone…' She looks away, as if checking the side mirror, but there's nobody on the road behind. 'Important. I told myself I was mad at you when you went away because you'd hidden how you were struggling, because you'd been putting on an act for me, for everyone. The truth is I don't think I ever fell for it. I could see that struggle; I just chose to ignore it and keep on pushing because I was getting what I wanted.'

'What we wanted,' Nathan corrects her.

'I think the real reason I was mad at you was because you couldn't go on…' She lifts her fingers from the steering wheel, bending them backwards. 'And because I knew that I wouldn't be able to go on without you.' Now she checks the rear-view mirror, and this time Nathan knows exactly what she's looking at. 'So, who's the monster really?'

Out of the corner of Nathan's eye he can see a plastic bag tucked down in the footwell behind the driver's seat: the bag that Katie took from the flat – the bag with contents he must never see. 'It's not Christian,' he says. 'We're not the same.'

'None of us knows what we're really capable of,' says Katie, her attention once again fixed on the road. 'And none of us is entirely the same. I always thought I was like my dad: driven, decent, moral…' She releases a long, uneven breath. 'But now…'

'Now you'd do anything to make this stop, maybe even take a life. Is that what you're trying to say?'

'Maybe.'

Nathan can see, even with her face turned away, that he's got it wrong. That wasn't what she'd meant at all. He can also see that she's not about to correct him with the truth. They sit in silence again, his previous elation now a gnawing worry for the only two people in his life he cares about. He starts to knead one hand inside the other, a burning sensation at the tips of his fingers and an itch related to the plastic bag behind him that he can't even bring himself to look at directly. The discomfort sharpens his thoughts, bringing them to a possibility that he had somehow overlooked.

'Markham's plan was to make Christian take the blame,' he says slowly, as his fear starts to build. 'So there's no way he could allow him to come forward and provide an alibi. He needed to make sure my brother was silent.'

'But he wasn't silent. You spoke to him on the phone.'

'Markham could have taken him since.' He pinches at the hardened skin of his scars.

'He's not dead,' says Katie.

'No,' Nathan agrees, his thumb now resting on the inside of his wrist, checking for a pulse which isn't hard to find. 'I'd know if he was.'

Katie takes her hand from the steering wheel and lightly places it on the back of his.

'If this is Markham, though…' she says. The *if* makes Nathan pull his hand away, turning towards the window. 'I'm sorry,' she continues, 'but we have to keep asking the right questions. Like, why would Markham be doing this to us? He has no connection to me as far as I can tell, and if anything, he should be grateful to you and your brother.'

He leans towards her, jabbing a finger into his temple. 'It doesn't have to make sense! You should know that. I definitely know that.'

'How did Markham end up working for you?'

'Christian put an ad in the paper.'

'When was this?'

'I don't know exactly. Not long after you and I had started working together, and so by that point,' his fingertips prickle and he gives his hands a shake, 'by then I'd decided I couldn't risk seeing Christian. He couldn't know what I was like.'

'Couldn't Christian have found your journal?'

'No,' he says sharply. 'He doesn't know about me.' He's run through the possibility so many times, piecing together old conversations, fleeting looks, unanswered questions, and not once has he suspected that his secret has got out. He'd given up everything to keep it that way: his friends, his name, even his relationship with his brother. Given that sacrifice, a lifetime of effort and a memory that can call up a million details of much less importance, it makes no sense that he can't remember where he last left the journal. But then the lingering ache at his temple where he'd jabbed it with his finger reminds him of his own words: *it doesn't have to make sense*.

Katie brakes hard before pulling over into a side road. There are no street lamps and he can see little more than her outline.

'I know you want me to trust your brother, but I have to work with the evidence. We've been here so many times before, and on each of those times you've been right, but we've always needed evidence, and when it's *this* close, when it's family…'

'I know,' says Nathan. 'I know.' He places a fist against his forehead, lightly tapping it over and over. 'Jesus, how often have we sat talking to family members, listening to them defend their loved ones to the last, blind to the evidence in front of them.' He stares at Katie, his eyes slowly adjusting to the dark, and he can see her lift her hand to her shoulder-length hair, tucking it behind her ear. It's something he remembers from before: an action that he'd recognised as a need for distraction. And this time it *has* distracted him, taking him away from concerns about his brother. He reaches up and switches on the light, catching the startled look from Katie as she retreats from his outstretched arm.

'It's okay,' he says, reaching towards her and pushing back the hair. It reminds him of a girl he'd known in his teens. She'd been clever, beautiful, funny, and he'd hoped that the light she brought to his life might somehow counteract the dark that was descending. For a while it had worked, and he'd started to believe he might be okay, but then had come the intimacy, the time spent alone, and he'd realised that breaking her heart by walking away was far better than what he was imagining doing to her.

Lost in the memory, he almost misses what he's exposed in this intimate moment with Katie. With her hair pushed back he can see that the line of chocolate icing on her neck is not only at the front. He follows it with his finger, and she lets him, until he reaches a point at the back where the two meeting lines are wrapped around each other.

'What is it?' she says.

'I don't know. A link to another case, perhaps.' He reaches under his hair, still held at the back by a single rubber band. 'I don't remember seeing it on the wall in your flat, but did any of the victims wear a necklace with a fastening like twisted wire?'

Katie reaches up instantly and turns off the light, but not before he catches the look of confusion quickly turning to terror.

'It's probably like the doll,' she says, shakily. 'It means that he didn't just want to cut my throat; maybe he had trouble getting the lines to meet at the back? Or maybe his hand was shaking?'

On the steering wheel he can see hers doing the same, and he wants to tell her that it's okay, that she doesn't need to share what she's really thinking, not yet. Instead he stays quiet and settles back into his seat, thinking of the first time he'd met this remarkable woman. She'd been so different back then; so self-assured, so in control. If there'd been doubt in anything she did she was able to hide it well, but with his eye for detail he'd also noticed a trace of something else, a sadness he couldn't ever pinpoint. He remembers going to her previous flat once – far larger, in a far better part of town – to pick up something on the way to a crime scene, and he couldn't help but absorb every detail of the immaculate interior around him. When he'd got home that night he'd played it back in his mind, finding himself living her life, behind her eyes, and eventually those eyes, or perhaps his eyes, had started to cry.

*

As they walk up the stairs to her current home, he watches the bright strips of material on the backs of obviously well-used trainers Katie had pulled out of her car. He starts to feel as if he's just finished one of the runs around his house in Scotland, a marathon that never took him more than a dozen metres from his front door. He doesn't notice Katie has stopped in front of him until he's very nearly walked into her, bashing instead into the plastic bag containing the Steven Fish file. He's about to ask what's wrong when she spins towards him, holding a finger to her lips, eyes wide. That same finger then points ahead, and when he leans to look past her he can see that the door to her flat is open.

'Probably me,' he says, as quietly as he can manage. 'I left in a hurry.'

This time her finger directs him to the floor just ahead. The lights in the stairwell are not the strongest but he can see the muddy marks leading up to the door. He makes the shape of a phone and holds it to his ear, but she shakes her head and starts moving on. Reaching the door, Katie pushes it open a fraction more, enough for them both to slip through. He's keeping close, but not so close he can't fling himself in front of her should there be an attack.

The flat is exactly as he had remembered, still a bit of a mess, still with the spare room door he'd shoulder-barged open hanging from one of its hinges. The light in the little room is still on, just as he had left it, but the broken door is blocking his view inside. Katie moves swiftly to the bedroom, leaping through the doorway and turning to her right into one of the few parts of the flat that can't be seen from the centre of the living room. She comes back out, eyes wide and shifting rapidly from side to side.

'Perhaps you left the mud and we just didn't notice it,' he whispers.

Katie says nothing, moving across and slamming the front door shut before fastening the chain.

'Or perhaps it was a neighbour who noticed the door was open and called in to check you were okay.'

She switches on the main light and, looking down, they can both see that the mud extends into the flat. They follow the footprints round to the kitchen. And it's there, in the centre of the table, that they spot the knife. It is the largest of the knives taken from the block on the side: the very knife that Katie had placed between them the night before. Alongside the blade are two small objects. From a distance they remind him of the chopped carrots he'd seen in Markham's kitchen. There's no pool of blood here, but they have a redness at one end that makes his stomach twist. He moves closer and Katie tries to block him off with her arm. It's too late; he can make them out clearly, as clearly as he can see his own fingers.

He pushes past her and steps in close, so close that he can see the white of the bone. Both fingers have been severed cleanly, cut off just below the second knuckle with a precision that suggests they were taken individually. Nathan stumbles backwards, slamming into something hard, then sliding down towards the floor.

'My brother,' he says.

'We don't know that for sure.'

'I felt it,' he says, squeezing the tips of his fingers where the burning and then the numbness had been. 'And I did that.' He points at the smallest of the fingers. 'I accidentally shut Christian's in the car door when he was seven. It broke and never straightened. I-I remember being horrified that we were no longer the same, that I'd made him different to me. I even thought about breaking my finger too.' His voice emerges so flat and cold he's almost convinced it's not his own.

'You'll have mentioned the broken finger in the journal,' says Katie, pushing herself up straight, then squatting down next to him, reaching out to touch his arm. 'He's just showing he knows things that he shouldn't, things that are secret and private. It doesn't mean that Christian is dead.'

Nathan reaches out for the connection to his brother, searching for comfort and finding pain. 'He's not,' he says, glancing across at the plastic bag that Katie had dropped upon entering the kitchen. 'But this is worse.'

CHAPTER TWENTY-SEVEN

Katie follows Nathan's glance at the bag and suddenly understands what he means by *this is worse*. It also reminds her that there are other murders and other pieces of evidence hidden in this flat. She moves quickly, almost tripping over Nathan's legs as she runs out of the kitchen through to the tiny room and instantly surrounds herself with the images that have filled her mind, her days and her nights for so long. But there's only one she's looking at now, pinned in the gap she had made to protect Nathan. And it's Nathan's face that fills that gap now.

She'd taken the photo with her mobile at the end of one of their biggest successes. He looks young and handsome, with close-cropped hair and a broad smile. She remembers that smile, remembers the effect it had on her before she'd pushed those feelings down. It's then that she spots the addition to the photo: the narrow line of what she's sure is chocolate icing drawn across Nathan's throat. She lifts a hand to her own throat, feeling the raised line before rushing into the bathroom and vomiting in the sink.

She throws water on her face, then, almost without thinking, starts to rub angrily at the chocolate icing on her neck. Even this past year, when she's never been more desperate to make things right, to find a way to get the results she craves, she's never tampered with or destroyed evidence. She's always followed the process and never been anything less than the policeman she'd always thought her dad had been. But now… She closes her eyes and releases a breath that seems to empty her of far more than a lungful of air.

Lifting her eyes to the mirror to check it has all been removed, she sees another version of herself reflected back. A second photo has been printed out and stuck up, this time of her from the early days, when she too looked younger, when she too could wear a smile. But that smile has been broken by a thick line of smeared chocolate icing running north to south across her lips.

'Oh, Jesus!' says Nathan, and she turns to see him standing in the doorway. 'What does that mean?'

Katie starts to work through the possibilities, alarmed at how easily her mind settles itself to the task. Although this feels like the lowest point, she also knows this has moved them forward, towards the end, somewhere closer to a final understanding. She reaches into her pocket and pulls out her mobile, starting to punch in the only number she's ever dialled of late. Then she looks at the photo of herself again and stops.

'He's warning us not to share what we've found here,' she says, lifting a finger to her lips and mirroring the line on her image. 'Did you see the other…?'

He nods.

'Maybe that will only happen if we don't do what he wants.'

'But it's evidence,' says Nathan, and she can see him on the fringes of the mirror. 'It's proof of Christian's innocence.'

'You know it's not that,' she says, looking down at the sink, seeing and feeling how her insides have been emptied out. 'Not definitive. And until they've done the tests they'll only have your word as to who the fingers in the kitchen belong to.' As she says this she realises the same applies to her. But she's finding the old trust now, shaping her thoughts and ambitions around it, even if those ambitions are forcing her to lie.

'Why would he want them knowing about this?'

She's still staring at the sink, seeing more than the contents of her stomach. There's the chocolate icing, too, evidence she has destroyed, and perhaps evidence of why she's been so quick to come up with this need for secrecy. She looks away and considers her flat, sees the room with the door ripped off its hinges.

'It would be the final straw,' says Nathan, as if reading her mind. 'If your colleagues discovered what you've got hidden here.'

'Which might explain Markham's need for silence,' she says. 'He wants us to keep working the case.'

'Or he wants us to keep working alone, not trusting the others. Not trusting anyone.' Nathan grabs her by the top of her bicep. 'We need the others. We've always needed them. And right now they're wasting time looking for the wrong man!'

'Hang on,' says Katie, lifting the phone again and typing in the same number.

'Uncanny,' says DS Peters, when the connection on the phone is made. 'I was literally about to give you a call. I know you should be sleeping but I thought you might want to hear this.'

'Go on.'

'He's never been married. At least not under the name of Markham. And when we dug a little deeper, things didn't stack up. The records aren't so good twenty-five years ago, but it appears he did change his name at some point.'

'So we don't know if he has any living relatives?'

'According to the neighbours he's a loner. Doesn't speak to them. Doesn't speak to anybody.'

'Markham is our man,' says Katie.

'Hang on,' says DS Peters. 'I know what you've been through, it was horrible, it was…'

She can hear him swallow and finds herself feeling a greater discomfort for what she seems to have put him through.

'But you didn't actually see him attack you, did you?'

The story is there – she's formed it in a flash. It's simple, simple enough to be believed. She only has to say that she saw more than the boots and the jeans after she'd been hit, that she caught a glimpse of him reflected in the television screen. The smack on the head will explain the confusion and the delay in the memory returning. And what harm could it do? It will simply steer the investigation in the direction she now knows is right, save her team time and effort in the background checks. Time that might even save Christian's life. She lifts a hand to the back of her head, carefully touching the spot where she was struck. It's just above the point where the chocolate lines crossed like barbed wire, just like the necklace she once saw in the hand of her dad.

'Are you still there, boss?'

She looks down at herself, wondering at the question. So much of her identity seems to have disappeared in this past year.

'No,' she says, firmly. 'I didn't see him. But there's still plenty to suggest that it was Markham. He was holding the likely weapon when I arrived. And it happened in his house: a house that he insisted I travel to alone; a house from which he has disappeared, with no evidence of any kind of struggle.' She's also thinking of the carrots, cut up carefully on the side in Markham's kitchen, so reminiscent of the fingers on the table behind her. 'Are his prints on the journal?'

'They are,' says DS Peters. 'Although they're not on our system. He can't have previous, name change or not.'

'Or he simply hasn't been caught.'

Out of the corner of her eye she'd seen Nathan shift uneasily at the mention of his journal.

'Listen,' she says, finding strength in her voice and in her convictions. 'You told me this was my case, mine to solve, and my instinct is telling me that it's Markham. Find him and we find our killer.'

'All right. It won't be easy convincing the Super to focus our efforts on finding Markham. You know what he thinks. You know what he believes. Every bit as strongly as you. But it's good...' He pauses. 'Good to have you sounding like your old self again.'

'Ring me if you have anything new.'

'Will do,' says DS Peters, and they both hang up.

She looks across at Nathan, who's been standing close enough to hear every word.

'This isn't your old self,' he says. 'You would never have kept quiet. You'd have been scared of the court case, of the omissions, of the lies. I'm not even sure,' he looks over her shoulder at the photo taped to the mirror, 'that we've read this right. What if it's not a warning of silence, but a prediction?'

She holds his stare, feeling her hand rise to the back of her neck. 'I'm trying to save your brother.'

'Are you?' he asks, as her hands start to rub at the skin.

She turns her back on him and stares at the image, seeing her old self, a self whose intentions he would never have doubted.

'What case were we celebrating?' she asks.

'Mark Todd, the guy who killed that homeless man in Isleworth.'

'That's right,' says Katie, and it all comes back to her in an avalanche of detail. 'It was snowing at his funeral.'

'And we were the only ones there.'

'That's because his only friend was still being held by us. Taylor was convinced.'

'Until you found the knife.'

'And you found Mark Todd. God, no wonder we were smiling: Taylor looked like such an idiot.'

'To us,' says Nathan. Katie glances over her shoulder and can see he's perched himself on the edge of the badly stained bathtub. 'But he soon made it look like another one of his successes.'

'We never did this for the plaudits,' says Katie. She's staring at the photo of herself again, her hair and make-up as immaculate as ever, although the shade of lipstick she always wore doesn't look quite right. She moves her head from side to side, checking that it isn't just an effect of the bare bulb hanging above them. And then she sees it.

'Shit!' she says, rushing out through the door and over to a desk on the far side of the living room, knocking over an empty wine bottle on the way.

There's a well-worn computer on top. She hits a button on the front of the base unit and it whirrs and whines as it starts up.

'What's going on?' asks Nathan, moving up close behind and peering at the far-from-flat-screen monitor.

'He used my printer for the photos. I could see the same faded strip that always shows.' She leans to one side and considers the USB port. 'But those photos weren't on the computer. I...'

'Removed them?' asks Nathan, and she replies with an embarrassed nod.

The prompt for a password appears in the middle of the screen and she hesitates before typing it in, fearing that Nathan will follow the movement of her fingers as they spell out his name and the name of the location where they first met. Over the years it had seemed to Katie like a place of birth, where she'd first started to be who she had wanted to be. She's a long way from there now, but at least she's thinking again, seeing things more clearly, making the connections that have eluded her in the past twelve months.

'How does he know all this?' she asks, loading up a search engine then checking the history. She gasps when she sees the last entry, quickly double-clicking to bring it back up. A route planner has been uploaded, showing an address in Yorkshire three hours' drive away, according to the website.

'We need to go,' she says, already peeling off her paper suit and moving towards the bedroom where she'll find more clothes for them both.

'Do you think he's made his first mistake?' Nathan calls out.

'We'll find out when we get there.'

CHAPTER TWENTY-EIGHT

Nathan sits up suddenly, causing Katie to flinch and send the car veering to the left. She pulls it back in line and looks across. Her head is throbbing, and the lights on the motorway seem painfully bright. Nathan stares out of the window, breathing deeply.

'Where are we?'

She's about to tell him they're ten miles out of London on the M4, before realising it's probably not specifics he's after, not having woken from twenty minutes' sleep. 'We're travelling to the address that Markham left on my computer.' A Google search on her phone had revealed nothing about the address, and she'd quickly decided against sharing with the rest of the team. DS Peters was already getting too protective and would never have kept the information to himself. The superintendent would have wondered why she was ignoring his orders, yet again.

'What happened to the BMW?' asks Nathan, and this time she doesn't look across.

'The same thing that happened to the flat.'

'Paying for your dad's care?'

'Yes.'

'You'd do anything for him, wouldn't you?'

She can't see his expression clearly in the low light, but she can hear something's different. When they'd got in the car and he'd slumped into the corner she'd likened it to a computer shutting down. Now it appears he's rebooted.

'You need to tell me,' he says.

'Tell you what?'

'About your dad.'

'What about him? He's ill. He's not getting better.'

'There's something else. What are you protecting him from?'

'We don't talk about family, remember?'

'And what the fuck do you think we've been doing these last two days?'

'This is different.'

'No, it's not. If there's a connection – and I think you know there is – then you have to trust me. My brother's life is at stake here.'

'It's not trust,' she says, realising the car's been picking up speed and taking her foot off the pedal. She sucks in several deep breaths to help ease the flow of words past her lips, but all it does is make her feel light-headed. 'You know all that running…' She spins a finger in the air between them, then snaps it down when she spots her mistake. 'The way you were shutting stuff out. Well, that's what I've been doing, trying to keep my distance from thoughts, from possibilities that threaten… from everything.'

She catches him glancing at the bag on the back seat again.

'Maybe it's time for us both to take a risk,' he says. 'I reckon I could now, now I know about Christian.'

'What if that's exactly what Markham wants? To push you over the edge.'

'What I want,' says Nathan, his words suddenly softening, 'what I *need*, is to be able to trust you. We had that before, but it was professional. It wasn't… it wasn't enough.'

'It wasn't,' she says. Then, after a long pause: 'The guy I've been talking to at my dad's new home said the same, told me I needed to start sharing with people I cared about. The problem was, I first needed to admit there were people I cared about.' She puts on the wipers, as if that's the reason she can no longer see the road ahead. 'I couldn't even tell Dad how important he was to me, not back when he would have understood. And then there was you…' She's glad for the low light, offering only little glimpses of her troubled face. 'I just left you in Scotland. Dumped you there without a word. Yeah, I was hurt that you hadn't trusted me enough to tell me how you were suffering. But I knew. I wasn't blind. Just like I saw the change in my dad thirty years ago. And yet I never asked him, and he never spoke about what he'd done, not until the Alzheimer's had torn away the barriers.'

'What had he done?'

'The right thing,' she says firmly. 'The only thing he could have done. He had no choice, I'm sure of it.' She slams a hand against the steering wheel. 'Jesus, he was always so principled, always so strong.' She looks across at Nathan. 'At least as strong as you.'

Nathan gives her a look of horror, starting to understand.

'The right thing,' she repeats.

'What did he tell you?'

'Next to nothing. I haven't really allowed him to. I went this evening, before I visited Markham.' As she mentions his name she reaches for her throat, feeling a slight tackiness where she's failed to wash off all the chocolate. 'But I've only been to the care home maybe half a dozen times, and when I'm there I spend more time talking to Dad's carer than Dad. He's a good listener, more like a therapist really.'

'Was that the guy you said you've been seeing?'

'Until I fucked things up.' She feels herself flush, remembering the drunken night she'd lost control. 'Then I went back to the work again, taking refuge in other people's nightmares.'

'Only now those nightmares aren't just other people's,' says Nathan.

She sighs, realising she's pushed the car back over the speed limit, as though if she drives fast enough she might leave her past behind. And maybe they could? They could carry on driving all the way to Scotland to live in a house and run rings around it. But what would it achieve?

'You need to tell me what you know about your dad's crime. It's important.'

'I don't know much.'

'I don't think that's true,' says Nathan. 'You couldn't have resisted.'

'I managed to resist looking into your past,' she says, glaring across, 'when I had similar doubts. And he's my dad. He made me who I am. This will potentially change who I am. That's why I've started to doubt my instinct. I mean, if I couldn't even see the truth about my own dad.'

'The truth is what you need,' says Nathan. 'Look at what I believed my brother had done.'

Katie pushes herself back in the seat, feeling the acceleration rising again, wondering if it's ever going to stop. Then she takes back control, lifting her foot from the pedal and allowing the car to cruise. 'A twelve-year-old girl was murdered. She went missing from the back garden of her parents' house. No witnesses, no clues, nothing to go on at all. Dad was part of the team that found the body. And then another girl disappeared, same age, same method. Of course, everyone was in a panic, desperate to find her before it was too late. My dad and his partner were good detectives. That's what everyone who's ever worked with them has told me. The trail took them to an old grain barn in the middle of nowhere. They found the girl alive, but the man who'd taken her died trying to get away.' She pauses, takes a breath, grips the steering wheel tightly. 'He had a fall.'

'And your dad changed after that?'

Katie nods. 'He was never the same. I'd always been troubled, angry, withdrawn, but it was like he gave up fighting me, stopped trying to tell me what I was doing was wrong. Jesus, he wouldn't even look me in the eye. I think he was just as cold with Angie, which is why she didn't hang around long after.'

'Angie?'

'She helped raise me. She was okay, I suppose, did what she was meant to with feeding me and keeping me safe, but like I say, as soon as Dad changed, and as soon as I was old enough to take care of myself, she was off.'

'What about your mum?' asks Nathan, tentatively.

'Left the world the same day I came into it.'

'I'm so sorry.'

She shrugs. 'It was far harder for Dad than me. I had no idea what I'd missed out on.'

'What makes you think he took someone's life?'

'Because he told me.' She runs a tongue across her drying lips. '"I murdered him", that's what he said. I looked across, and he was standing at the window staring down, his two hands pressed against it. I asked him what he was talking about, but he'd slipped away again. It wasn't hard to figure out what case he was referring to – I'd seen how it had affected him at the time and I guess I'd always had my doubts.' She pushes herself back in her seat, sucking in a long breath and lifting her chin.

'What about the chocolate icing on your throat? What was the significance of that mark?'

'I skipped school once, more than once, but on this occasion I followed Dad, desperately wanting to see what he did with his days, all the things he wouldn't share with me when he got home. I wanted to see why he'd been acting so strange. Only, he didn't go to work. He went into town and met up with a girl – a girl who didn't look much older than me. I remember thinking… Jesus, I remember thinking all kinds of things!

'I confronted him that evening. I asked him if he was some kind of pervert. I asked him if I had a sister he wasn't telling me about. I thought that might explain why he'd been so cold towards me. He just told me it was to do with the murder case he'd been working on, someone he had saved.'

Katie thumps the door, letting out a fraction of her frustration. 'Christ, I said some horrible things in return, things I'd somehow managed to forget until now… But there were two things I'll never forget: Maclean was the name of the man Dad had saved the young girl from, I got a glimpse of the case notes on his desk. There was also a necklace in a box there, a necklace with a twisted fastening. I thought at first it was for me, his own way of saying sorry, of proving that I was more important than anything at work, but the next time I followed him I saw him give it to the girl.'

'Markham knows this,' says Nathan. 'Which means he must have something to do with the Maclean case. And we have evidence.' He turns to look at her. 'Or rather, we did. You washed it away.' He's holding his throat, although it feels very much like he's squeezing hers. 'We need to share this with your team.'

'The photo back at the flat warned us to keep quiet,' she says, lifting a finger to her lips.

'You're protecting your dad.'

'Of course I fucking am! It would destroy him. His reputation is all he has left. He might have lost who he is in the present, but I can protect his past. I owe him that. I owe him everything.'

'But my brother!'

'I know,' she says, 'I know. But you also have to remember that Markham gave us the clue. This is what he wants: to hurt us the way he's hurt the other families.' She slows a little and looks across at Nathan, seeing his frustration, feeling his pain.

'Fuck it!' she says, pulling her mobile out of the centre console. 'Let's do what's right. Alex Maclean, 1987. Tell them to look into it, just in case. Tell them about the mark on my neck. Tell them I destroyed it. Tell them…'

Nathan looks up at her, then down at the phone, the screen illuminating his face. 'No,' he says eventually. 'You're right. We can't risk telling them anything yet.' He lifts a finger to his lips and holds it there. 'Let's wait and see what's at this address first.'

Katie nods and takes back the phone, the speed building under her foot again. She tries to convince herself she really was doing what was right in offering Nathan the phone, in risking everything, but the truth is she'd always known he wouldn't make the call. Worse still is the sense that they're using each other. He needs her to help find the man who may have already killed his brother. She needs him to shut that man up for good.

CHAPTER TWENTY-NINE

There can no longer be any doubt. Nathan knows exactly where he's heading. It's where he would always head when he couldn't find a way to distract himself. He's just never, in all his endless imaginings, come up with a murder that felt so justified.

He's pulled out of his thoughts by the phone between them buzzing into life. Katie snatches it from under the dashboard and opens up a message. It's almost four in the morning, so Nathan expects it can only be work-related, but the twist in Katie's face says otherwise.

'What is it?' he asks.

Katie throws the phone down and it bounces off the centre console and disappears into the footwell ahead of him. He thinks about reaching for it, but he hears her bark an order to open the glove box as she swerves towards the hard shoulder.

He does as instructed, confused and a little scared, suddenly imagining another part of his brother's body will be in there – a tongue, an ear, a curl of skin sliced from his back. But instead there's a book. He pulls it out and she snatches it from him, bringing the car to a stop and switching on the light above them. It's not at all what he'd expected: it's a children's book with a brightly coloured illustration of a Christmas tree on the cover and a title he can't make out. Katie sits with it on her lap, her eyes wide, her hands shaking. It reminds Nathan of the books he escaped into in the early days up at his cottage in Scotland. But this is not one of his. Katie carefully opens the book and, with a trembling finger, follows the handwritten inscription:

YOUR FATHER SAYS IT'S TOO EARLY FOR PRESENTS, BUT I JUST CAN'T WAIT FOR YOU TO COME, MY LITTLE KATIE. WE'RE GOING TO HAVE SO MUCH FUN TOGETHER!

The bottom right-hand corner of the page is blackened with yellowing fringes, a clear sign that someone has tried to set it alight. Above that are words written in a smaller hand. He needs to lean in closer to make them out, his head only a couple of inches from Katie's. It's not the same writing as on the notes they've found before, but far more upright and angular:

I don't make mistakes. See you at the end.

CHAPTER THIRTY

It's started to get light outside. It's also started to rain. The wipers on Katie's dad's old car are struggling to keep the windscreen clear. How could Markham have known about the book from her mum? *She* hadn't known about it until she was in her teens, finding it in a pile in the attic. She'd waved it at her dad, and he'd told her he'd never seen it before. She'd kept its contents a secret, the only secret she had ever shared with her mum until, one day, when she'd let her temper get the better of her, she'd taken a lit cigarette (one of the many secrets she kept from her dad) and put it to the corner. She hadn't let it burn for long.

When she thinks about Markham touching it, she feels what little control she has left starting to slip, hammering her hands against the steering wheel. Nathan has his head pressed into the glass of the passenger door. He hasn't moved for a few minutes.

'You think it's a trap?' he says, without lifting his head.

Katie finds herself looking across at the glove box to where the precious but now defiled book has been returned. 'Of course.'

'Do you think he means see you at the end of the journey?'

'I'm not sure.'

'Do you think Christian will be there?'

'Again, I don't know.'

'What do you think he's done to Christian?'

'Don't!' she says sharply. 'We need to keep our focus.'

'You think I don't have focus?' says Nathan, turning to look at her.

It's when she looks back at him that Katie really sees the torment and the bubbling rage, and she finally understands. She's calm because one of them needs to be. It's how they've always worked, it's *why* they've worked, because they're opposites, because they're a team.

The closer they get to the address they've been given the more privilege they see, until eventually they find themselves crawling down a tree-lined street of huge detached houses. They find the number seventeen on a tall brick gatepost at the end of a snaking drive. Although there's a gate with a keypad, it's not shut and they drive straight in, deep gravel crackling under the tyres. In front of the house, a 1970s red-brick building that must have at least half a dozen bedrooms, is a tall, broad man with swept-back grey hair. He's standing next to a bag of golf clubs he's loading into a shiny black BMW. The sight of the clubs takes Katie back to the twisted body of Sarah Cleve.

She pulls alongside and winds down the window and asks warily: 'Who are you?'

'You're fucking kidding me!' he says, a rough voice that speaks of sixty a day and a whole lot of shouting.

She almost smiles: it's exactly what her dad would have said.

'You drive onto my property and ask who I am?' continues the stranger, his face reddening. He pulls a club from his golf bag.

'Feel free to take a swing,' she says. 'It might iron out a few of the dents.'

There's something about him that seems familiar: the way he carries himself; the way he's peering into the car, as if assessing who he's up against. He's confident, and his broad shoulders and solid arms suggest he might be right. But that confidence suddenly disappears and he takes several steps back, stumbling on the gravel.

'I know you!'

At first Katie thinks he's talking to her and that she was right, he's recognised her from an old case and it's more than the bonnet of her car she should be worried about. But she turns for a split second to Nathan and sees he's pressed his back into the door and lowered his head right down.

'I'm a police officer,' she says, reaching into her pocket and pulling out her warrant card. The man has moved round to the front of the car, and she has to press the card up against the windscreen to show him. He barely looks at it, so she pops open the door and half-steps out, leaving the engine running, ready to slip back in and throw the car into reverse if need be. 'This is not who you think it is. And we are no threat to you. We just want to talk.'

This time her words seem to have broken through, and he glances across at her, the club now resting on his shoulder.

'What about?'

She'd like to be honest and say she doesn't have a clue, but not before she knows who she's talking to.

'As you will have seen from my card, I'm DS Katie Rhodes. I work Serious Crimes back in London, and—'

She was intending to continue, to offer up her own story in the hope of hearing his, but from the very mention of her name his mouth has fallen open and the golf club has slipped from his hand and slapped against the gravel. He takes a step forward, staring intently at her.

'Christ, I can see it!' he says. 'How did I not see it before? And this is the profiler?' He glances across at Nathan. 'The one who always shied away from the papers, but whose face is now plastered across every single one?'

Once more Katie considers the age of the man, the vague familiarity and the level of aggression and comes to a new conclusion.

'You worked with my dad,' she says, trying to make it sound like she'd known all along.

'I was his partner for fifteen years,' he says. 'He talked about you all the time. Sadly we never got to meet.'

She reaches for the name and is relieved when it comes to her.

'Detective Sergeant Barclay,' she says with a smile.

'It was Detective Chief Inspector when I retired a few years back, but don't you worry about that. Your dad was always very particular about authority, a real stickler for the rules...' He slows, taking in her crumpled appearance. 'But you can call me Malcolm.' He matches her smile, but it doesn't linger. 'Now you didn't come out here just to say hello. In fact, you shouldn't have been able to come out here for any reason. This address is only known to a select few, seeing as I've made some pretty high-profile enemies over the years.' While he says this his eyes are darting left and right. Katie's do the same, and she finds there's not much to see except for a wood on the other side of the road and a glimpse of the neighbouring properties.

She decides to take a punt. It's not that she has nothing to lose – pretty much everything is on the line here – but whatever might have held her back before seems to have frayed and now finally snapped.

'Superintendent Taylor,' she says, and leaves it at that. From the way the man's head tilts and offers the tiniest nod she knows she's guessed well.

'How is he?' asks Barclay.

'Better than my dad,' says Katie.

The old detective's face twists in discomfort and he releases a long breath. 'I heard about that. I'm so sorry. I should have gone to visit Simon.'

Simon. She hasn't heard him called that in a long time; even in the care home it's always Mr Rhodes.

'I wanted to go. But...' Barclay stops to search for the words.

'I understand,' she says, thinking of her own reluctance, her own regret.

'I lost my own dad to dementia. When he was younger than I am now. And some days…' He reaches up and rubs the side of his balding head. 'Some days when things aren't coming to me clearly…' He seems to have lost some of his original size. 'I was never scared of anything at work, and we came across so many truly terrible things—'

'That's what I came here for,' Katie jumps in, spotting her chance to move things along. 'I need to know about the Maclean case.'

'Really?' he says casually, slipping the golf club back into the bag and avoiding her gaze. 'Why?'

'Because my dad has been talking. Not much, and not cohesively, but it's clearly causing him a lot of distress. I hoped you might be able to help.'

He lifts the bag and carries it towards the boot of the BMW. It's a car built for speed more than practicality, and once again Katie finds her anger building. This is the retirement her dad should have enjoyed.

'It's all in the papers,' he says, looking up briefly.

'All of it?'

'The important bits are. Your dad was a bloody hero.'

'Do you remember what happened? Only, he said a few things—' She breaks off, hoping that Barclay might fill in the rest.

'I remember,' he replies. 'I don't mind discussing this with you, but we should probably go inside.'

'You're worried someone might overhear?'

He smiles at this suggestion. 'My concern is about keeping dry,' he says, pointing to the dark clouds gathering above and moving for the door, beckoning her to follow.

'Is he helping with your investigation?' he asks, nodding towards the car.

'Offering a perspective. It's not personal to him, unlike…'
She moves in closer and lowers her voice. 'He's looking to be
occupied, as well you can imagine.'

'But shouldn't *that* be the case you're working on? Shouldn't
you be searching for his brother?'

'Superintendent Taylor has given me time to recharge my bat-
teries. These past few days have been…' she looks down, unable
to find the words. 'I'm sure you understand, sir.'

'Malcolm,' he corrects her, pushing open the front door at
the same time as Nathan climbs out of the car. 'Can I get you
both a cup of tea?'

'That would be great,' she says with a genuine smile. She wishes
she'd come to see this man sooner, and on her own terms, if only
to talk about Dad. Nathan catches up and declines a drink and a
handshake, keeping his arms fixed tight to his sides.

The living room is just as she'd pictured it from the outside,
dominated by a huge stone fireplace filled with dried flowers,
not logs, and with an even bigger television hung above it. The
carpets are thick and obviously new, and they've been asked to
take their shoes off. Katie feels rather embarrassed; in the rush
to get out last night she threw on the first pair of socks she could
find, which happen to have an enormous hole in the toe.

They sit next to each other on a deep sofa in the middle of the
room, twisting to look across at Malcolm Barclay on a reclining
armchair. He has it upright now, his posture even more so, a cup
and saucer balanced on his knee. Katie can't help but laugh to
herself at how ridiculous he looks, not at all the man he would
have been when her dad was working with him. Back then, she's
sure it would have been a polystyrene cup and a bacon butty.
Here he's offering Duchy Original biscuits carefully arranged on
a bone china plate.

While he'd been organising all this, possibly buying himself
time to prepare his story, Katie and Nathan had looked around

the room, focusing on the detail rather than the impression it was intended to give. On a table in the corner there were more than a dozen silver-framed photos showing Barclay and his wife, the children, the grandchildren and the dog, which appears not to be around anymore. The one that had instantly caught Katie's eye was of two young men standing with their arms around each other's shoulders, smiling broadly into the camera. Katie had gasped the moment she saw it; it had been so long since she had dared look at a photo of her dad as he used to be. By her calculation he must have been about her age in the photo, tall and fit and with a full head of hair.

'So, your dad's been talking?' says Barclay.

'Indeed,' says Katie. 'There was something he said a while back, out of nowhere: one of the few things he has said in the last few months that has made any sense. It was like he was himself again, for maybe thirty seconds, nothing more. He took me by the hand and made me swear that I'd do it, like it was the most important thing in the world to him.' She glances over Barclay's shoulder, giving the impression she's reliving the moment. 'He said he had doubts over Maclean's guilt. Said I had to look for him, to do all I could to be certain myself.'

'Well, tell him not to worry. There was more than sufficient evidence. He found him standing over the girl with a knife in his hand, chased him and the bastard slipped and fell.'

'But you weren't there?' asks Katie, and for the first time she can see discomfort in his face.

'Yes, I was,' he says, quickly. Too quickly. 'Of course I was. Check the report if you want. I saw it all.'

'Fine,' says Katie, not wanting to push too hard too early on. 'What can you tell me about Emma Pritchard?'

'The first girl?' Barclay starts to stir his tea very slowly with a silver spoon. 'About her, very little. She was from a good family. I used to see a lot of bad ones, so I always noticed when the love was there. And as far as we were ever able to discern there was no motive beyond the lust of that sick bastard.'

'There were never any other suspects? No footprints, no fingerprints, no DNA?'

'None of the first two, but I imagine plenty of the latter. We've not gone back to check it, though. We had no need. We found the right guy.'

'How do you know that?' asks Nathan, a sudden and unwelcome interruption that brings a glare from Katie.

'Because we caught him at it,' he snaps, 'with another little girl.'

Katie allows a moment of silence, as she has done in so many formal interviews, finding the perfect point at which to change direction. She studies her hands, considers the scratches and scrapes she's received in the last few days. 'Are you ready to tell me the truth now?' she says finally, calmly. 'Trust me, it doesn't need to go any further.'

'What the hell are you on about?'

'I'm sorry, Malcolm, but I think it's time.'

Barclay opens his mouth to protest, then closes it again. His broad shoulders rise and fall, sinking lower with every breath. 'They said you were like him, always following every rule, but never knowing when to stop, always pushing for the answer...'

'No matter the cost,' says Katie, nodding for him to continue.

'I did it for Simon,' he says eventually. 'And for you. You were everything to him.' He reaches for his tea, but his hand stops short. 'Your dad and I went there on a hunch; he always had such good instincts. We got separated looking around the farm, and when I walked into the grain barn and saw your dad holding the girl, I thought he'd just untied her and that monster had got away. But then he nodded up towards a metal gantry by the roof. "Call it in," he said. "One man. Dead." I asked him if he was sure, and this time he looked towards the ground outside the window. I didn't bother to go and check if he was right. I asked if he'd fallen, and your dad just shook his head. I couldn't believe it. Or rather, I could believe it because of the way he'd been talking in the days before. The death of Emma Pritchard, a girl the same age as you, had done something to him, made him… different.'

'What about the second girl?' says Katie, feeling the need to move things along. 'She must have kept quiet too.'

'She'd been drugged, and only came round a few minutes later.'

'By which time you'd agreed to make up a story?'

'Listen, I don't feel any guilt about it. The guy deserved to die. He would have killed Tracy, there can be no doubt. And he had previous, plenty of it: violence, drug use, assault, even rape of a minor.' He catches her eye and tries to summon up a smile. 'I think your dad used to meet up with her sometimes.'

Katie nods but doesn't say a word, her hand coming up to her throat again, her fingers following the line of an imaginary necklace.

'We both used to get Christmas cards,' Malcolm Barclay continues. 'I guess they stopped when she wanted to stop thinking about it and move on with her life. Which is a good life from what I can tell, from my own enquiries.'

'So you know where she is now?' asks Nathan.

'I do. She's got a wonderful family. Two lovely girls.'

Both Katie and Nathan look at each other at the same time, eyes wide, mouths partly open, as if about to say something but not daring to do so. Malcolm pushes himself forward in his seat.

'What the fuck is this?' he asks. 'What haven't you told me? Does this have something to do with his brother?' He looks across at Nathan, eyes narrowing.

'No,' says Katie, with a calming gesture. 'I promise you this is purely to do with my dad. It's just,' she shakes her head, 'we couldn't help thinking… when you hear about a young woman with two kids…'

Malcolm sits back in his chair, still not looking convinced but less agitated than he was before.

'Somebody needs to catch that monster,' he says, his eyes not leaving Nathan.

'I don't know what you've seen in the press,' says Nathan, holding his stare. 'But that monster is not my brother.'

Katie worries for a moment that he's about to give the game away, but he appears to have pulled himself back under control and the only damage done is to a biscuit he'd been holding out of politeness that is now a pile of crumbs in his palm.

'I don't suppose you could give us Tracy's address?' she says.

'No,' says Malcolm, firmly. 'She took on a new identity and a new life. Nobody is supposed to know what she went through. I'm not even sure her husband does.'

'We will be discreet,' says Katie, trying not to let the desperation seep into her voice. 'We'll wait until the husband and kids are out. Or maybe we could ring ahead?'

'I don't have the number. Look, I'd love to help you, but—'

'Please, Malcolm.' She waits for the tears to come, wiping her nose with her sleeve. 'I promised him; I promised Dad I would find her and see for myself that she was okay, that some good had come out of what happened. And he understood. It made him smile. Such a rare thing. Such a beautiful thing.'

Malcolm Barclay smiles too. There's plenty about him that reminds her of her dad: a big man, a strong man with a good heart. He looks across at the family photos again, then back at Katie.

'You swear you won't let her see you?'

'I swear,' she says, placing a hand on her chest, covering the moles that started all of this.

He gets up and leaves the room, returning a couple of minutes later with a Post-it note and a hastily written street name. He passes it to her, then places his hand on her shoulder, giving it a squeeze. She looks up, and he looks away. 'Say hello to your dad from me. I'll try and make it across there very soon.'

They thank him and leave, walking down the long gravel drive and back to the car. It has started to rain heavily now and they both make a show of wanting to get out of it, picking their pace up, aware that they're being watched from the living room window.

*

Back in the car they're forced to endure a seemingly endless drive out of the estate, passing over the speed bumps and sticking to the twenty-mile-an-hour limit. Once clear of that, Katie hammers her foot to the floor.

'I'm sure she'll be fine,' she says over the scream of the engine.

'Markham can't have known we'd get Tracy's address,' says Nathan, his body shifting backwards and forwards in the seat, as if that might help the old car to go faster. 'Or make the possible connection.'

'No,' says Katie, then again for reassurance. 'No.' Her driving is reckless, but they're making good time. Then, suddenly, she takes her foot off the pedal. 'What if the address was what Markham needed? What if he's using *us* to find out where Tracy lives?'

'I don't think he needs us to help him with any information,' says Nathan, gesturing for her to pick up speed again. 'That bastard already knows *everything*.'

'This is going to be like Mark Brooks all over again,' says Katie quietly, remembering the little girl's face as she clung onto the doll. 'Markham's found a whole new way to torture.'

They reach the outskirts of High Wycombe in just over an hour and a half, and five minutes later, thanks to directions from her mobile, pull up outside the address Malcolm Barclay had written down. The house is a small semi with a neat front lawn and a people carrier in the drive.

They rush up the pathway, passing a row of roses, and hammer on the door. Katie had thought about asking Nathan to stay in the car to avoid being seen, worried about how Tracy might react, but he was out of the car before she even had the chance to speak. Instead, she pulls out her warrant card, holding it up ahead of her so that Tracy might know from the outset that there isn't a threat. There's no response. She tries again and reaches forward to try to grab the handle, finding it locked. She presses her face up to the frosted glass, then steps out onto the front lawn to peer through the living room window, spotting no movement inside.

'She might be out,' says Nathan.

They both look back at the car in the drive, then hear a key in the lock. Katie moves in front of Nathan and lifts her card again. She's so tired she's struggling to hold it there, almost as much as she's struggling to hold her smile.

The door opens and a petite blonde woman of around forty-five peers past the edge of the door. Katie can't help but stare, carried back all those years to the time she'd seen her dad with this same person, then just a girl. She remains silent, only vaguely aware of Tracy's eyes flicking from her to Nathan and back again. It's only when Tracy takes in the warrant card that her face drops.

'What's happened?' she says, lifting a hand to her mouth. 'Not the children!'

'No,' says Katie, snapping out of her daydream. 'It's nothing like that. And I'm so sorry if we startled you. As you can see I am DI Rhodes, and this is my colleague, Nathan—' She cuts herself off before it emerges. 'My dad was a policeman, DS Simon Rhodes. You perhaps know him from a few years back?'

The door has swung open further, revealing dirty knees, a pair of gardening gloves and a mud-encrusted gardening fork which Tracy is holding out like a weapon.

'What's this about?'

'My dad's not very well. He hasn't been for a while. We can no longer… communicate. One thing he did say was that he wanted to know how you are doing.' Any guilt she might feel at yet another lie is soon eased by the relaxation on Tracy's face.

'You'd better come in.'

Katie checks over her shoulder. It's the middle of the day now and there's nobody around apart from an elderly woman in the distance and a teenage boy being dragged along by a German shepherd. It's not enough to let herself relax, even when she sees the interior and feels the warmth of the family photos lining the brightly coloured walls. Even when she sinks into the comfortable sofa and hears the soft purring of a cat sleeping in the corner. Why have they been led here? What interest is this to Markham after all these years? She finds herself searching the photos again, desperate for an answer to present itself. Out of the corner of her eye she can see Nathan is doing the same, sucking up the details, absorbing the life and no doubt processing all that information at a frightening speed. She hopes he's going to be the first one to talk, that he'll spot something that will send them racing off elsewhere, as far away from all this as they can possibly get. But it's Tracy who speaks first, returning from the kitchen with a pot of tea and three mugs decorated with roughly painted animals.

'I should have gone to visit him,' she says. 'But he told me not to. He said I should focus on…' She lifts her arms and offers a broad sweep of the room. 'Still, I wish I had done. I wanted to, and I definitely would have if I'd known he was ill.'

'He would have understood,' says Katie, instantly regretting her choice of tense. 'When was the last time you saw him?'

'At least a decade ago. I remember you'd just got a promotion. He always talked about you when I saw him. He was so proud.'

She smiles, and Katie tries to match it, but these are things about her dad that she didn't know and will never hear about from him. She only vaguely remembers the promotion, and her dad had never expressed anything other than disappointment at her ignoring his advice and joining the force.

'He was like a dad to me,' Tracy continues, before holding a hand up to her mouth. 'I mean, not like… he only dropped in every month or so.'

More frequently than he did for me, thinks Katie, looking away to try and hide her distress. Her attention falls again on the photos in the corner, and she finds herself unable to shake off the sense that she's close to something important. Climbing to her feet, she heads for a photo of a young girl that Katie had originally taken to be one of Tracy's daughters. The closer she gets, the tighter the cold grip on her heart squeezes. It's actually a photo of Tracy, she can see that now, and she can also see that hanging round the then teenager's neck is a chain she suspects had a twisted fastening at the back. Worse still, there's a resemblance she hadn't noticed before.

'I'm glad my dad was able to help,' Katie says, fighting to keep her voice flat and calm. 'Is yours not around anymore?'

'No,' says Tracy, failing to hide the shift in her own emotions. 'He left when I was young.'

'Went back up North?'

'How did you know…?'

'I thought I heard a trace of an accent in you,' says Katie, forcing a smile.

'That's impossible. We moved down when I was a baby.'

'My mistake.' Katie moves across to a table full of photos, leaning forward and carefully making her way through each one. 'Is he anywhere here?'

'Mum wouldn't allow it.'

Katie doesn't want to push too hard. She knows she's already making Tracy suspicious of her. This woman is a survivor, has built a life far more stable and, she's certain, more rewarding than her own. She could very easily, and selfishly, damage it by being too reckless and too desperate for answers. She knows now that this is what Markham will have so carefully worked out: the next stage of his plan. But perhaps she can resist.

'There are no photos of him at all?' It's Nathan that's broken the silence, leaning in close.

'Why?' Tracy's voice tightens. 'Why are you so interested in my dad?' She's retreating to the far side of the room, giving herself time and space to think, looking at Nathan properly for the very first time. Katie is waiting for the penny to drop, but there's nothing.

'Do you watch the news?' she asks, already thinking she knows both the answer and the reason.

'Why? Are you saying my dad's been on there?'

Katie's thoughts are tumbling over and over. She wishes she didn't have to do this, and again she wonders if she might just walk away, forget about it all and give up for once. She's so caught up in the possibility that she misses Nathan moving across to the sofa. When she turns, she can see he's holding up a remote control. He punches in the number for a twenty-four-hour news channel and of course the story of 'The Cartoonist' is there, headline news.

Tracy stares at the screen for a few seconds, eyes not blinking, not moving an inch. Then she's staggering away, folding her arms across herself, her back pressed up against the patio windows leading out to her garden. All the time she's looking back at the screen, at the photos and at the banner headlines scrolling across the screen and spelling out the terrible crimes that have been committed. The photo used was of Nathan as he'd been a few years earlier, cut from an image of Katie's investigations team. He'd stood apart, barely in frame; the reluctance to be there was written all over his face.

'This is the man we're after's brother,' says Katie, pointing at the TV and then at Nathan. 'He is a criminal psychologist. He works with the police and is helping us to find both his brother and—' She cuts herself off, realising there's no need to continue.

The image of Markham has already flashed up on the screen. It's an old photo of a younger man, likely the only photo her colleagues could get their hands on. It might not be ideal for a public response, but Tracy's is immediate.

'You're wrong,' she says, grabbing at the curtain behind her as if that might hold her up. 'Whatever you think he's done.' She turns her attention to Nathan. 'He would never…' Her breathing has quickened. 'He promised me.'

'Promised what?' says Katie. 'When?'

Tracy spins suddenly, trying to get a look at the garden as if she's heard a noise out there, her hands shaking uncontrollably against the glass. Katie wants to pull her close, but she can tell she's petrified of everything and everyone.

'Do you know what this will do to your father?' says Tracy, with a desperate stare in Katie's direction.

'Please,' says Katie. 'We just need to know where he is.'

'I don't know,' she replies, sinking down. 'I haven't seen him since…' she pauses again, grips the curtain tighter, 'since a long time ago.'

'Perhaps your mother?'

'My mother is dead.' She sinks further so she's curled into a ball, her arms wrapped around her legs, dragging them in. 'But you're wrong. He wouldn't… He promised. He swore on his life it wouldn't happen again. That's why your father…'

'What happened?' says Nathan firmly when she doesn't go on. 'You have to tell us.'

But she doesn't speak. Nathan's hands are stretched out towards Tracy, but Katie moves across and blocks his path, her mind suddenly clear – the way it always was when they were approaching a solution.

'Your dad was there, wasn't he?' she says, unable to prevent a gasp as she finally recognises the truth. 'He was in the barn the night you were attacked.'

Tracy pulls her limbs in further; before she lowers her head to her chest she offers a single nod.

'Did he attack you?'

'No,' she says, her voice childlike.

'Who was the man that died?' asks Katie.

'Evil.' She looks up suddenly, eyes wide. 'Pure evil. He killed the other girl. It was like that bastard had control over Dad, could make him do whatever he wanted. Dad never actually touched me on that day, he just stood there like a zombie, like he couldn't believe who he had become. He was never like that before. He was a good dad.' The tears come again, and Katie needs to know more before she can console her.

'How did Alex Maclean die?'

Tracy visibly shakes at hearing the name. 'Like they said,' she manages eventually. 'Your dad chased him up to the roof. And then…' One hand comes up towards her ear, as if to try and block the sound she's reliving. 'There was a scream.'

Katie has interviewed enough witnesses over the years to know when they're holding back, and she knows she must push on, right to the end.

'You heard more,' she says.

Again Tracy tries to deny it, but there's something surging to every corner of Katie's body that convinces her to ask again, finally cracking Tracy.

'Not really. I was drugged and confused. He said something about giving up, just before… I mean, he might have meant he was giving up on life, readying himself to jump, because I just can't see your dad doing that… Maybe Maclean wanted him to do it, took control of him somehow, like he was a devil or something, the same way he had with my dad.'

'And what happened to your dad?'

'He'd been cuffed, but I begged for him to be let go. Not so much for him, but for my mum. I couldn't bear her knowing that

Dad had been there, had stood and watched his own daughter being abused.' Tracy wraps her arms defensively around her chest. 'Of course, she had to live with him leaving her, and she was never the same, had no fight left when… when she got sick.' She sucks in another uneven breath. 'But it was better than her knowing the truth. That was why I threatened your dad, told him I'd heard everything that had happened, told him I could get him in the shit.' She stares at Katie, blinking back the tears. 'I didn't know he had a daughter too. I guess that was the reason he agreed in the end.'

'To what?'

'He made my dad swear he would leave home as soon as he could without it seeming suspicious, and he said if there was any evidence he'd committed more crimes he would hunt him down and finish him off like the other guy.' She pulls the curtain across, trying to cover her face, trying to block the path between them. 'It was just words, it didn't mean…'

Katie knows exactly what it meant, there can be no doubt now; not when she remembers the change that had taken place in him, and the horror on his face in the care home when his darkest secret had broken free. Another possibility crawls unbidden into Katie's consciousness, something she quickly suppresses. A resolution is close, though, she's certain of that much; they're coming to an understanding, or at least being guided towards one.

Katie wants to sit down on the floor next to Tracy, to curl up and wait until she feels her strength return, but Nathan's there too and when she looks back at him she can see the expectation in his face.

'What now?' he says.

She has no answer. She is exhausted and in shock. Her phone starts to buzz. She struggles to squeeze it out of her trouser pocket, working through the possibilities and settling on it being DS Peters back at the office with news. But when she finally gets to look at the screen she can see that she's wrong: it's a message from an unknown number, the same number that had texted her in the car.

LOOK AT WHAT YOU'VE DONE TO MY POOR LITTLE GIRL.

The calculation is quick, as is the following movement. She lowers the phone and rushes over to the patio window, standing over Tracy as she draws the curtains fully back and peers out into the garden. The edges are lined with carefully maintained shrubs, some of which have grown higher than the surrounding wall. She determines it would be possible to climb the other side and see but not be seen. Her eyes dart around, looking for the slightest trace of movement, but there's only a light breeze moving the leaves on a big oak tree in the far corner. When she looks down she can see that Tracy is cowering even more, as if fearing she is about to strike her, and suddenly she pictures her as a little girl, down on the floor of the warehouse, her own policeman dad standing over her, perhaps offering a hand as he lifts her to her feet.

'Is there someone out there?' says Tracy, twisting awkwardly to look outside. 'Is it Dad?'

'Just wait here,' Katie barks, grabbing an open-mouthed Nathan by the arm as she hurriedly draws back the patio door. 'And once we've gone, keep everything locked!'

CHAPTER THIRTY-ONE

'What the fuck is going on?' asks Nathan as they rush across Tracy's back garden, heading for the stone wall at the bottom end.

'He's been watching us,' Katie says breathlessly, her boot crushing the stem of a rose to place her foot on a much lower side wall so she can spring up and throw herself over the top. Nathan follows close behind and lands heavily on the other side into a bed of brambles and two-foot nettles that haven't been maintained in a long time. He ignores their sting and the shooting pain in his ankle, heading across the unmown lawn towards the back of a small red brick house. He's scanning around for movement, but all he can see is Katie, several strides ahead. They arrive at the back door and find it open.

'Stay behind me,' Katie whispers, shooting him a look that says *no argument*. He nods and they enter, the tiniest groan as the door is pushed open.

At first he finds nothing, no sound, no evidence of life, until his nose picks out a smell, sickly sweet and unmistakable, the finishing touch on his most realistic of fantasies. He follows the smell to the living room, where the body of a man has been laid out across the carpet. Nathan's heart freezes, desperate to look but unable to do so.

'It's not him,' says Katie, and he hears himself breathe.

It's obvious now: he's too tall and too far gone, his unfamiliar face turned a terrible blue. Dressed in black, his legs are bound together and his arms are extended equally on either side, as though his head, covered in thick black hair, is the tip of an arrow, pointing back to where they've just run from. It's a comparison supported by the words written in baked beans on the floor alongside:

Location Location Location

'Is he here?' asks Nathan. 'Markham, I mean.'

'We'd better check,' says Katie, already heading out of the room.

When they've both carefully searched the sparsely furnished two-bedroomed house – Nathan fearful of finding his brother's body, or bits of that body, at every turn – they push past the mountain of post, open the front door and slump down next to each other on the doorstep. They had intended to call it in and race back to Tracy's to make sure she was okay, but from the upstairs window they could see that the local police had already arrived.

'We'll have to go and face the music soon,' says Katie. 'Jesus, when Taylor hears about this, when he finds I've gone off on my own again—'

'Not on your own,' says Nathan.

'No,' says Katie, and he's aware of her hand resting on the step between them, just a few inches away from his own. The memories are returning now. His connection with Christian had been there from birth, it was natural and unshakeable, but with Katie it was different; their relationship was something they had formed together, and it could be broken.

He looks up at the sky, spotting a buzzard circling above them, a sight that reminds him of his time in Scotland, a sight that reminds him why he can't take that hand in his again. This might not be his last day on earth, but that last day is still coming. He cannot afford to think that just because his desire to kill at this moment is focused – normal, even – that it won't return to how it was before. If anything, it's likely to be far worse.

'He killed the poor sod simply to be able to watch us,' says Katie, finally pulling the hand away and tucking it in her lap.

'More of a reason than any of the others.'

'Why didn't any of his neighbours suspect there was something wrong?' She pushes herself up and peers over a hornbeam hedge at an identical-looking house with a white van in the drive.

'Why didn't his family? By the state of him I'd say he's been dead for weeks.'

'Is that how long Markham's been planning this?' Katie asks, as much to herself as him.

'Years would be my guess. He's certainly had time to figure everything out.'

'But I still don't understand why he's targeting us. What have we done to him? He should be fucking grateful to my dad for letting him go.'

'Your dad killed Maclean.'

'But he can't have been a true friend of Markham's. Maclean was a monster.'

'And that's what Markham has become now. Maybe promising to stay away from his family, threatened and watched by your dad, brought about a terrible change. Perhaps he can only find comfort in destroying families. Even his own.' Nathan breathes out slowly, a tingle in his fingertips as he thinks about his brother. 'Is he done?'

Katie doesn't answer, rising to her feet and tentatively rubbing the dull ache at the back of her head where Markham had struck her. Nathan closes his eyes and presses his knuckles against his temples, trying to trigger the positive side of his affliction – the ability to see inside a killer's mind – but as had been the case in the last few months before he'd run to Scotland, he finds it almost impossible to escape from his own.

'Shit!'

He hears the word and opens his eyes, but Katie's already off, running up the drive. He follows close behind.

'Where are we going?' he calls out.

'He was never in there,' she shouts back, without slowing. 'There was no mud on the carpet, no side gate, no window open, and therefore no chance he could have got out the front door without disturbing the pile of mail.'

He's almost alongside her now, running effortlessly, his body seemingly delighted at the chance to do so. 'So, the guy back there died for nothing after all?'

'I think he died to keep us occupied for a while,' says Katie, picking up her pace. 'It was *location, location, location*, all right – ours and fucking his!'

They arrive back at Tracy's house two minutes later, both twisting and turning to try and take in everything around them, to try and spot what Markham has been up to while they were away. Two police cars are parked haphazardly on the pavement and a fresh-faced PC has stepped out of the front door and is making his way towards them.

'Have you seen anyone?' says Katie, holding up her warrant card.

The PC stops, nods and looks round. 'Sorry, ma'am, but what's going on?'

'There's a dead man in number five of the road behind this one, Chilcott Way, I think it's called. You need to get round there and secure the scene. My colleague and I,' she nods towards Nathan and cuts off the question when she sees the young officer's mouth fall open, 'the brother of the man you will no doubt have been told to keep an eye out for, came to talk to the woman here,' she gestures towards Tracy's house, 'about something related to—' Suddenly Katie breaks off.

Nathan imagines she's hurriedly working through what she does and doesn't want to say, a last desperate attempt to protect

Tracy's identity. He imagines Tracy must have been the one to call the police, but from the PC's confusion it appears she isn't talking now.

Katie pulls Nathan to one side, needing to talk, to share, to find one of those moments of revelation that brought them so much success.

'He brought us here to have his fun,' she says breathlessly, aware of the curtain twitching at Tracy's house. 'But there must have been something else, another reason he wanted us out of London.'

'Another murder?' says Nathan. He poses it as a question, but he's already working through the possibilities. 'But why would he need us out of the way for that? It seems his previous victims were entirely random. There's no way we could have predicted who they would be.'

'Which is what's worrying me,' says Katie. 'He doesn't need to pretend to be your brother anymore. He might still have Taylor fooled, but I don't think he expects that to last long.'

'So, what? So he can kill who he really wants to now, rather than just trying to hurt us?' Again the question is out there, hanging in the air between them, but both are already working it through, weighing up the evidence, thinking of the man whose identity they have finally revealed.

They come to the answer at the very same time, Nathan turning to warn Katie only to find her standing frozen, staring at the old Rover. Then she starts to run, arriving at the car in a few seconds, Nathan just behind. Thirty seconds later they're accelerating hard, as a bewildered-looking PC shrinks in the mirror.

'He must blame Dad for failing to stop him,' she says. 'For making him into the monster he is now.'

'How far?'

'Too far,' she responds, placing her warrant on the dashboard, ready, he imagines, to be waved at any police car that might try to flag them down. 'Maybe an hour.'

'He'll be okay,' he says, reaching for the warrant to stop it sliding off. He wonders if this is it; if they're racing for an ending that's already mapped out. Or whether, for once, they're moving ahead of Markham.

'He was there,' he says, as the old car takes a pothole badly. 'The timing of the text told us that, proved that he was watching Tracy. And he's not matching these speeds. He can't afford to get stopped, not now his photo is everywhere.'

'Maybe,' Katie says, fighting the gears as hard as her thoughts.

'Shouldn't we phone ahead?'

'But what if this is what he was telling us to keep quiet about? You wouldn't risk hurting Christian, and I can't risk him hurting Dad.' He can see her knuckles whiten on the steering wheel. 'If he has…'

Nathan nods, falling back into his seat. He knows exactly what she means, reminded of the truth he'd shared right back at the beginning: *it ends the way it has to end for us.*

'Do you think Christian might be there too?' He can hear the desperation in his voice, embarrassed that for once he can't predict Markham's actions.

'I don't think so.'

'Do you think he's still alive?'

'I don't know,' she says, slipping out past the back of a lorry, barely a foot between them.

He stares at the side of her face; it's beautiful, there's no denying it, not anymore, but it also has a tell, a tiny twitch at the corner of her mouth. She's holding back. He tries to reassure himself that he's mistaken, that it's simply his imagination trying to make him doubt everything, and everyone, and lead him down the darkest path.

He twists to have a look behind Katie's seat, seeing the plastic bag with the evidence from the Steven Fish case that he still hasn't looked at, that he will never look at for fear of becoming as bad as the person they're after. They had been wrong about the murder of Steven Fish being the beginning for 'The Cartoonist'. The beginning had been the day Markham had stood in front of another man attacking his own daughter and had done nothing other than absorb the evil.

Nathan closes his eyes and seeks out the words of one of his favourite children's books, but instead he finds the words that come are from the book he read in his youth, the book that spoke to him like no other, that made him feel like he was not alone. If only his mother could have shared her secret with him. If only Katie's dad could have done the same before it was too late. If only they'd known what their silence would cost so many people. Nathan slumps back in his seat and lets the darkness take him without a fight.

When he opens his eyes again, everything is different. He's surrounded by trees, manicured lawns, carefully tended rose beds and, in the distance, a gently meandering river. The rain has gone, replaced by a soft sunlight that seems focused on the large Victorian building at the top of the narrow drive ahead.

What is this place? he's about to say, but to his right is a sign stating they have arrived at GREEN ACRES, a private care home.

Katie has slowed, perhaps not to the ten-mile-an-hour limit, but close enough. They continue up the drive before arriving at a car park in front of the huge building. She pulls into the nearest free spot and kills the engine. It feels strange to suddenly have silence and stillness, almost as though the chase is over, but then Katie pops open her seat belt, opens the door and is running towards an entrance at the back before he's had a chance to ask what's going on. What help can he be? Is he even ready to take on the man who's outsmarted them at every turn? He hardly has the strength left to get out of the car.

Looking around him, he almost expects to see men in white coats coming to take him carefully by the arm and lead him to his room, where he can stare out of the window at circling birds and draw patterns on the walls with dirty fingers. The truth is, he broke a long time ago; not when standing in the centre of an horrendous crime scene had started to give him pleasure, not even when he stood in the kitchen of his family home staring down at his mother's lifeless body. But with his first, terrible thought. Everything that followed that moment had been madness. He'd solved a few cases, built a reputation, but it was nothing to be proud of; it was something to be feared. And what of his brother? The connection he senses between them has faded to the point where he's not certain it was ever there at all. Does Katie know? Has she weighed up the evidence like she's always done, meticulously piecing it all together, while he's been lost in his fantasy?

The sun is on him, a great shaft that's cut between the oaks above that does nothing to stop him shivering. He's holding onto the door handle as if they're doing ninety again. He looks up the pathway to where Katie disappeared; of course she had to keep the truth from him, she needed to focus on saving her dad. But does he even want to save him? That's the real question; the question that's most likely kept him in his seat. Maybe he feels the same as Markham: that Katie's dad is to blame for all of this, for creating the monster. Nathan squeezes his fingers, feeling the blood, feeling the pain. 'But he did it for family,' he says quietly to himself, before repeating it louder, 'he did it for family!' He's thinking only of Katie now, as he throws open the door and jumps to his feet, sprinting towards the point where he'd last seen her.

Everything about the care home screams money. He can see now how someone on Katie's wage would have had to downsize her life to afford it. The likelihood is her dad is totally oblivious to it, but if it makes Katie feel better… They've obviously spent money on security, too – CCTV cameras are fixed above many of the doors.

The door that Katie went through is locked with a keypad, and there's nobody sitting behind the desk he can see when he presses his face up against the glass. He starts to run again in a desperate search for another entrance and eventually finds an open door round the back. He moves quickly through it, expecting to be accosted at any moment by someone who's been watching the news and wants to act the hero, fearful of what he might do if they get in his way. But the place is empty. There's no sound beyond the soft tick of a clock somewhere nearby. It reminds him of the clock in the Brooks' kitchen; it reminds him he's taken far too long already.

He feels the urge to run but he has no idea where he's heading. There is a maze of corridors ahead with no signs. He wonders about calling out to Katie, but he doesn't want to warn Markham of his location. If he had a phone he would ring her; if he could find a member of staff he would ask for the location of her dad's room. He feels like a child lost in a supermarket, trying to be brave but on the verge of tears.

Suddenly he hears a scream. He tells himself it could be anybody, but something in his core knows that it's Katie. He runs towards the sound, bouncing off the wall as he takes a corner too fast. And suddenly he's not alone: a young man is moving quickly alongside him, and this man seems to know where he's heading. They don't say anything to each other, saving their breath for a huge flight of stairs ahead. At the top, Nathan feels his legs start to give way, but still he carries on, following the young man who he spots is wearing a polo shirt bearing a logo matching the one on the sign out the front. As they sprint down a seemingly endless corridor he pictures Katie laid out in a pool of blood, her limbs twisted, her beautiful face pale and still. He shakes his head, forcing the vision away and, as they skid to a stop in the doorway of the furthest room, the reality presents itself. Katie is standing over by a table in the corner of the room, almost fully obscuring whoever is sitting beside her. The only thing Nathan can make out is an arm, hanging down and horribly slack. He rushes forward, almost tripping over the edge of a thick rug, desperate to see whose body it might be.

She steps out of the way, and he looks down at the elderly man slumped over the small table, his head twisted sideways, his left cheek flat on the surface. Poorly arranged above his pale, skinny face is a shoulder-length blonde wig. In front of him, at the centre of the table, is an empty container of pills. The whole scene is almost exactly as Nathan remembers it: the pale blue blouse and loose black trousers; the tights with the heel missing on one side; even the smell, the distinctive, sweet scent of his mum's perfume. And then there are the final details: the note on lined paper, words written in bold, and a photo he'd somehow overlooked before, as if it wasn't there, as if it couldn't be there. He starts to blink over and over, his brain unable to process the information, or perhaps over-processing, adding things that cannot be, blending two different moments in time.

'It's impossible,' says the young man he'd run to the room with, and all Nathan can do is nod his agreement. 'I was here half an hour ago. Mr Rhodes was sitting by the window. He was fine.'

'He still is,' says Nathan, finally taking in the additional details; the very things that were missing from the day he'd found his mum, even though he'd prayed for them over and over.

Katie spins round to look at him with tear-stained eyes turning to anger. 'What the hell are you—?'

'He's breathing,' he says, cutting her off, still feeling disconnected from the scene as he continues to struggle with how so much of it, just as the young man next to him had suggested, is impossible. He sees a flash of movement out of the corner of his eye as Katie reaches down towards her dad's neck, fingers fumbling for a pulse. Then she's pulling him up and off the chair, falling onto the floor with the big man on top of her. It looks – remarkably, appallingly – as Nathan imagines it must have done when he'd grabbed his mum twenty years ago to the very day. Only there's movement here; the old man, who Nathan can now see looks a lot like his daughter, lets out a sound, and his eyes slowly open, settling flatly on a point somewhere in the far corner of the room.

'Dad!' cries Katie, pressing her face against his, soaking him in tears that he clearly doesn't understand. 'Oh, thank God!'

'No,' says Nathan, as he takes a step back, staring at the single object on the desk that shouldn't be there, that *cannot* be there no matter how carefully he works things through in his head. 'Not God.'

CHAPTER THIRTY-TWO

The two of them are slumped down on yet another step. It's narrow and their legs are touching. Katie wonders if Nathan's even noticed. He's clearly churning things through in his mind, troubled by something he's yet to explain. She has her own questions, her own impossibilities – like how could Markham have got to the care home ahead of them and found time to arrange such an elaborate scene? He can't have set it up in advance, not if the young care home worker had seen her dad just half an hour before. And what was the meaning to all of this? Is the final, terrible message soon to be delivered?

She didn't think she could hate Markham any more; she'd happily take a knife to his neck and draw it slowly across while smiling and staring into his cold dark eyes. Fuck the law, there's no place for that here. Now she totally understands what led her dad to kill a man all those years ago, and she wants to go upstairs and tell him once again that she understands, that they're – she hesitates as the feeling takes her – the same.

The moment she rises to her feet a voice barks across at her.

'Are you *insane*, DI Rhodes?'

She sighs and doesn't look up.

'This is a mess, a diabolical mess, and you know full well who has to clean it up. It's all right for you, running around with your mad little friend, finding bodies then fleeing the scene, but I—'

'Don't know what you're talking about,' she says, cutting him off and closing her eyes to feel the warmth of the sun on her forehead. She knows she'll only get a few moments rest before the chase is on again. Unless they arrest her, physically prevent her from looking, she'll be following this through to the end. No matter what. 'I came here to try and save my dad.' She finally turns and faces her boss's rage. 'Do you remember your old friend?'

'Very well,' he says. 'I reckon I've been here more than you have.' He's said this proudly, shoulders back, but it's clear he's seen the change in Katie because he leans forward, face flushing, not with rage, but with something that almost makes him look human. 'I understand you may have been right about Markham,' he says softly. He pauses and casts a look up towards the second floor. 'What on earth possessed your father to let him go?'

'*Possessed* might be the right word,' she says, following his gaze. She wonders if Superintendent Taylor has heard the whole of the story – how her dad threw a man from the top of a building – and she feels the tiniest fizz of excitement, believing there could be a way to keep it under wraps. Until, that is, she realises it doesn't matter anymore because her dad will always be held to account for a greater crime: as the man who let 'The Cartoonist' go free.

'This needs to stop,' says the superintendent. 'Today.'

'I think it was always intended to,' says Katie.

'Why the hell didn't you tell us what you were doing?'

'We were warned. He said he had Christian.' She hesitates, looking at Nathan, motionless on the step ahead. 'And he left proof that he has him, back in my flat.' She knows she's giving away far more than the location of the fingers; that her colleagues will wander through that poky little place, littered with the evidence of a life of which she's not proud, and find the room that will likely guarantee the end of her career.

'What the hell is Markham up to?' says Superintendent Taylor, turning away, hat as always tucked under his arm. 'And more importantly, where is he?'

'He could be anywhere. He's already doing the impossible. There's no way he could have got from High Wycombe to here and arranged that hideous display before we arrived.' She keeps her back to the building, trying to shake off the memory of the moment she'd found her dad.

'Hideous indeed,' says Taylor, a hand tightening on sharply pressed trousers.

'He had to be near Tracy's house,' she continues, 'to know when to text to tell me he was watching, and no doubt enjoying, the unravelling of his own daughter's life once again.'

'He could have used a camera. We're currently checking the neighbour's house.'

'Maybe,' she says, sensing Nathan's discomfort on the step below her. And it's his discomfort that's now holding her back, keeping her from sharing her strengthening belief that she knows exactly how 'The Cartoonist' could be in two places at once. Yet again, she finds she's deceiving her colleagues, deceiving her boss, and risking lives in doing so. Yet again it seems she cannot resist.

'Any joy on the family doctor?' she asks.

'We've discovered he was formerly a surgeon.'

'What sort?'

'Plastic. Supposedly a good one, too, but the misdiagnosis and death of Nathan's father, a family friend, seems to have put an end to his career. He went to live abroad, in the South of France and then Spain, before disappearing off the radar completely a decade ago.'

Katie releases a long breath. The pieces are almost all in place now, and yet there's something simple eluding her amid all the bluff and deception from Markham. At moments like these on previous cases she's had a chance to talk to Nathan and together they've found the solution, but he's the very last person she would talk to now. She looks across, feeling a mix of frustration and sympathy for the man sitting on the step, legs tucked up close to his chest, head pressed into his knees. She's about to turn away and speak to her colleagues when his head shoots up and he looks at her with such a glare that she stumbles back and almost topples off the edge of the steps. She's certain he's seen it too, worked through the few facts that are known to them and come to the same unbearable conclusion.

'It's impossible,' he says, now facing the superintendent.

'What is?' asks Taylor, as alarmed by this interruption as Katie.

'It's the photo, you see,' he says, seeming not to care that they don't see, or that his voice is barely a whisper. 'Markham couldn't possibly have known about that. Nobody knew about it.'

'What are you talking about?' asks Katie, unable to soften the question, wondering, hoping, that she's somehow read it all wrong. 'The photo on the table up there?' She jabs a thumb over her shoulder at the building behind. 'You said that was nothing, meant nothing.' If she hadn't been distracted by her dad, by the relief of finding him alive, she might have spotted the lie. It would have been there in Nathan's horror, the very horror she's seeing now. He draws his legs in even further and wraps his arms around them as if suddenly cold. And he does now seem to be shaking, despite the warmth of the midday sun. 'I'm sure you've figured out why your dad was dressed up like that.' He pauses, but neither takes the chance to draw a breath. 'And Markham got it almost exactly right. Including the note with "So sorry to have left you alone".' He starts to shake his head violently. 'But it's the photo. The photo is an impossibility.' He looks up at her now, his eyes wide and once again childlike, desperate for understanding. 'I took it away the moment I found her in the kitchen. I slipped it into my pocket.'

'It was a photo of your brother and your dad,' says the superintendent. 'Might it have been a warning? You said he's being held.'

'It wasn't Christian in the photo. It was me. Just me. That's why I couldn't leave it there for my brother to discover. It was madness, I know, an overreaction, but I couldn't bear to think of Christian believing he'd been excluded, not right at the end. I didn't even dare to write about it in my journal, so Markham couldn't have known, he couldn't…'

'Is it *exactly* the same photo?' asks Katie, inching along so she can get a better view of Nathan.

'No. I burnt the original,' he says, instantly reminding Katie of the inscription in the children's book from her mum. 'Every time I looked at it I could see Mum lying there. Or Dad with his arm around my shoulders, strong, unbreakable, the man I always wanted to be.' She watches Nathan's shoulders rise and fall as he sucks in a long and unsteady breath. 'But the photo Markham left was close enough, close enough to tell me he must have been there the day Mum died.' He lifts his head again, shielding his eyes from the sunlight then turning to Katie. 'I do *this*, or whatever it was I used to do, because of that day, because I simply hadn't seen it coming. But what if it was all a lie? What if she had no intention of taking her life?'

'You're suggesting Markham killed her?' She can't help but shake her head, can't help but dismiss his theory, while risking giving her own away. 'Your mum died more than fourteen years before he started working for you and your brother.'

'But what if that's *why* he started working for us? He wanted to come back, to revisit the scene of his crime, to see us, to see what he'd done. He's most likely been watching his daughter, too, and not just over the neighbour's wall.'

'What's the connection, though?' says Superintendent Taylor. 'What could he have had against your family back then? It seems a terrible coincidence.'

Nathan shrugs. 'The novels? Maybe he knew. Maybe he blamed her for putting those ideas in his head, same as he blamed Katie's dad for giving him the opportunity to act them out.'

'What novels?' asks Superintendent Taylor.

Katie looks across at Nathan, and he nods assent. 'Nathan's mum was J.M. Priest.'

The superintendent's surprise is clear, and he stands in stunned silence for a moment before slowly shaking his head. 'It's seems like too much coincidence that you two were linked to this guy all the way back then.'

'I agree,' says Katie, biting her lip and turning away, the growing sense of certainty in her own deductions threatening to overwhelm her. She needs distance, some time and space to breathe and think, and she needs to do what she was intending to do before: to go and hold her dad and tell him how proud she is of him, how much she loves him.

She's heading towards the open door, no hesitation, no explanation, when her phone starts to ring. She pulls the mobile out of her pocket, somehow hearing the voice before she's even accepted the call.

'That were cruel of me, lassie.' She turns back towards the others, pressing the speakerphone button, with an expression on her face that tells them they need to shut up and listen. 'I think I might have got a little carried away. But your dad didn't seem to mind. Not much of talker, to be honest. Being a murderer must have taken its toll.'

Katie is surprised at how calm she sounds when she speaks. 'The greater crime was letting you go.'

'I'll admit that has turned out badly for a few people. Tracy were convinced that Alex Maclean was the evil one, that he had a kind of control over me. I guess kids are a bit blind to their parents' faults. A bit like you, eh, Nathan, not seeing what your mum was really like. Funny how she was happy to share her darkest thoughts with millions, and to make millions from it, while leaving you to think you were all alone.'

Katie turns to stare out across the vast expanse of lawn to the surrounding trees, desperately trying to find the calm of before.

She has at least managed to maintain her professionalism, helped perhaps by the proximity of her boss, who's moved in close to the phone, hat in his hand. Perhaps she's also been helped in a strange way by Markham, because for all the terrible things he's saying his voice has remained flat and emotionless throughout, like they aren't his words. Like he's possessed.

'What do you want?' she says.

'I want the two of you, to be honest. I want you to become who you were always destined to be. You're just like your dad, Katie, you want to take the law into your own hands and—'

'You're right,' says Katie, cutting him off, certain Markham was going to reveal the truth about Maclean's death to the superintendent, 'like my dad – I'm very keen to do what's best for your family.'

'Whereas Nathan…' Markham starts up again, his voice uncertain for just a moment, 'Nathan wants to live out the pages of that wonderful journal of his I found. God, it's so much better than his mum's work. It feels so real. And, of course, it could so easily be real.' He draws in a long, nasal breath. 'Come on, Nathan, you wouldn't believe how liberating it feels.'

'Is that what you do it for, the liberation?' says Katie.

'That and the immortality. You've seen the press. Hell, you started the press. I'm "The Cartoonist"! I don't have to hide away anymore, no name, no family, no reason to hide who I am. It's all out there now for the whole world to enjoy.'

'Are you going to come out for us to enjoy?' she says before she can stop herself, the blood-soaked image of a slashed throat flashing up in her mind, her hand on her neck where the chocolate icing had been, where the knife might have been. And then there are the girls, and Felix and little Tate, still smiling, still fuelling her rage.

'That's more like it, detective,' says Markham. 'What about Nathan, though? Not hearing anything from him. You sure he's okay? He doesn't look too good, slumped down on the steps like that.'

Katie and Taylor's eyes are scanning the trees in the distance, but her instinct tells her they're wasting their time.

'I hope that poor lad doesn't go the way of his mother. Nasty business that was, to leave two young 'uns without so much as a word. Well, without those few words and a silly little photo. I mean, it's fair enough if an individual like myself decides it's time for Mum to go, but...'

Katie is only aware that Nathan's risen when she feels the phone being snatched from her hand.

'How did you know about that photo?'

'Don't you forget, lad, that I know everything. You, on the other hand, seem to know nowt.'

'Where is my brother?!!' he screams. 'I swear, if you touch another fucking hair on his head, I will, I will...' There is saliva hanging from the corner of Nathan's mouth as the phone slips from his fingers.

'*There* you are,' says Markham, with the same emotionless delivery. 'I knew it was in you. Your book described all that wonderful potential. And don't you worry – you couldn't put all that hate into words. Trust me, action is far more important, and far more fun. I think you'd find it easy, too. I bet if I came over there now there wouldn't be no hesitation.'

'Why don't we see if that's true,' says Katie.

'Part of me would love to, lassie. It would be worth risking death to see the same excitement in someone else's eyes. But I think I've played with you two for long enough. It's time for me to head for new horizons.'

'What about Christian?' Nathan shouts, his grip tightening again.

'Do you really need me to spell it out for you?'

'No,' says Katie, grabbing the phone back and ending the call.

'What have you done?' says Nathan, with a disbelieving stare. 'What the fuck have you done?' He raises an arm as though he's about to strike her, then something seems to switch off behind his eyes and he stumbles backwards and falls heavily to the floor. She wants to rush forward and grab him, to whisper in his ear and convince him that she's not the cold-hearted bitch he must think she is, but the superintendent has blocked her path.

'Your career is over, DI Rhodes,' he says, holding her stare.

'Has been for a while,' she says, with a sigh.

'But why would you…? Why?'

Katie draws herself upright and keeps her voice nice and steady. 'He was giving us nothing.'

Taylor grabs her roughly by the arm, mouthing, *what about his brother?*

'Do *I* have to spell it out?'

'How can you be like this?' says the superintendent, and again something inside of her starts to slip. 'If we'd kept him talking he might have made a mistake.'

'He doesn't make mistakes,' she says, certain this is true. The last piece of the puzzle had not been given by accident. Nathan would have spotted it too if he hadn't been so distracted. She knows she shouldn't keep it to herself, it's exactly what 'The Cartoonist' would want, but that stubbornness is rising inside of her again; the need to get the result, no matter what the cost. Only this time it's not just about catching a killer – it's about creating a future that both she and Nathan can live with. 'You heard him,' she continues. 'Every word carefully delivered. No emotion. No slip-ups. He knew exactly what he was doing.'

Superintendent Taylor shakes his head, but the anger is leaving him, only to be replaced by resignation and fatigue. He looks his age: the same age as her dad. 'So, what next?' he asks, reaching down to pick up his hat and weakly dusting it off with the back of his hand.

'Not my problem,' she says. 'My career is over. I'm going up to see my dad.'

She turns her back on him and walks away, not once looking over her shoulder, stopping only very briefly in the doorway to the care home to order PC Kieran Smith – who hasn't heard their conversation – not to take his eyes off Nathan.

Five minutes later and she's kneeling next to her dad's chair, lightly holding his hand. She'd needed to say goodbye first, just in case she didn't get another chance. She also needed to express her intent out loud, as if that might help to make it real.

'I'm going to kill him,' she says. 'For Nathan. And for you.'

She believes for a moment that she might have seen a response, the tiniest twitch to tell her he's listening, but she's been fooled that way many times before. She gets up and walks slowly to the window, the very window her dad had been looking out of when he'd let his own confession slip out. As she stands there, leaning heavily on the sill, she turns back to the remaining doubts, to the reason she hasn't yet left. Is it selfish to risk so many lives to try and protect just two? Is it possible without anyone else ever finding out? Doesn't an attempt to kill and never get caught make her the same as the monsters she hunts? At this point, it seems she's unable to resist. She takes another look at her dad, picturing him all those years ago telling Markham he could walk away. Perhaps it's in her nature. Perhaps it's in her blood.

A movement in the car park below catches her eye. Everywhere police cars and officers are racing in and out, but this is different; it's steady, it's calm, as is the face looking up at her. Martin Coates offers a nod and a comforting smile, and she steps quickly back, as if he might somehow have read her thoughts and understand what she's about to do. Then she steps forward again, realising that his presence might be exactly what she needs. The carer can help her see things more clearly, just as he had done before a drunken night ruined everything. She's never felt more sober than she feels right now, and just a few words from him might make all the difference, guiding her away from such a reckless plan.

She heads for the door, stopping very briefly to kiss her dad on the top of his head, reminded, not for the first time, of how the tables have turned. Each time he left for work when she was a child he used to stop and kiss her on the top of the head and tell her he'd be back before she knew it.

She heads down the stairs and through the fire exit. She doesn't want to be seen by anyone, not yet, not until she's come to her final decision. The closer she gets to Martin the more convinced she is that she won't go through with her plan; she's not going to risk everything for the sake of two people. She feels a sudden sense of guilt, like she's cheating on Nathan, like she's deserting her dad.

She makes it to the car park without being spotted by any of her colleagues. At first she thinks she may have missed Martin, but then he appears from alongside a large black saloon car.

'Are you okay?' he asks. 'I understand from my colleague that someone was attacked here.'

'Yes,' she says, as the memory flashes up in her mind. 'My dad. He was humiliated.'

'Jesus! I'm so sorry, Katie. Who would do a thing like that?'

'Have you heard of "The Cartoonist"?'

Martin's face visibly pales. 'He's been here?' He looks up at her dad's room again. 'Why?'

'To hurt me. And now I'm going to hurt him. I'm going to find him, and I'm going to kill him.' The confession takes her by surprise, more proof that she's starting to lose control. 'I'm sorry, but I have to go.'

Martin stands between two cars, not a tall man but wide enough to block her path. She knows he'll be worried by what she's said and will want to try and stop her, so she starts backing up to find a way to walk around.

'Wait,' he says, and she doesn't want to.

He has this way about him that makes her suspect he could talk her into, or out of, anything. He'd been the only carer to ever make any impact with her dad, triggering tiny movements in him whenever he was nearby. Initially giving her so much hope. 'I might be able to help,' he says, and suddenly she's listening. 'There was someone here. I caught him hovering near your father's room the other day. I didn't get a good look as he ran away, but I had a photo taken from the CCTV. I was going to ring the police about it, I was going to ring you, but then…' He looks away, face reddening again, and starts to move towards the back of the car. 'It's tucked in one of my files. Come and look.'

Katie follows as if in a daze. If the photo is good then it changes everything, ruins everything. She steps past the raised boot of the car, glancing up at Martin; his hair is a mess, his clothes the same: a crumpled shirt and an old pair of cords. He's tucked one hand out of sight as if he's holding something he doesn't want her to see, but that's not the hand she's staring at, it's the other one. A jacket had been covering it before, but now the jacket has slipped back to reveal a bloodied bandage wrapped around his fingers. Katie feels the world tilt, reaching out a hand to the corner of his car to steady herself. The boot is empty, except for a rope that already feels like it's coiling round her neck, stopping her from shouting out, stopping her from running. Even if she could move, she knows it's too late. Just as it had been back in Markham's house, she waits for the blinding light, then darkness.

CHAPTER THIRTY-THREE

Christian is dead. For Nathan there can no longer be any doubt. The moment he'd heard those words, *Do you really need me to spell it out for you?* he'd known all trace had gone. Katie had known it too, cutting off the phone call because she knew it was all over.

He's not moved from the steps for half an hour, maybe more, working his way through the words of the children's books in his mind, repeating each sentence to calm his burning desire to kill. If he waits just a little longer he'll finally be able to answer it, or at least die trying. Every muscle in his body is aching to run, in a straight line at last, right to the place where he knows Markham is waiting for him.

Why didn't Katie spot the clue? So many hours spent staring at it in that tiny room in her flat. He fears she's given up. He'd never believed she could quit anything, not in all the years they'd worked together, but so much is different this time around. If he could, he'd go and speak to her and explain why he cannot be there to help her anymore. He must remain silent for his plan to succeed. This is how his mum must have felt at the end; he cannot deny the irresistible parallels.

He feels his feet starting to twitch, feels the words of the children's books losing their effect. But it's all right; he'll be able to slip away from the slowly dwindling numbers of police soon. He knows there's one still watching him, but now he has a plan to escape. He rises slowly and unsteadily from the steps before pretending to gag into his hand.

'Toilet,' says Nathan to his only guard before stumbling towards the building, the young PC following close behind. He'd noticed the signs for the toilet on the mad rush up to Katie's dad's room, and had figured out since that it backed on to the car park.

Once he's inside, he climbs out the window with the minimum of effort and starts to move quickly between the cars. It's only as he's passing a rusty old Rover that he realises he doesn't need to run all the way to Markham's location. The keys are still in the ignition. He slips into the driver's seat, praying the old car will start and that Katie's not watching him from the window of her dad's room. The Rover bursts into life on the second attempt, and his brain is flooded with images of what might be waiting for him at the end of his journey.

CHAPTER THIRTY-FOUR

Katie opens her eyes, but her head is covered by a hood and the only light is a flash of pain through her head like a lightning strike. She whimpers, wanting to reach up and touch the pain but finding her arms are pulled tight behind her back. Her feet aren't moving either; her knees are drawn up towards her face, her body numb. She knows her time is up. All that's left to do is wonder what it's going to say in her speech bubble, what message her colleagues will read when they look down at her contorted body. COP-OUT, POLICE CUTS, or, with a tiny slice to a vein in her neck, NICKED. Unless, like Steven Fish, there's still a lot more to endure before then.

It makes sense to her now, horrible sense; the way the two of them had been able to talk, the connection she'd felt, how she'd finally found a solace for her separation from Nathan. Even the killer's knowledge of her dad's secret and of the book from her mum she had tried to burn. She pushes against her restraints. If his intention in exposing the Maclean case had been to ruin her relationship with her dad then he had, for once, read things very wrong; she feels closer to her dad than she has ever done. If only she could free herself from these restraints, she would show them how alike she and her dad really are. There would be no witty comments written on the floor, no careful arrangement of the bodies. She's often wondered how Nathan's imagination could seem so real to him, but this one, now, soaked in red and framed by a huge surge of adrenaline, seems so close to life the only thing missing is the satisfaction of knowing her victim is feeling that reality too.

She silences her thoughts at the creak of a door opening, followed by footsteps on an uncarpeted floor that only stop when they seem to be beside her. She readies herself for another blow.

'How are you, lassie?'

She sinks back. It's not the voice she'd expected, even though she'd known that Markham would be there too. She wants to reply, to show both of them that she's not scared, but her mouth feels like it's only good for biting, tearing and spitting out flesh. If she's scared of anything it's of who she's about to become.

The hood – and she's certain now that's what's blocking her view – has been pulled a little too tight around her neck, restricting her breathing. Markham reaches down to loosen the string.

'I hope that hasn't hurt you,' he says, retreating a few steps. Through the fabric, she searches for shapes but finds none, only the images of all the victims she's come here to avenge.

'Why?' she says, with a dry rasp.

'I didn't know. Not until it was too late.'

'It's not too late now.'

'I'm afraid it is.'

'You can help me,' she says, lowering her voice but still fighting against the ties around her wrists.

'There's nothing I can do,' Markham whispers back. 'We shouldn't even be talking.'

'Free me.' She twists her wrists again, completely unable to tell how much he can see of this desperate attempt. 'If you don't, we will both be victims today.'

'Maybe it's for the best,' says Markham.

She wants more than anything to see his face, to know if there's any chance of winning him round. As if reading her mind, he steps over, and she feels hands fumbling at her neck and the material is lifted clear. She blinks for a few moments, but there's little difference; the space around her is so dark it seems endless, not a wall in sight, no objects to give scale. Perhaps she is dead already.

She looks for Markham, rolling over stiffly when she realises he's behind her from the sound of his breathing. She loses him again, and after a moment of readjusting to deal with the pain in her head and cramped legs, she determines he's now standing above her head, remaining just out of sight.

'I can't do anything,' he says. 'But I just needed you to know that this isn't me. This isn't who I am. I never got a chance to talk to my daughter, to try and explain…'

She feels the need to close her eyes despite the darkness. The hope is leaving her and taking her anger with it. All that's left now are questions, many of which she knows will never be answered.

'How did he find you?' she asks.

'Through you. He's been watching you for years, lassie, ever since you started working with his brother. He has this way of reading people. He must have spotted something when you were with your dad… I didn't think he knew about me when he called me about a job. He said he'd been impressed with my work, and I thought he were talking about the gardening.'

'But why did he need to work at the care home if he already knew about the Maclean case?'

'He likes to know everything,' says Markham. 'Helps him control people. Knowledge of who or what they care about. Knowledge of what they've done.'

She's seeing it now, the tiny signals from her dad, the connection that she'd seen that had given her so much hope.

'When did you find out what he was really like?' she asks, through gritted teeth.

'Only a few days back. I hadn't seen him in years, and suddenly he turns up at my home. He don't look the same; he don't act the same, neither. He weren't aggressive or nowt, but he made it clear what I had to do if I wanted to keep my past life secret. I thought he were just playing games at first. And when I found out different, when I found out what were really going on, well…' He retreats a few steps more, but she can still hear him swallow. 'After that his threats were different. Far worse. I just pray he doesn't…' He coughs to clear his throat, then moves in close again. 'How did you know it weren't just me?'

'Because of your daughter, Tracy,' she says. 'She told me you weren't capable of doing these things.' Katie stops, once again thinking of her own dad, thinking of his own crime. If she's honest with herself, and she sees no reason not to be now, she'd always suspected what her dad might have done, had seen the guilt Christian had seen. 'I believed her. And once I'd believed her there could only be one explanation.'

'Thank you,' says Markham, his voice thick with emotion. 'And if it makes a difference, you should know that Maclean were an evil bastard. Your dad shouldn't have felt bad. He did the world a favour.'

'I would have liked to have done it another favour with Christian,' says Katie, softly, once again testing her restraints. 'Why did he come to get me from the home? I was already on my way to him.' She searches the darkness again for even the faintest outline.

'He said he needed you here first.'

First. That single word that brings so much pain. She knows what he means; he doesn't need to say any more. Of course Nathan will have spotted the clue; he never misses a thing. And, of course, he will try to come on his own, to answer his own desire to kill. But does he know who is here, waiting? Or does he still believe it's just Markham? Markham has gone quiet; she can't see him and can't even hear him moving around anymore. She's certain he's played his part now – they both have. What's left is for the two brothers to resolve. She feels herself sink down, as if the hard floor beneath her is swallowing her up.

Then she hears three words spoken from such a short distance away that she can smell the accompanying breath. It's a familiar smell and a familiar voice, soft and low and smooth as silk. A voice that had once provided comfort in the darkest of times, but now it brings ice to her veins.

'Thank you, Katie.'

She's been tricked again, and Markham has been used again to deliver carefully scripted lines. She knows without seeing that Christian is standing over her. Her fear is everywhere.

'My brother is on his way.'

Two spotlights burst into life above her, blinding, horrifying. Over in the distance she can see Markham reaching through an endless black curtain towards the switch. Then, finally, she forces herself to look at Christian. He's put on the glasses that had always been there, glasses that she now doubts he needs at all. They're thick, but she can see no distortion through the lenses. His hair is dyed paler than Nathan's and has been cut so that it looks thin at the scalp. And then there's the face, the marks of his surgery suddenly clear; the un-straightened nose, the narrowed jawline, the too-thin lips. It's only when she looks hard that she can see the similarity.

'I know,' he says, revealing uneven teeth that cannot be real. 'You're thinking about that wonderful night. Do you know you accidentally called out my brother's name at one point?' He holds his good hand over his chest with a look of mock distress. 'I couldn't help but take offence. It's so pathetic how much you love him.'

The words take her by surprise.

'And you think that he loves you?' laughs Christian, slapping his bandaged hand hard against his chest. 'I know all the feelings inside my brother. And *none* of them is love.'

He slips his hand into his pocket and draws out a six-inch blade. Katie suddenly finds herself trying to recite the words of the children's book left by her mum, but instead all she can remember are those added by Christian: *See you at the end.* She looks up at him. He's removed his glasses and seems to be carefully studying her. She can clearly see his piercing eyes, the one bit of his face he hasn't changed, and within them a horribly familiar intelligence. Then, as if he's read her thoughts yet again, he starts to grin and slowly shake his head. 'Not yet, Katie,' he says. 'I'm going to let you watch the birth of something beautiful first.'

CHAPTER THIRTY-FIVE

The 'N' and the 'R' have all but rubbed off and the rest is partly eaten by rust. The sign had been newer on the photo in Katie's tiny room, but it's the same sign and the same place Markham had referred to at the end of his call – 'heading for new horizons' – the place he had wanted him to come to, there can be no doubt. Nathan is holding the photo in his hand, pulled from the bag behind the seat in Katie's dad's car.

Markham must know he's here. The factory where Steven Fish was killed is on a derelict industrial estate way out in the country, and he'll have seen the car a mile away. But Nathan doesn't give a damn as he jumps out of the car, his head jerking left and right, searching for movement and a chance to begin. He places his palm lightly on the bonnet of the dark saloon parked alongside, feeling the warmth spread up his arm and across his chest. *Recently arrived*, he thinks. *Soon to be departed.*

There's a gap in the fence which leads down to the dull grey factory building surrounded by weeds higher than the smashed-in first-storey windows. Stepping over a pile of abandoned scaffolding poles, he reaches down to pick one up, feeling the weight of it, feeling the potential. It doesn't matter what Markham has in store, as long as Nathan gets to see him die first, before *he* does: horribly, painfully – wonderfully.

As Nathan steps into the building his entire body is trembling. It's dark inside, and he worries that unless he finds a light switch he will miss everything that is about to happen. He slides his hands along the wall but quickly gives up. Turning round, he lets the door swing shut behind him and walks into the darkness until, suddenly, the scaffolding bar knocks against something. It moves. He lunges forward taking a great swing, as if the darkness itself could be broken. And it is. A tiny split of light appears somewhere near the floor as the obstruction reveals itself to be no more than a thick, heavy curtain.

He wants to push on, he wants to push through, but his imagination is holding him back, assembling every little detail: the vivid colours, the sharpened silence, the smell of fear, of sweat, of blood. But Christian's body could be just a few feet away; he could walk through this curtain and find him contorted into another hideous joke, his fingers severed, the flesh peeled from his back. The thought of that makes Nathan hesitate, and then do something he's never been able to do before, not in his forty years of life: he turns it off. Only reality lies ahead of him as he pushes back the curtain and slips through.

The man Nathan has come to kill is standing in the middle of a blinding circle of light. A flash of brilliant pain slices Nathan's brain in two as he propels himself forward, letting out a scream that falls dead against the darkness. The old man doesn't respond, just stands there carefully folding what looks like clothes. The metal pole is raised high above Nathan, and his eyes are locked on his target's head. A single strike and it will all be over. A single strike and it will have begun.

And yet that strike doesn't come. It's not that Nathan wants an explanation, it's not that he wants to hear him speak – they've heard more than enough from him already – the problem is… the problem is … Nathan doesn't know what the problem is. All he knows is that his body is in revolt. He's lost control. Or has he found it?

'You have to do it,' says Markham, without turning. It's the same voice as the one on the phone just an hour before, but it's even flatter and more lifeless than it was back then. 'If you don't, she'll die.'

Nathan's arm is still frozen above him and starting to ache. It would be so easy to bring it down, break the man's head the way his own head feels like it's breaking – he's done it before a thousand times in his imagination – but suddenly he's lost.

'*She?*' he says.

There's no response. He wants the old man to turn round so he can see the truth in his eyes. Perhaps that's what's holding him back? He reaches forward to grab Markham's shirt, but the tips of his fingers start to tingle and he finds he can get no closer. All he has is his voice.

'Who will die?'

Nathan lowers his arms and draws in a deep breath, desperate to summon up the strength. All those years of dreaming about killing without reason and yet now, with a man who deserves to die more than anyone ever could, he feels utterly impotent.

He looks at Markham, trying to harden his gaze and focus. Here is the man who killed two mothers, who tortured and beheaded a dad, who killed a stranger for simply living in the wrong place, and a doctor to try and frame his brother. Here is the man who has killed his brother! And yet… He hears the pole clang to the floor before he's even realised he's let it go. He's a coward, nothing more. A fraud, who has built his reputation on being able to read the darkness in the minds of others and totally misread the darkness in his own.

He's alongside Markham now, staring at the side of the old man's face, and he's amazed to see that there are tears running down his cheek. It looks real, as does the expression of utter hopelessness. Markham is not looking back at him, just staring at that curtain of darkness ahead, and Nathan finds himself doing the same. The two of them stand shoulder to shoulder, with no understanding of the situation they are in.

The room is silent, save for the laboured breathing of Markham and the occasional shuffle of birds up on the roof. Nathan finds himself starting to drift, but not to the usual places his mind would wander. Instead, he's thinking about the warmth he'd felt being near Katie, and how the strength he found in their connection is being re-established. It feels, in part, like a betrayal of his brother, but he lets it in. He lets Katie in to the hole that his brother's absence has made in his heart. He knows she is nearby. And that she is in danger.

He grips the old man's shoulder. 'Where is Katie?'

'You haven't totally lost it, then!'

The voice is unmistakable – an echo of his own. He spins round, but there's only endless darkness.

'I'm sorry,' Markham says in a trembling voice. 'I did what you asked. I've done everything you asked. Please! Please don't hurt her!'

The curtain is drawn back and a man steps through, only, he looks nothing like Christian: big features, all bloated, fat and twisted. And yet… and yet… Nathan can't help but draw in every disgusting detail until the reality finally dawns. The last time he saw his brother was six years ago, and when he said goodbye on that day he believed with the heaviest of hearts that it was for the last time. Now with every fibre of his body he wishes it had been.

'You look like you've seen a ghost, big bro,' says Christian.

And there can be no doubt now, not with that voice and those eyes and that smile. The years fall away and so does the mask created by the hand of a plastic surgeon, perhaps the same surgeon whose body was found in their basement. The last couple of days have been horrific, one nightmare after another, but this goes far beyond anything he's had to deal with.

To believe that his brother might be 'The Cartoonist' is hard, but not impossible, given their family history, but to try and accept that Christian is capable of this… He'd thought there was no limit to his imaginings, no depth to which he couldn't descend, but Christian has proven him wrong.

'Why?'

'That's your problem, Nathan; you're always asking stupid questions. Does there need to be a *why*? Can't you just do what feels right?'

'How can what you've done *ever* feel right?'

'Okay,' says Christian, holding up his hands defensively. One of them is wrapped heavily in a bandage, and Nathan is reminded of what his brother has been willing to put himself through just to bring them to this point and get his attention. 'We were born this way.' The crooked smile on that crooked face starts to grow. 'Plus, it's fun. A game. A challenge.'

His brother's eyes dance with madness. For so many years he's wanted to be like him, to be living that life on the beach with the wife and child. Now he can see the lie laid bare, and his anger builds as rapidly as it left him when he'd stood behind Markham with a metal pole in his hand. He bends to pick up the pole again. Had he somehow known the truth even then? Was that what had held him back?

'That's right,' says Christian, calmly. 'You see? You *do* have it in you. You just need a little… motivation. We could be unstoppable, you and me. Which is why…' He reaches behind the curtain and drags Katie out by her hair and pulls her across the concrete floor. Her mouth is taped up, her arms tied behind her back.

'You're probably a little angry with me now, big bro,' he says, letting go of Katie and pulling a long blade out of the back of his trousers. He crouches down and lowers the point to just an inch or two from Katie's neck. Nathan can see Katie's eyes bulge as she struggles to get away, but Christian has one boot on her hair, holding her firmly in place. 'You'll forgive me when all this is done. In fact, you'll be grateful I helped you to be who you were always destined to be. Now, the scenario is very simple. You need to do what you should have done just a few minutes ago. You need to turn Markham's head to pulp. If you manage that, and I know deep down you're desperate to, then in taking one life you will have saved two. First, our little girlfriend here.' He pauses to let that information sink in. 'Second, the life of Markham's daughter, who I believe you ran into and…' Christian tries to twist his face in mock concern, but the skin is tight and resists, 'caused some distress.'

'Please,' says Markham, palms pressed together as if in prayer. 'You promised not to hurt Tracy. I'm begging you.'

'He really is begging,' says Christian, keeping his eyes on Nathan. 'Strange, if you ask me, coming from a man who was happy to stand back and watch his daughter being assaulted all those years ago. But there you go – some people are a little strange.' He lifts the knife from Katie's neck and tugs his sleeve back with his teeth, revealing a small black watch. 'Now, I'm sure you didn't tell anyone else you were coming here. You were, after all, desperate to commit a murder. I know the look you had in your eyes when you ran in here, so why don't you just hurry up and get it done, then we can be on our way.'

Nathan's mind is starting to swim, backwards and forwards, memories from his childhood washing into the present day. He's still gripping the pole, but more for support than in threat.

'I saw it,' he says, thinking of the bag he's left in Katie's car. 'I stood on the edge a year ago and stared right into the heart of my darkness. I resisted then, and I'm going to resist now.'

'Are you sure?' Christian places the knife against Katie's throat again.

Nathan's whirling mind suddenly finds focus in Katie's eyes. She's staring up at him, unblinking, and although she can't talk he knows what she's trying to say. She wants him to let her die.

'I can't do that,' he says to her softly. He bends down slowly and places the pole on the ground again. When he rises back up he takes a single step towards his brother.

'I don't know what happened to you,' he says.

'Nothing happened to me!' Christian snaps back. 'Other than what was supposed to happen. You think you're better, but you're not. You're just less honest.'

A long breath leaves Nathan. 'What about Mum? You were there, weren't you? You were the first home.'

Christian shakes his head. 'I don't want to talk about her.'

'Why not?' Nathan takes another step forward, holding his brother's gaze. 'Surely this is the perfect day to talk about her, to talk about what happened exactly twenty years ago.'

It's Christian's turn to move, retreating a step and brushing the thick curtain. His boot is no longer on Katie's hair, and his knife is no longer at her neck, but he could still reach her if he wanted to, long before Nathan could stop him. 'I didn't kill her, if that's what you're saying.'

Nathan is calling on his memory, drawing up every detail of the room on that day. Had her body been arranged like those he's seen recently? He shakes his head, dismissing the thought. 'You spoke to her about your problem?'

'I spoke to her about who *we* were,' says Christian. 'She told me all I needed was to follow her lead and find an outlet.' He shakes his head. 'She showed me those pathetic books, said it was enough to put things down on the page.' He steps forward and lowers the knife towards Katie, drawing a line just an inch in front of her nose. 'I think I convinced her in the end that it would never be enough. Sadly she chose to take the coward's way out.'

Nathan can see his mum's lifeless form, and he can feel in his fingertips the coldness of her skin. He can also see those words. After all those millions she had written for strangers, just six left for them.

'You found my journal?'

'Found it. Read it. Loved it. I think that's when I first started to feel the connection between us. It was so good to have proof that we were the same.'

'Just words,' says Nathan quietly, repeating those spoken by Katie. 'What about the photo?' he asks. 'Why was it just me?'

'Because she was deluded,' Christian spits, dragging the knife across Katie's face, cutting a deep slice into her cheek.

'You can't!' Nathan cries out, disbelievingly. 'You can't.'

'Mum thought one could be different to the other,' Christian continues, as if he hasn't heard his brother. 'She thought your darkness wasn't the same. But I know better. And so, deep down, do you.'

Nathan takes another step, his hands now behind his back. He's just a few feet from Christian, and it's like he can feel the connection between them rising and disappearing like a wave.

'You want to know why I'm not going to take anybody's life today,' he says. 'It's because whatever it was that existed between us has gone. You killed it. You killed it the moment you did this.' He looks down at Katie, at all that blood that for once he cannot bear to see. 'You did what I would never have done. You hurt the person I love.' One more step, and he's almost in touching distance, but Nathan's arms remain behind his back. 'In that one stroke of a knife you've proven the absolute difference between us. You've shown me that I am better than you.' He feels himself straightening, towering over his brother. 'All the years I stayed away because I thought I was the sick one, the one that might contaminate *you*…' He twists his neck, feeling the ripple of tension across his shoulders. 'I would have given up my life for you – I was going to, on this very day – so that you might never know. A cowardly thing to do, perhaps, but it felt right.' He looks at the knife, at the sharpened edge covered in Katie's blood. 'It still does. I'm sorry, little brother, so sorry to have to leave you alone, but you and I are, and always will be, different.'

Christian makes as if to speak, but nothing comes out.

Nathan no longer sees the person he spent twenty years of his life with as he carefully dismantles him with his eyes: the loss of fingers that had once tickled him, pinched him, punched him, and the one finger he had shut in a car door, the first change, the first superficial difference between them.

Without taking his eyes off Nathan's, Christian draws the knife across Katie's other cheek.

'You love her,' he says. It sounds like an accusation.

'Yes,' says Nathan, trembling as he watches the blood streaming out of Katie.

'More than me?'

'More than you.'

Christian stares in disbelief, then looks down at Katie, taking the knife and sinking it into her stomach.

'No!' Nathan screams.

'You know this is your fault. You know that you're killing her with these lies.'

'Fine!' says Nathan, desperately. 'You're right. I don't feel a thing. I was lying. I was just trying to hurt you.'

'It's too late,' says Christian. 'I've seen enough.' He tips his head back, staring up at the spotlights, barking a laugh that falls dead as it hits the surrounding curtains. 'Mum never found love, either.'

'She died because of it,' says Nathan tentatively.

'Don't you dare try and take her away too!' Christian snaps. 'We were the same. The same thoughts. The same desires. It was all written down. The whole fucking world saw it!'

'Just words,' says Nathan again, staring at Katie, making sure she is still conscious, taking comfort in the increasing distance between the knife and her. 'Just her imagination. She would never have done the things you've done. You'd have to be a monster. Jesus, look at Steven Fish: I stood on the edge of that insanity.'

'I think you'll be standing on the edge of it again,' says Christian, with a sneer. 'Long after this is over. There's plenty still to reveal about *that* particular case.' He pushes out a breath and then starts to smile. 'But believe what you like for now, big bro. I know the truth about Mum and me. Twenty years ago today. The symmetry is impossible to resist.' Suddenly his face transforms. 'So sorry to leave you alone,' he says, lifting the knife.

Nathan reaches out desperately, realising what's about to happen. But it's too late. An arching spray of blood covers him, and he can feel the warmth of a few specks striking his face. Then the darkness rises and takes him, both brothers crumpling to the floor in perfect synchronicity.

CHAPTER THIRTY-SIX

Darkness. Endless darkness. At least it had seemed that way. But now there's a sound, the faintest whisper, which is growing louder. It cuts through everything, all the doubt, all the fear, all the emptiness. It cuts through everything like a razor-sharp blade, even though the sound is anything but sharp; it is soft and warm and without any edges at all. She wants to reach for it, to pull it closer still so that it envelops her, embraces her and lifts her out of the darkness, but she knows there is no need. It's coming anyway. It cannot be stopped. All she needs to do is wait a few seconds more.

She opens her eyes then closes them again. It's too much, too bright, too real. She follows this routine several times, each time managing to hold her eyes open for a little bit longer, until eventually she's drawing in shapes as well. They're moving over her and they're saying things, kind things. She wants to talk back to them, whoever they are, to tell them she's okay, but there's something in her mouth, something of which she's becoming increasingly aware. She's also becoming aware, despite the light, that she might not be okay. She's remembering what happened. Something is blocking the physical pain, and when she moves her arm she can feel the tubes, but nothing can stop the images flashing up in her mind, several of which are telling her that she shouldn't try and touch her stomach or her face.

As she lies there, oblivious to time, it's like she's trying to rediscover who she is. She tries to imagine who she might be now it's over. There had been occasions when her looks had been a curse, preventing others from taking her seriously, preventing them from seeing who she wanted to be. Now it will be so much worse. Everyone will see her face and feel horror, or even worse still – pity, perhaps even the one man she most wants to see. She doesn't allow herself to cry. If she retains nothing else from her previous existence she can at least be strong. And if she isn't strong, if she doesn't survive, if she doesn't get over what has gone before, then the unforgiveable will have happened: the evil that did this to her will have won.

Not that this case has ever been about winning. From the very start she's known it was about degrees of losing. There are other differences from previous cases, too, priorities that seem to have been realigned. It's always been about catching the culprit, but right now her primary concern is for the victims: for the sons, the daughters, the mothers, the fathers and for one person in particular.

'Nathan?' The tape and narrow tube in her mouth stop the name from emerging, but she continues to try until it is finally removed. It leaves her throat burning. Perhaps they see the focus in her eyes or the tightness of her grip on the white sheets, but they soon stop asking.

*

The answer does not come till later that evening. He stands in the doorway with a bunch of flowers, and a smile on his face that is wonderful to see and yet far from convincing. Nathan places the flowers at the end of the bed and moves around and close to her. He looks hesitant about getting too close, as if she might be scared of him, but from somewhere she suddenly finds the strength to reach out and grab his sleeve and drag him in. The pain is extraordinary, right across her stomach, in her core. But it's worth it. He leans over and kisses her lightly on the crown of her head, then looks at her, just as he had back in the disused factory. She returns that look, strengthening it, strengthening them.

'Always,' he says.

But the word offers no comfort, not when she thinks about where they might be heading from here. She wishes she could turn to her judgement, to her instinct, to find the answer there, but that can't be relied on now, not since she discovered the truth about her dad. She's not confident of anything anymore. It's possible they won't be together. It's possible they only have a few days left. It's possible this is it right now; the final word that will come back to haunt her.

Always.

She grips his sleeve again, even tighter, not daring to find the scars on his wrist. Instead she says what she says to victims when she's lost and confused and running out of hope.

'I'm sorry.'

'I'm not,' says Nathan, moving his foot to touch a narrow shaft of sunlight slipping through the curtains she'd insisted are kept drawn. 'It's the only way it could end.'

She thinks of that end. She hadn't been able to see the final cut, but her view of Nathan's face had been clear. She'd seen the horror. She'd felt it too. And then, almost at the same time as the two brothers had fallen to the floor, she'd slipped into darkness. She knows she's heading that way soon – the medication is dragging her under once more – but before she goes there are a few more things she needs to ask.

'Markham?'

'Called the ambulance and the police himself. Probably kept you alive.'

'And my dad's crime?'

'He's keeping silent about that at the moment. As are Barclay and Tracy. But we have a decision to make in the future.'

This brings her directly to her final question, to her greatest concern. 'The future?'

He leans over, the trace of a smile as he brushes a hair from in front of her face, revealing the damage and not flinching in the slightest. 'We have work to do.'

It takes a moment for the words to translate, and to make sure that she's not already dreaming the impossible. 'So you're not…?'

'No,' he says softly, as her eyelids fall and she slips into the warm embrace of sleep and certainty, 'not the same.'

A LETTER FROM NICK

Hi,

I wanted to let you know how grateful I am that you chose to read my debut novel *Dark Lies*. If you liked it, and want to keep up to date with my next release, please sign up at the following link. Your email address will never be shared, and you can unsubscribe at any time.

www.bookouture.com/nick-hollin

Dark Lies came to me in a rush, a story I couldn't wait to tell, with characters I felt connected to from the very start. The second book has proved equally rewarding, and I've loved returning to Nathan and Katie, to push them even harder and test their remarkable detective skills.

It would be wonderful if you could find time to write a review of *Dark Lies*. It's obviously helpful in finding new readers, but also fantastic for me, after so long locked away with only a keyboard and my thoughts for company, to hear your views. Should you be social-media minded, I would also be delighted to hear from you on Twitter @vonmaraus. This is just the start of my writing adventure, and it would be great to have your company on the way.

Best wishes,
Nick

ACKNOWLEDGEMENTS

It hasn't been easy to reach this point. So much frustration, confusion and doubt, so many early starts, so many late finishes, near misses, rewrites galore, whole chapters thrown out. But one of the loveliest things about getting here, in finally achieving this lifelong dream, is that I get a chance to recognise those who've helped me along the way.

I'll start with those that have suffered the most: my family. To my partner, Amanda, I can't thank you enough for your patience and faith. To my parents and my brother, your support has been immense, and something for which I will for ever be grateful. To my son, Ethan, your arrival has given me far less time but far more focus (oh, and please don't read this book for many more years). I hope this is some justification for the time I've stolen from you all.

To my agent, Sarah Manning, and my editor, Jessie Botterill, you have been extraordinary. Thank you for your passion, your commitment and your belief in my writing. You are everything an agent and an editor should be.

To those friends who have given encouragement over the years, and even to those who clearly doubted I'd make it, you have been invaluable. A special mention to Kim Curran, a brilliant writer and the most wonderful source of sage advice. We've come a long way since the RWC.

And finally, thank *you*! The reader. Much as I love the writing process, it's brilliant to be able to share my efforts with you.

Lightning Source UK Ltd.
Milton Keynes UK
UKHW02f0634170418
321178UK00011B/794/P

9 781786 813374